Six Sisters

P. J. Lazos

Dedication

~

For my mother, Rita, the Lioness. You set me on the path when you taught me to read.

Acknowledgments

~

How do I thank the world, or at least those players in my part of it? There are so many people, too numerous to count, who have encouraged my writing along the way, and in my mind, I've thanked you time and again. Since everything is communicated telepathically, I'm hoping you got the message. In addition, I'd like to give ginormous thanks to Duncan Alderson and the Rabbit Hill Writers, how I miss you all; my extremely talented friend, illustrator and graphic designer, Robert J. Puzauskie; my editor, Gaspare Perrello who never tired of reading yet another *slightly altered* version; my friends, Debbe Bosin and Randy Myer for suffering through first drafts without complaint; eagle-eye Jan Nation, my punctuation hero; my blog partner and California Dreamer, Cynthia Gregory; my mom who says everything I write is fabulous, even when she hasn't read it; my kids, Morgan, Ian, and Arianna, who test my mettle with their interruptions and save me from myself time and again; and last, but definitely not least, my husband, Scott Eberly, who tutors me on topics I can never hope to fully understand.

p.s. A special thanks to the angels who had a hand in creating these little works of fiction. You know who you are. 🕊

A Gathering of One

~

Patrice wasn't sure when her fascination with opera began. Perhaps it was the night in intensive care, not the night she and her sister were born, but the night when Patrice's mother, Kassie, sat a grim and weary watch, holding tight to the invisible cord that tethered Danielle to the earth. Danielle the exuberant one. Danielle the daredevil. Danielle the clown. Danielle the troublemaker. Kassie had many names for Danielle, but that night it was critical.

Exhaustion had overtaken Kassie, and she half-sat, half-lay, leaning over the guard rail of her daughters' hospital bed, her head resting in the nook of her elbow, a tiger waiting to pounce, albeit a sleepy one. Luciano Pavarotti's melodious tenor drifted from the tinny speakers of the small transistor radio that Kassie had placed on the hospital table, infiltrating her subconscious as she dozed and providing a bit of solace. The table was loaded with cups of melting ice chips, a half-eaten

1

container of strawberry jello, several sponges for swabbing parched mouths and lips, two coloring books, two small packs of crayons, and a spare blanket which Kassie had folded and refolded half a dozen times while contemplating the vicissitudes of that inevitable Change her mother's instinct told her was coming, no, charging, at a rate of 186,000 miles per second, or 700 million miles an hour, depending on how you counted Time. Change was the uninvited dinner guest at a swanky restaurant who drank and talked excessively then bailed on the check, a nefarious six-letter word that entered like a hurricane scattering roofs and dreams, downing all electrical connections, and leaving ruin in its wake. She waited for Change now, hoping for a good one, dreading a drastic one, praying for a just one, knowing she'd be forced to surrender to whatever came because in the end, that's all anyone can do.

The strength of Pavarotti's voice conquered the crappy little speakers and although Kassie had no idea what he was singing about, distorted as it was, and in Italian, the timbre of his voice was enough to lull her into the much needed sleep that had eluded her since all the horror began. While Kassie slept, the twins, Danielle and Patrice, did the same, lying side-by-side in the hospital bed, their faces close, their 5-year old limbs, intertwined like pretzels. Patrice wasn't sick, unless you counted sick at heart, yet she refused to leave Danielle's side and Kassie appreciated the show of camaraderie.

Kassie roused herself and sat up in the straight-backed chair. Her hair stood at weird angles surrounding a face creased with the imprint of her arm. She stretched her upper torso over the railing, listening to her daughters' breathing. Danielle's was raspy, grasping, as if she couldn't pull enough of the invisible stuff into herself. Kassie felt her stomach do a little somersault. She was certain that the air passing back and forth between their nostrils hadn't had a chance to recycle itself, and the girls would suffocate from too much carbon dioxide. She knew this with absolute certainty, thirty-five years before the topic of global warming was even in vogue, because she had studied chemistry and because it made sense. Years later, she would shake her head and laugh sardonically at the politicians who debated such issues, as if

2

there were a question, when any high school student could see it was an absolute. Our ozone was running out, holding hands with Time, scurrying out the back door like the Dish and the Spoon.

She thrust a finger between their noses and felt the warmth and condensation as the girls breathed – toxins out, clean air in – then poked Patrice in the ribs. Her oldest daughter by two minutes and fifty-seven seconds flinched and rolled over onto her back. Kassie took a deep, relieved breath and sat back in the chair. A moment later the room went still when Danielle stopped breathing. Kassie lurched forward as if drunk and lowered her head to her daughter's face while the guard rail cut into her stomach. Nothing. She had another small panic attack as she placed two fingers at the base of Danielle's throat, a panic that stayed with her long after she felt the gentle thump, thump, thump, rise up to meet the tips of her fingers, and heard Danielle's sharp intake of air followed by her more or less regular, but labored breath.

Kassie sat back and resumed her vigil, feeling neither relieved nor lucky. No one would have blamed her. Not since the twins were born, all blue and slimy and no bigger than the palm of her hand, a full 14-weeks early, had she had a complete and satisfying night's sleep. The memory of that heart pounding trip to the hospital nestled in the hallways and back rooms of her cerebral cortex where she caught glimpses of it from time to time, appearing in shadow, but now, since this latest latest mishap, crisp, clear and center stage.

One minute she had been shuffling off to the bathroom for a 4 a.m. pee-break and the next her water broke. She remembered being relieved that it broke on the toilet and not while she was still in bed. It was all so civilized until reality hit, and her heart registered the information: time in utero – 26 weeks! Kassie couldn't remember how long she sat on the toilet, holding her heart and belly simultaneously, as if they were having a dialogue and she was the mediator. The next thing she knew she felt a movement down below, like someone was clawing their way out, and she screamed, a hair-raising, toe-curling scream that propelled Dylan, like a catapult, out of bed. Before she knew what was happening, he'd cleaned her up and bundled her into the car with the front seat extended all the way down and a towel between her legs, hoping to hold in whichever one of their children had other plans for that evening.

Kassie felt a head sticking out between her legs. She knew that wasn't possible, but in her terror all she could do was squeeze and pray. Since her water had broken – actually, it was more like a slow leak – the babies were more susceptible to infection. The alternative could be much more dire, born prematurely at 26 weeks, what chance would those babies have? So Kassie kept squeezing, so hard her inner thigh muscles screamed with the strain of it, and praying until her mind numbed into submission, into oblivion. *Hail Mary, full of grace, the Lord is with thee....*

Somehow it had worked, and when she arrived at the hospital, breathless and terrified, the nurses jumped to as if waiting just for them, put her in a wheelchair, and raced her down the hall to a private room. They inserted two IVs, administered drugs, the names of which Kassie could no longer recall, but which stopped the contractions and the leaking, and put her belly to rest for the night. The rest lasted six days. Patrice was born first, then Danielle, slipping out one after the other, like spilled milk, small as peanuts, and thirteen weeks early. To Kassie it seemed that they'd slipped out; Patrice would later claim that she was pushed.

Five years later, Kassie could still recall the pressure on her bladder, the uncomfortable push against the back of her spine. She felt a pain shoot through her abdomen, and realized it wasn't just a memory – she really did have to pee – and she laughed out loud at herself. Patrice flinched and jerked once in her sleep, jarred by the noise, but Danielle didn't move, just kept breathing those raspy, haggard breaths. Kassie thought she could see the ghost-like threads of the luminous cord that connected Patrice to earth, a faint, shimmery thing, starting at the heart and floating upward like fairy wings in a column of light. But when she reached for Danielle's, her hands came up empty. *Danielle's cord was gone!* She sat for a fear-filled moment, staring at her sleeping daughters, the pressure on her bladder growing exponentially. She wished Dylan were here to dismiss her ludicrous fears, but Dylan was

4

making rounds in this very hospital while his daughters lay here sleeping, one of them possibly dying. . .

"Ridiculous," she said, leaned over and presented them with a fleeting brush of a kiss against their damp cheeks. "Don't go anywhere," Kassie said, hesitating before scurrying off. "I'll be right back."

Crouched over the toilet – she never sat down on a toilet seat unless it was in her own house – a fully formed thought displaced the relief she felt as she emptied her bladder: Danielle was not a good listener.

❧

Patrice and Danielle were in the backyard, hovering over the sandbox, building castles, when their mother called: "Dinner."

"Awwww, Mom," Patrice called back. But ever the obedient daughter, she tossed in the toys, the shovels, diggers and sifters that they had used at the beach, and which, now that summer was over, had taken residence in the sandbox, then grabbed the buckets and threw them on top, decimating Danielle's sand castle.

"Look what you did, you dummy," Danielle spat. "You've ruined my townhouses. Now I'll have to start all over."

"You heard Mom. Let's go."

"You go. I'm staying until I finish this housing development.

"You're nine. What do you know about housing developments?"

Danielle shrugged. Patrice brushed her hands and stood up, arms akimbo, staring at her sister.

"Daniellle," Patrice said. "Mom's going to be mad."

"Mom's always mad."

Patrice nudged her younger sister with the tip of her sneaker, cocked her head toward the house. Danielle shook her head.

"I don't have to go if I don't want to."

"Fine. But I'm not going to get into trouble with you." Patrice shot Danielle an angry look, wheeled on her heel, and stomped off toward the house, slamming the kitchen door behind her. She peeked out the window the whole time she washed her hands and intermittently as she set the table and filled the water glasses. Danielle remained exactly as

Patrice left her, crouched over the sandbox, reconstructing her "housing development," but what looked to Patrice to be just a big pile of stupid sand.

Her mother never said a word. Not when she strained then whipped the mashed potatoes or pulled the roasted chicken out of the oven, not when she dressed the salad, using too much vinegar as she always did, or even when she sliced the bread, all the while humming a tune that Patrice recognized as opera, something from Carmen, only because her mother had the record and she would often put it on the stereo. The stereo was a massive piece of oak furniture. The turntable sat in the middle under a hinged lid while the attached speakers, fully covered with a resilient mesh fabric design that moved when you poked them, flanked the turntable. Kassie played the record on Sunday mornings before church while the family was eating breakfast. They were sad, mournful melodies and sometimes her Mom got tears in her eyes.

"Go tell your father to leave the world of information and come eat dinner," Patrice told her daughter.

"What about Danielle?" Patrice asked. "She's still out at the sandbox."

Kasssie looked out the back window and drew her lips in tight, straining against her teeth until her lips all but disappeared. Patrice knew what that look meant, knew not to ask again, and went off in search of her father.

She found him in the living room, simultaneously reading the newspaper, watching the evening news, and listening to the baseball game on the radio. The TV anchor man droned on about how it was the end of the Vietnam War and how Americans needed to stand behind their boys who were finally coming home. Patrice watched as American soldiers were evacuated by helicopter. Something about what the man was saying didn't sit well with her, but she couldn't have said what it was so she shrugged it off, too young to understand as her father always said.

Her father was an E.R. doctor who, on the occasions he was home, always seemed tired. She watched his profile – he hadn't even noticed her entry into the room – and wondered what he was thinking, or even if he was thinking at all, what with everything he was doing at one time. She thought that one day she would walk into the living room and find her father's brains exploded all over the tawny shag rug, a victim of what her mother called information overload. She tapped her father on the shoulder: "Dinner."

He looked vacantly at her for several seconds. Patrice returned his gaze, wondering if it was the sight of her that made him so unhappy. He asked, "Is dinner ready?" Patrice nodded, her large grey eyes absorbing the 5 o'clock shadow, the prematurely receding hairline, the vacant, grey eyes, identical to her own, the slight, half-smile he now tried to give her as her reward for coming to get him. She stood still, hoping he would reach out to her, pat her shoulder, or her head, squeeze her arm, maybe even give her a kiss, but he just nodded and said, "okay then," before rising from his seat to turn off the television, the forgotten newspaper scattering in several directions as he stood. Patrice shuddered as he walked past, his gloominess trailing him like a funeral procession. By the time he cleared the space and she could follow him, she'd become as glum as he.

Kassie frowned, but didn't ask Patrice what was the matter. "Wash your hands," was all her mother said. Patrice craned her neck, looking out the window at Danielle as she turned on the water, practically scalding herself with180 degrees of heat flowing right from the furnace in this turn-of-the century Victorian house. She stifled a yelp and added some cold water to regulate the temperature, then took another peek out the window. Danielle had moved to the swing and was happily pumping her feet up and back, rising higher into the air with each successive pump. Patrice glanced over at her mother, about to raise another objection, but Kassie spoke before Patrice could.

"Patrice, would you please sit down. I didn't spend all afternoon cooking so we could eat everything cold."

The words, "but Mom," died in her throat and she took her place at the table she'd set, the plates arranged, one on each side of the rectangle, even though that meant they were so far apart that you had to get up to pass a bowl. She'd done this purposely, though, knowing that if you drew a straight line between the plates you'd form a crucifix. She pictured herself at the top of it, right where Jesus's head would be. Patrice glanced over at Danielle's place setting, right where Jesus's left arm would be. "Why doesn't Danielle have to come in for dinner?" she asked, mixing her green beans in with her mashed potatoes, hoping to hide the taste, and shoving a giant forkful into her mouth. Her father cleared his throat and her mother's face took on that strained, pinched expression. She watched her parents exchange a look Patrice couldn't decipher before continuing their dinner in silence.

"It's not fair," Patrice said again at dessert, shoving a bite of her mom's famous cherry pie into her delicate mouth. Her mother baked a dozen of them each year for St. Francis's yearly summer flea market and bake sale and the pies were the first to sell out. Patrice knew she should be grateful to have a mother who baked such delicious pies, but as she chewed, staring at Danielle's empty chair and empty plate, her anger grew and spread, obliterating the sweet cherry taste so much so that Patrice didn't notice the blood that squirted into the pocket of her mouth when she bit into a piece of the crust and caught her tongue instead.

∾

"Go fish," Patrice shouted.

"You think you're so smart, Miss Sassy Pants." Kassie gave her 10-year old daughter a wide smile, then picked seven straight cards before she could lay a pair down. Patrice counted the cards in her mother's hand. Unlucky 13. She squirmed in her seat with the anticipation of winning. Patrice had only three cards and she laid two of them down, smiling.

"You can't win. You never do," Danielle's voice banged into the side of Patrice's head like a floe stopped by the glacier. She turned and scowled at her sister who sat in the corner, arms crossed, looking sullen.

"Shut up," Patrice whispered.

"Hmm?" Kassie said, pulling another card.

8

"Nothing," Patrice replied.

Patrice looked up to see her father walk in and shuffle over to the closet. After a minute of his rooting around, Patrice asked, "What are you looking for, Daddy?" Dylan mumbled a response into the back of the closet where he was crouched. When he emerged, he gave her the same sad smile that always graced his face when she spoke to him.

"I finished the bills," he said to Kassie. "They're on the counter."

Patrice noticed him fingering something bulky in his pocket, but she couldn't make out what it was.

"I paid three months ahead. They just need stamps."

"Why'd you pay ahead?" Kassie asked. She didn't look up.

Dylan shrugged, fixed on Kassie with his eyes.

"What's wrong, Daddy?"

Dylan shifted his gaze to Patrice and took a tentative step forward, raising his hand as if to touch her, but she sat halfway across the room and Patrice could tell from his face that the journey looked to him like a million miles. He sighed, nodded in resignation, and walked out without another word. Patrice looked at her mother, who was gazing at the empty space Dylan had left as if she could divine something from the swirling dust particles that remained.

After a few moments, Kassie turned back to her daughter and asked, "Any eights?"

"Go fish," Patrice said. Her response was punctuated by the noise a gun makes when it discharges into someone's skull.

❧

Patrice stood with dry cheeks in front of the open casket; she stood tall and exceptionally straight, like an exclamation point, teetering on itself. The last time she stood before an open casket, her mother told her to stop crying and stand up straight. She was ten and it was her father's funeral. Thank God for Andrea Bocelli. His voice provided the soothing background she needed to counteract the sorrowful din in the house and her head. The few dozen people who had come to pay their last respects to Kassie Davis had been kind, bringing food and their concerns, and the thought reminded Patrice that she hadn't eaten since last night's dinner. Someone touched her shoulder and she jerked back before turning to look into a face as ancient as dirt. A gnarled, arthritic hand touched her cheek.

"You're a good daughter," the face said. "A comfort to your mother all those years."

The hand stroking her cheek felt like sandpaper, rubbing across her cheekbone, but starved as she was for a physical connection, Patrice accepted it gratefully. The woman's words lodged in her throat like a wad of cotton. The last thirty-five years had more to do with servitude, her daughterly duty, a duty she still had not shed, and the thought made her glance involuntarily toward the kitchen. While the conflicting thoughts duked it out for dominion over her larynx, Patrice nodded and tried to smile. She found it harder than it should be given that a face uses twelve muscles to accomplish the task. All those muscles and all they could do was quiver.

The old woman touched her arm and this time Patrice did not jump. She examined the woman's attire, wrinkled and out-of-date, then moved up to the weathered, liver-spotted face, the lines running from her yellow, watery eyes in rivulets, the crevices, yawning to life like scorched earth along the sides of her mouth. The woman smiled, revealing a mouth full of silver fillings and yellow, coffee-stained teeth. Patrice contrasted this figure with the one lying stretched out in her best dress, nestled in the satin lining like expensive chocolates. Her mother looked small and insignificant now, not the force she remembered, in a dress that was two sizes too big after all the chemotherapy and radiation. They had taken part of her mother's left lung, but failed to take the sorrow that had caused it to wither and die prematurely. So the sorrow stayed, slaking its thirst on the very air her mother breathed, sucking the life out of her until she surrendered. Patrice turned to leave, but the boney fingers dug into her forearm, holding her back.

"Duty's done now, dear. Don't waste another minute. Find yourself a nice man to marry. After all," she said, her unencumbered arm spreading in a wide arc that encompassed the room, the house, and quite possibly, Patrice's last thirty-five years, "this is too much."

"What?" Patrice said.

"This," the woman responded as if it couldn't be clearer. Patrice felt the anger rise past her cheeks all the way to her eyebrows. Stupid old woman. I don't care if you are my mother's aunt.

"We'll manage just fine, Thea."

Thea raised her eyebrows and pursed her lips in a manner reminiscent of Patrice's dead mother, but made no move to stop Patrice as she extricated her arm and turned toward the kitchen, mumbling apologies, a small smile plastered on her lips.

She found Danielle in the kitchen, slathering Vicks Vapor Rub on her throat. "That stuff stinks," Patrice said. "Get away from the food."

Danielle looked at the cured hams and turkeys and salamis as if they were the offenders her sister spoke of, uncrossed her legs and dipped her fingers in the jar. Danielle moved onto her chest, rubbing in slow, lazy circles. Patrice thought she could almost see the vapors rise in hazy tendrils toward the ceiling. Danielle had rubbed herself into such a languid state that she dropped the jar of Vicks into the potato salad.

"Ugh," Patrice said, turning away in disgust. She grabbed a spoon and fished the contaminated potato salad out. "Why are you such a pig?" She glared at Danielle before throwing the whole mess in the trash can. Danielle snorted in response.

Patrice pulled out the Vicks and rinsed off the jar. "Oh, forget it," she said, slammed down the jar and walked out of the room.

It had been a rhetorical question anyway.

∾

A week after the funeral, the neighbors' casseroles ran out and Patrice needed to make a grocery run. Danielle insisted on going. The two sisters, Patrice, long, lean and sinewy with the grace and agility of an athlete, and Danielle, plump and delicious like overripe fruit, could not be more dissimilar as they made their way through the produce aisle. Patrice stopped the cart at the pineapples and grabbed one of the spiny, cactus-like leaves. It pulled out easily, a sign that it was ripe, so she put the pineapple in the cart. She added a plastic container of blueberries.

"I wouldn't buy them," Danielle said, squeezing a peach between menthol fingers. "They're too damn expensive."

"Too expensive is when you don't have the money to buy things in the first place." Patrice placed a container of raspberries next to the blueberries.

"Ach. Those are even worse."

"I don't notice you saying anything about it when you're busy stuffing your cheeks with them," Patrice said, placing a honeydew in the cart. She followed it with some red grapes, the color of a fine, aged wine. "Besides, when you work," Patrice put the emphasis on the word, "you can afford a few luxuries." She gave her sister a sideways glance and half a smirk before moving on to the bananas, still as green as the tree they grew on.

Danielle shuffled after her. "What's that supposed to mean?"

"It means what it means."

"Which is?"

"Just shut up, Danielle, would you? What is your problem today?" Patrice said, placing a package of feta cheese and some cured black olives in the cart.

"Don't make this about me," Danielle whispered, somewhat viciously. She looked down at the cart. "I don't like olives."

"Well, I do."

Danielle poked at the cheese. "I don't like that kind of cheese, either. I want that." She pointed to a package of American cheese, each slice individually wrapped with a piece of cellophane as if to keep the slices from consorting with each other.

Patrice picked it up. "It's completely over-packaged. Do you know it takes 1,000 years for plastic to break down into something the planet can recycle?"

Danielle pantomimed Patrice as she spoke. "How would they know that?" Danielle asked. "Has anybody lived 1,000 years to confirm the exact moment when microscopic pieces of plastic go scattering to the four winds?" Danielle raised an eyebrow and set her lip, blocking

Patrice's cart. Patrice gripped the cheese so tightly it looked destined to become string cheese.

Patrice pulled back and around her, but Danielle stepped in front of the cart again. They continued this dance for half a minute, each time with Danielle blocking her path. In frustration, Patrice threw the American cheese into the cart.

"Hey, watch out. You'll bruise it."

"Cheese doesn't bruise."

"Does so."

"It does not. Fruit bruises. Hearts bruise. Cheese just gets moldy."

"Kind of like you," Danielle said.

Patrice scowled at her sister and pushed off toward the coffee aisle.

"You forgot soda," Danielle said.

"I don't want soda," Patrice replied.

"I do."

Patrice raised an eyebrow in her sister's direction, and shrugged a shoulder. "So get a job."

Danielle looked truly hurt. "Don't you think I'd get one if I could," she said breathlessly. "It's just that my condition...."

Patrice pressed her lips together tight against her teeth, forming a thin white line.

"You look like Mom," Danielle said.

"Listen," Patrice said, using her patient voice, the one she used to talk to Richard's irate clients. "I don't care, all right. Just stop whining."

Danielle started with a small whimper and before Patrice knew it, she'd escalated it to a full-throttle, all out wail. Patrice hurriedly pushed the cart down the chip aisle, leaving Danielle sobbing in front of large plastic bottles of Pepsi, Coca Cola, and Mountain Dew. Patrice was shaking as she hurried the cart along, trying to put as much distance between them as she could, her eyes blurring with embarrassment as she click, click, clicked away from the noise. She emerged from the chip aisle and peeked around the corner. Danielle stood, hands clenched at her sides, her mouth open, crying silent tears. She was less than five feet away. On any other day, Patrice would have rushed to her, taken her hand, guided her back to reality. Yet today was different: her mother was dead and she no longer needed to cater to her sister for her mother's sake.

"It would be a comical scene," thought Patrice, "if she weren't my sister." She pushed on, catching the edge of the end cap with her cart. The end cap shook slightly, and a jar of pickles teetered before crashing to the floor, the pungent, vinegary juice spraying everywhere. The smell made Patrice's mouth water involuntarily and she hesitated, straining not to look at the mess she would never voluntarily walk away from, but Danielle had caught a glimpse of Patrice and begun her shrill wailing anew. Patrice knew that Danielle's antics were about to draw some assistance and inevitably, the broken pickle jar would be discovered.

Danielle would give her up. She'd tell the manager that her older sister by two minutes and fifty-seven seconds had abandoned her and busted a jar of pickles, too. Danielle had been calling the shots since before they were born, since they were in the womb and Danielle had kicked her so hard that Patrice's lovely warm sack had burst and all that soothing liquid filtered out, leaving Patrice cold and shivering and very much on her own. She could have made the best of it. Even without the sack it was much warmer than the world ever would be, but Danielle was relentless, kicking and pushing until she practically shoved Patrice through the hole and out into the light. Since then, as far as she remembered, Patrice had never really made a decision without taking Danielle into account, so it was a bit of a surprise that Patrice had gotten all the way to the chip aisle before patterning caught up with her.

She was running now, back to the produce aisle as Danielle's screams grew more intense. A cold sweat broke out on Patrice's brow – it had a distinct smell, like the fear that precipitates a loss of control – and her cheeks glowed crimson. As she rounded the corner, she saw a small crowd that included, according to their name tags, the manager, the assistant manager, and the deli meat supervisor. They had gathered near Danielle, but closer to the pickles, deliberating. A woman arrived with a mop and someone pointed at Patrice. A "caution wet floor" sign had been placed next to the spill. The mop lady gave

Patrice a smoldering look, but said nothing as she bent to the task of cleaning up spilled pickle juice. Patrice bristled. Danielle was screaming her head off in the middle of the store and all these people could do was stand around and gawk because Patrice had broken a stupid jar of pickles.

She motioned to Danielle to come, careful not to look at the store employees, staring after her with a common eye as she darted past the wailing Danielle, scurrying to keep up with her. When they were out of range of eyesight and standing in front of the chips, Danielle stopped crying.

"Mmmm, Cheetos. Can we get some?"

Patrice bit her tongue and rolled her eyes to heaven. It was some kind of punishment, she was sure, but for what she didn't know. God didn't send stuff like this down unless you deserved it, that's what her father always said, and he must have done something awful, too, so awful that he couldn't bear to face it anymore, which is why he chose a bullet to the brain over dinner with his wife and kids. It had taken her mother weeks to get the blood stains out of the carpet. Patrice thought, had it been her husband, she'd have just as soon replaced it, but her mother insisted on cleaning up the mess as if it were some kind of penance. Her father had never been the same since Danielle's accident, none of them were, but sometimes bad things happened and you learned to deal with them.

Danielle reached for the bag of Cheetos, but Patrice grabbed her arm. Patrice jumped when Danielle grabbed her arm back and they stood there a moment, locked in a checkerboard square embrace.

"Promise you'll never leave me again," Danielle said. She shuddered and leaned in close to her sister, breathing the words in her ear, "'cause sometimes I'm scared."

Patrice looked into the eyes of her twin – right now 5-year old eyes – and the valves of her heart squeezed themselves tight while a thousand spots of darkness swam in the fine liquid covering her cornea, obliterating the rays from the florescent lights, twitching overhead and traveling at a rate of 186,000 miles per second. She clutched at her heart while the opening strands of *The Prayer*, a duet with Andrea Bocelli and Celine

Dion, wafted through her ear canal and on to the tympanic membrane, the drum that calls the bones to life, wrapping around them and stimulating them to movement, the tiny cilia, picking up the rhythm and translating it to words and sounds and music. She thought it odd that the grocery store would be playing Bocelli and wondered if maybe she weren't dead, but the music swelled and already the dark spots were retreating, the light returning. She opened her eyes to find Danielle staring at her, mouth agape, clutching her throat.

"Are you all right?" Patrice asked, forgetting her own angina. Danielle nodded and Patrice breathed in relief. She laughed once nervously, straightened her blouse, and smoothed out the wrinkles out of her skirt. "C'mon. Let's go. You can push."

Patrice held fast to the side while Danielle pushed the cart down the aisle, proud and smiling and without further incident, until, that is, they reached frozen foods.

"Oh, would you look at that!" Danielle said.

A woman was walking toward them, about 25, with big, blond hair. She teetered on stiletto heels, her breasts as big as watermelons and looking equally as ponderous to manage. She stopped in front of the frozen dinners.

"Stop staring, Danielle."

"How can I? She looks like she's going to fall over any minute."

"I doubt you'll be able to catch her if she does."

"No, but I can be there to watch and laugh and maybe even point."

"Stop it, Danielle," Patrice said. "You're embarrassing me."

The woman glanced at Patrice, a curious look on her face, but said nothing and went back to scanning the freezer shelves. Her black halter dress was so tight one could see the outline of her naval piercing.

"Would you look at that dress? You couldn't squeeze a silk worm in there."

"Shush!" Patrice whispered.

The woman had made a selection and began clickety-clicking toward them.

"Oh my God. Look at those things. She probably has to tamp them down just to get her dress on in the morning. There's no way they're real."

"Shut up, Danielle," Patrice hissed.

"They're a choking hazard."

"Shut up, Danielle!"

Patrice said this just loud enough to draw the woman's attention away from staying upright on her stilettos. She stared at Patrice, making sure to keep her distance as she moved unsteadily past them. Danielle started after her, the clicking receding as the woman turned the corner.

∽

"It's quiet without Mom bossing us around," Danielle said.

"What would you know about it? She never bossed you around." Patrice put a scoop of macaroni and cheese on Danielle's plate and then her own. She took two hot dogs out of a small sauce pan of boiling water, placed them in buns and set them on the plates.

Danielle grabbed hers and held it up accusingly. "Ketchup?"

"Most people have it with mustard."

Patrice put ketchup on Danielle's, mustard on hers. Danielle made a face, but said nothing. Patrice drained the broccoli and put a few pieces on each plate.

"I'm not eating that."

"Do what you want."

Patrice sat down and put some olive oil and balsamic vinaigrette on her salad.

"I'm not eating that either."

"Suit yourself."

"How can you eat it anyway? It's so. . . . salad-y."

"That's it," Patrice said. She took her plate to the trash and tilted it in. She whisked Danielle's food away and threw it in after.

"What'cha do that for? I wasn't finished," Danielle protested.

"No, but I was," Patrice said, and stomped from the room.

The human heart has four chambers, two for receiving blood and two for discharging. It weighs about ten ounces and beats seventy-two times per minute. It's the size of a fist, but manages to pump about five liters of pure, life-giving blood throughout the body every minute whether sunny or cloudy, hot or cold, windy or rainy -- or broken. Patrice had no way of knowing that her heart had been broken since she was 5-years old, that the valves and vessels and muscles, ostensibly operating normally, had lost a certain amount of elasticity as well as the immeasurable things: resonance, happiness, joy.

The day her sister snatched the open can of drain cleaner from Patrice's hands, the one stored under the bathroom sink, tilted her head back and took a man-sized swig, all before Patrice knew what was happening, was the day Patrice's heart was cleaved in two. She had no way of knowing that it wasn't her fault even as she sat in the back seat during the terror-ridden drive to the hospital, muttering over, and over again, "I'm sorry, I'm so sorry, I'm sorry, I'm so sorry," like a mantra or a prayer, and then the days in the hospital, Patrice holding Danielle's hand, lying by her side . . . "I'm so sorry".

It had been Patrice's intention to smell what was in the bottle, but Danielle had swiped it from her. Patrice could still remember her own feeling of frozen horror as she watched in slow motion: Danielle's lips parting, raising the bottle, her Adams apple bobbing up and down as the life-sucking juice cascaded down her throat and into the esophagus where it scorched and incinerated every last cilia. Her terror was palpable as she cupped her hands beneath Danielle's arms, wet with perspiration and poison and the shadow of death, and hoisted her up and over to the toilet where their mother found them, Danielle hunched and vomiting up a yellow bile and Patrice, patting her back and crying, "I'm sorry," even though she knew that if Danielle would have just minded her own business for once in her life she wouldn't be in this mess right now. Patrice didn't know this business about hearts and the way they continued to work even after they were broken as the blood vessels transported blood and oxygen to places far and wide. She did know about the trachea and the esophagus and how a simple, ordinary household cleaner could burn the life out of them, making them unsuitable for future use. She started to feel sorry now for throwing Danielle's food away, knowing how often Danielle's throat bothered her and how she had trouble swallowing.

Patrice put on her nightgown, brushed her teeth and combed her hair to glistening before padding down the hall to knock lightly on Danielle's door. She smelled the Vicks, heard the TV going, or maybe it was Danielle talking to herself. She leaned against the door a moment, straining to hear, but a sudden wave of silence, filled with its own vibration, overtook her. She sighed and turned back toward her room, toward bed.

༄

"Where do thoughts go when you're done thinking them?"

"Don't you knock?" Patrice was in the bathroom, hand-washing several pairs of pantyhose in the sink. The water was rising, so hot it almost scalded Patrice's hands.

"Can you get me some Woolite?"

"In there?"

"No, in the kitchen. Duh. Yes, in there."

Danielle looked warily at the cupboard under the bathroom sink. Ever since the Drano incident, Danielle made it a point not to open that cabinet.

"Oh for Godsakes." Patrice sighed, shook her wet hands, spraying water everywhere, and opened the cabinet. "Right there. Grab it." Patrice nodded at the bottle, water dripping from her hands. Danielle shook her off like a catcher behind home plate, then leaned back and studied the cracks in the ceiling. Patrice stifled a curse, and grabbed the bottle of soap.

"You left the door open," Danielle quipped.

"So I did," Patrice said. She poured a capful of liquid soap under the running water. Bubbles floated up to the top of the sink.

Danielle glanced down at the open cabinet door then jerked her head away as if the contents of the shelves might reach out and bite her. She bit the side of her lip, rubbed her chest, and rocked back several times before continuing. "So what about the thoughts?"

"What about them?"

"Where do they go? You know, after you're done thinking them?"

"Danielle, I have no clue what you're talking about."

"When you eat dinner, and the next day you go to the bathroom, well, the dinner went down the toilet, right? Same with the water you drink, right? And if you breathe air in, it comes out as carbon dioxide. And if you speak words, the sound goes into someone's ears. But what about the thoughts you think? Where do they go after you're done thinking them?"

Patrice crinkled her brow, then opened her mouth. The question was neither dumb nor rhetorical, yet Patrice simply didn't have an answer.

"I don't know, Danielle. Maybe they go into a great big pile of thoughts somewhere. Or maybe they just float around in the atmosphere. You can't see them, so you wouldn't even know if you banged into one. Unless you started thinking it, but if it wasn't a thought you'd usually think, you probably would never know that you'd banged into someone else's thought. I'm just not sure."

Danielle crinkled her nose and scrunched up her eyebrows, contemplating. After a moment she nodded, smiled, and disappeared as quickly a she'd entered.

∽

Dawn loomed, large and imposing, cracking its one sleep-encrusted eye open a smidgen, enough for a peek, a glimpse, a short foray into the future. Patrice cast it a baleful look before slamming her own two eyes shut, refusing to acknowledge dawn's arrival. After what seemed like 10 minutes, but was really two hours, Patrice rolled over for a glance at the clock. 8:30 a.m.! She threw off the covers and scrambled into her day.

Forty-five minutes later, Patrice sat at her desk, Bocelli playing in her left ear, Richard's voice droning on in her right. For Patrice, it was Bocelli and no other. He was the Pavarotti of his day and she used him like a tonic, an elixir and cure-all, the remedy for sadness and happiness alike, better than meat loaf and mashed potatoes. She housed Bocelli in the left ear because the left side of the body was where the world's passion and intuition and beauty came through, integrating with her own cells and heart and sinew before floating out into the world from her right.

Richard was garbling again. She released the pressure of her foot on the pedal of the transcription machine and rewound the tape, replaying the last sentence: "After considering your proposal, my clients have decided . . . garble, garble, garble . . . firm decision. . . . garble . . . intend to fight this matter. . . ."

She'd been twenty-two years at the law offices of Tretorn, Hewitt and Lipscomb where, on her mother's urging, Patrice had started in the secretarial pool. She worked her way up the ladder, took night classes and become a paralegal, but a few scant months into her new job, the second-named partner, Richard Hewitt, snatched her up, offered her the position of paralegal and personal administrative assistant and paid her for both. Patrice kept both his business and personal calendars, making sure he was fully aware, and prepared for all depositions, court proceedings, client meetings and important business lunches – she devised a computerized tickler system so advanced that Richard sent all the new girls to her for instruction – as well as his wife's birthdays, their anniversaries and the children's soccer games. She knew when to send flowers and when to send the more expensive gifts, the perfumes from France, the diamond solitaire necklace (20th anniversary), the little cards that said, "I love you" in a dozen languages. She did this for Richard's wife, and Richard's family, but not for Richard's mistress because she disapproved. To his credit, he only asked her once. As a result of such fine care taking, Patrice commanded a six figure salary, one she knew to be more than some of the new associates at the firm.

To say she worked hard for the money would be an understatement. There were weeks when Richard was so busy that she had to come in on both Saturday and Sunday just to keep up with all the dictation. She could have farmed it out, letting some of the younger staff handle the typing while she dealt with more of the administrivia, but Patrice didn't operate that way. She needed complete control and handing out dictation tapes like playing cards would have surely eroded her power base, maybe not initially, but somewhere down the road. The only bad part about being indispensable was that you were, well, indispensable. Had she a family, that is to say a husband and children at home – she wasn't counting Danielle who, although still acting the part of the 5-year old, was completely capable of taking care of herself – she wouldn't have been able to keep these hours.

Richard's throaty baritone floated up through the transcription machine's cord and into the microphone inserted snugly into her ear canal, his voice leap-frogging, syllable by syllable, into Patrice's left temporal lobe, and then on to the motor cortex, her central dispatch that barked out commands for the head to turn, the eyes to blink, the mouth to swallow, the lips to kiss, and which now, along with the basal ganglia, cerebellum and countless neurons told her fingers to type, moving at a speed of 135 words per minute. As she hit the gas and her stride, the early morning confusion dissipated and she felt the freedom that comes with performing a job well. The weight of her familial obligations, which generally washed over her like a tsunami, fell away leaving nothing but lightness and open space around her.

When the tape snapped, so did Patrice's reverie.

"Damn," she muttered, extricating the crinkly brown cellophane from the cassette holder. It would have to be repaired because she hadn't finished and Richard was out of town, on vacation in Europe with the mistress, having left strict instructions not to call. She'd take it down to the mail room and give it to Bruce, the closest thing the law office had to a handyman and see if he could splice it. A thrill ran through her belly at the thought of approaching him directly, but she shoved it back down, grabbed the tape and stood to go. Halfway down the hall, she ran back to her desk and grabbled Bocelli.

∾

Bruce. Patrice shuddered as she approached the stairwell intending to walk from the 22nd to the 18th floor where the mail room was located. She always took the stairs, preferring them to the fickle and unpredictable elevators in this spectacular, but old building, partially because she wanted the exercise – four floors were four floors – and partially because she couldn't stand to wait. Each of the stairwell doors had the same small sign, the international symbol for a fire exit. The sign, like hieroglyphics, depicted a single flame for the "fire," and the stick-figure silhouette of a man, walking down a flight of stairs. She chuckled every time she saw the sign on the 22nd floor because someone had used an Exacto knife to remove the man's head and place it three steps below his body. Patrice was so flustered today, the heat of the blood rising in her cheeks as it climbed, that when she saw the sign she laughed out loud.

She inserted her earphones before she opened the stairwell door – it might help hide her embarrassment if initially she couldn't hear what Bruce was saying – and the first strains of Andrea Bocelli's *Sogno* spilled into her ears. She drew a deep and relaxing breath and recounted what she knew about Bruce. He'd taken early retirement from the fire department and although Patrice never got the full story, she understood that he'd left a hero, having saved more than his share of lives in the twenty-four years he'd been there. They'd offered him the position of Fire Chief, a position he could have easily filled, but on his last tour of duty before the shift from the laboring to administrative end of things, a burning beam collapsed on him as he made his way out of the building, breaking his hip bone and femur. It was only by some miracle that his partner had managed to remove the beam and drag Bruce to safety. Bruce had taken the whole incident as a sign, some kind of Divine Intervention, and after six months of convalescing and rehab, and with the Fire Chief's position being no longer available, he took the early retirement they offered him as a consolation prize. Patrice practically swooned every time she saw him, thinking of his courage, wondering what it would be like to kiss those lips, to be held in the arms that had saved so many. Having become so adept at hiding her feelings, Firefighter Bruce, saver of many, currently lover of none, or so she'd been told, didn't have a clue Patrice was interested.

She remembered the first time she'd looked at him two years ago. It had been Bruce's first day on the job. The transcription tape containing days of Richard's dictation had split so Patrice headed down to the mail room to have it repaired. Bruce had been hired as a runner and all around handy man so the job fell to him. Never mind that when Patrice walked in, Bruce had migrated toward her like water to the lowlands. He told her a joke as he spliced the tape and laughed at his own humor, a double-breasted laugh that seemed to emanate from every pore of his body, so much that Patrice found herself laughing, too. After that, he'd sought her out whenever he was on her floor.

When Patrice finally realized he was flirting with her, she made herself scarce. It's not that she wasn't interested, she was. Yet despite her forty years, Patrice had never been with a man. She had only kissed a few, if you counted the awkward ones in high school and her father, and as a result of her anxiety, had turned down countless offers over the years, citing familial obligations. Of course, it didn't help that she still lived with her mother, but whatever the reason, she'd never known a man completely, and the shame of that, of having to explain, far outweighed whatever joy she could foresee coming from it.

So it was with trepidation in her heart that she placed her hand on the handle of the 18th floor stairwell door and as she pushed down and the handle gave, but the door did not, she realized for the first time since she'd left her desk that she'd forgotten her access card and was stuck in the stairwell.

Bruce Danetti pushed the mail cart at a fast clip, finishing the deliveries on the 22nd floor, the one he always saved for last. He had a routine. By the time the post office brought the mail and he'd sorted and delivered it, it was almost the end of the day. He hoped one of these days his timing would be impeccable and he would be at Patrice's desk at the stroke of five, or maybe a quarter 'til, offhandedly asking if she would like to have dinner with him.

He'd met Patrice his first day two years ago and still hadn't asked her out. She was beautiful and smart and much needed by the head partner. She was no lightweight. Yet, neither was he. Bruce had never been married – his profession discouraged it. He knew plenty of guys who'd been perfectly happy until the kids started coming and their wive's started complaining that they were always at the station. The 72-hour shifts were the worst and that kind of lifestyle was just not conducive to raising a family. It got a little lonely at times, but he had his buddies at the fire station, and he never wanted for women. Seems he couldn't leave a bar or a Home Depot without getting a phone number. He must have those pheromones, the feral ones that attract members of the opposite sex. His were super-sized and they screamed: Bruce Danetti isn't afraid of anything, not fire, not smoke, not twenty-car pile ups on the turnpike. Women sensed this, even those happily married, and this is what attracted them. Bruce would keep them safe.

Then the sands shifted and the tide pulled out. A beam had fallen and broken his spirit, and although he had fully recovered, but for the aches and pains that came with the weather, he harbored fears that weren't there before, fears that woke him up from a deep sleep with a slap to the face. To hell with the 401(k). These were fears of life and self-worth and his own mortality. It was that last one that really got him. The one that kept him staring at the ceiling long after his lids should have closed or woke him up in an icy cold sweat that sometimes sat on his chest all day long making it hard to catch his breath. His friends said it was a mid-life crisis, but how the hell could he be middle-aged when a minute ago he was twenty and had the world by the balls on a downward roll? But that was before. Before the beam. Before he met Patrice. He had operated under the assumption that there wasn't a woman he couldn't have if he so desired her, the operative word being before.

Bruce took a deep breath. He had a good retirement package, enough, along with Social Security, to take him comfortably into old age if he lived right, and he wouldn't even have to skimp on the good vacations. He didn't need this job. Richard Freedman, the senior partner had offered it to him. They'd gone to high school together and Richard had seen the write-up in the paper after the beam collapsed. He'd called Bruce after he got out of the hospital to ask if he might not be ready for a less glamorous career that might let him make it to retirement. Bruce laughed, the first since the fiery beam had derailed his prior plans, and took the job on a whim. Two years later he was still here. The job was ridiculously easy compared to his former line of work, the people friendly. Then there was Patrice....

He was still physically very fit with a chest and forearms some would even call ripped, capable of benching 150 pounds without flinching. His dark hair had just a few strands of grey – no big deal – you could barely see them. His olive complexion was smooth and unblemished. Women had told him that they'd kill for his skin, but so far she hadn't noticed. It was easy to see why. She had a face sculpted to perfection, with high cheekbones, and wide open eyes that had a gravitational pull all their own. Her hair was a light brown with flecks of gold in it, ones that you couldn't buy at the beauty salon. Her body was long and lithe and moved like a whisper, gathering attention to her almost sublimi-nally, and he wanted to keep watching her, minute after minute, day after day.

He rounded the corner and his heart fell. Patrice wasn't at her desk. He made a show of rooting around on the cart for something that wasn't really there, stalling for time. Adele, at the next secretarial station, looked briefly at him before returning to her dictation, a small, knowing smile plastered to her face. Bruce knew he'd been nailed and reddened at the thought of how far he'd fallen. He continued with the ruse for another half a minute, mumbled something about leaving a package in the mail room and coming back later. Adele's smile grew wider, Bruce's cheeks more sanguine, but neither said a thing as Bruce handed Adele her mail and continued down the hall.

David, Adele's boss, rushed out of his office, practically bouncing off Bruce as he passed. "Oh, geez. I'm sorry," Bruce said. David stopped to catch his balance and adjust his glasses while Bruce stood there like the impenetrable Rock of Gibraltar.

"Oh. It's you. I just called down to the mail room for you, but they said you were making rounds. I need you to hand-deliver this immediately to Judge Brennan's chambers. He's waiting for it."

"Court closes in fifteen minutes." Bruce raised his eyebrows and waited.

"I know. I have faith in you." Bruce grabbed the envelope and turned to look at the mail-laden cart.

"Leave it," David said. "You can finish in the morning." Bruce stuffed the envelope in the back pocket of his Dockers.

"Take the elevator," David said. "It'll be faster."

∾

Patrice felt the panic rising; she was beginning to doubt anyone would come. She shut off her iPod, sat down and contemplated her options. She couldn't go down the stairs and out of the building because the building was officially closed to outsiders after 5 o'clock and the single guard left on duty wouldn't let her back in without her access card, especially with no one to retrieve her from the lobby. Without her purse, she had no money and no car keys. She stood up and tried the door again. Still locked. She could bang, yell and hope someone would hear her, but with two doors to be heard through, the chances of that weren't great. She banged once, said "Hello?", but it came out as a whimper. Geez, how stupid. The firm took up six floors of the building and employed hundreds of people. Am I the only one in this place that uses the stairs?

She sat back down. No, her best bet was to sit tight until someone came through on their way home for the day. Ah, but it already is past the end of the day. She dropped her head to her hands. Danielle

would be anxious, waiting for dinner. Maybe she'd call the office looking for Patrice or maybe she was still too mad to talk to her. Patrice
sighed, pushed the play button and prepared to wait. Bocelli's voice
flooded her senses. That's what it always came down to anyway: him
and her.

She listened to two entire CDs and when they were done, started on
the opera collection, her back propped against the concrete wall, her
head lolling to the side when she dozed off. She shook herself awake,
stood and stretched. She banged half-heartedly on the door and sat
down again. Her mind drifted to the first time she'd met Bruce. She
liked the way his muscles bulged against the fabric of his polo shirt,
how a few of the small hairs on his chest peeked out just below the
neck. She noted that he had grey hair on his chest, yet the hair on his
head was still mostly black. When he caught her checking him out,
he smiled, but she, humiliated, blushed and turned away. She'd been
turning away ever since. If asked why, she couldn't have said it was due
to anything but Fear – the great immobilizer – something she knew
better than anyone. She leaned on the step and rested her head on
her arm. There were plenty of tears hanging around the periphery
of her ducts, waiting for the command from her brain to be released,
but she wouldn't give it. Instead she turned up the volume and let
Bocelli's voice thunder into her, lifting and defining her, enveloping
her with a euphoria she never felt in the gloom that defined her real
life. Bocelli's voice overrode her mental clutter and broke through to
a heart needing to slake its thirst. Patrice lay twisted, half on her side,
half on her back, clutching her head with one hand, her heart with
the other when the tears broke through. Her mouth moved in silent
prayer, and whether born of pain or ecstasy a casual observer would
have been hard-pressed to say.

❧

Bruce hadn't meant to go back to the office after delivering the letter to the judge's chambers, but he needed his workout clothes and
didn't want to go home first to get other gear. He flashed his badge

to the lone guard left on duty – during the day there were as many as six – and took the elevator up to eighteen. He grabbed his gym bag and returned to the elevator, pressing the button for down. His finger lingered a moment when he remembered the mail cart on the 22nd floor. He sighed and pressed the up button as well. Maybe by some obscene stroke of luck Patrice would still be at her desk. When he got there, the cart he'd abandoned was gone. He returned to the elevator, but after half a minute, his impatience propelled him to the stairs.

Bruce generally didn't take the stairs because of all the surveillance involved. At street level a video camera beamed your visage directly to the front desk and a monitor set off an alarm when you exited at the street rather than on the second floor where you were supposed to walk down, sign out with the guard, and then exit the building. Then there were the signs. Oh, the signs! No less than three between the first floor and street level, red signs that screamed "Warning - Not an Exit" at you in the hopes you'd return to the elevators and the guard-monitored doors. Bruce blamed it on 9/11 which is when life got weird in metropolises all over America. He once counted a dozen video surveillance cameras on top of the taller buildings in a three block area. Bruce didn't like his picture being taken much less stored on anybody's hard drive, but today he just wanted to get the hell out of work and over to the gym so warnings be damned, he was going out the side door. He threw the stairwell door open and started down, taking the stairs two at a time. He flew around a corner, down, and around again, his braided arms hoisting him over the bannister, 21, 20, 19, but when his feet landed on 18, his heart stuttered, and he dropped his gym bag. *Patrice!*

She was lying across four or five stairs, one hand clutching her heart, her arm above her head, her face contorted as if in pain. Before Bruce consciously knew what he was doing, he was down on his knees next to her, administering CPR, three quick pumps to the chest, followed by mouth-to-mouth resuscitation, letting instinct and years of training take over — pump, breathe, pump, breathe — until he felt hands, delicate yet strong, pushing against his own chest. He stopped and found himself looking directly into the eyes of love. Unfortunately, love's eyes were obscured by storm clouds.

"Get OFF of me!"

"Oh, Jesus. I'm sorry. I'm. . . so. . . sorry." The words came out in bursts and his heart was beating so fast he could barely hear what Patrice was saying as she removed her earphones and stared at him with a mixture of admonishment and fear.

"I thought you were having a heart attack."

Patrice crinkled her brows and pressed her lips so tightly together they turned white. Bruce laughed and Patrice turned the color of the red rocks of Sedona before turning away to hide her embarrassment. Bruce grabbed her hand in apology and it froze like marble inside his own.

"I'm really sorry. I didn't . . . What are you doing here, anyway?"

He heard Patrice's shallow breathing replaced by something more regular, but her hand remained stiff, and quivered in his own. Her frightened, rabbit-like quality only increased her allure and he wanted to sweep her up in his arms and kiss every part of her. Instead he squeezed her hand again and when she squeezed back ever so slightly he felt his own parts stiffen. He cleared his throat, withdrew his hand and sat next to her on the stair.

"I was coming to see you." She held up the split dictation tape. "I was hoping you could splice it for me, but I left my access card on my desk."

"How long have you been here?"

Patrice shrugged. "Couple hours. Maybe more, I don't know. I've been listening to Andrea for a while now." She wrung her hands together, adjusted her blouse, and stole a glimpse of him before turning her gaze to the small screen where she pointedly scrolled through album covers.

"I was thinking about all kinds of things. Like work, and life insurance, and what my sis – what my relatives would do if I died. I was thinking that I've never seen the Grand Canyon, that I never learned to paint, and that I'm too old to be trapped in a stairwell. I was thinking what it must have been like for the people in the World Trade Center."

Her voice fell like shards of glass at odd angles around Bruce's feet, nicking his ankles and drawing blood. He'd been here a thousand times before, listening to the people who had stared Death down in its amorphous face, pouring out the contents of their souls and laying them before him. He always accepted their gifts, like a priest, hearing confession in grace and gratitude, but today it was Patrice doing the confessing, the unflappable, transcendent, impenetrable Patrice. He squirmed on the stair and reached for her hand again. She nodded, did not withdraw; rather the action seemed to spur her into monologue.

"I was thinking about death. What it would be like. To be dead, I mean. When the time comes and I do die, will anyone remember me or even care?" Patrice blushed and fell silent. "Would my obit be one of those long, glowing tributes or something short and perfunctory: name, address, next of kin? What if I don't want 'in lieu of flowers, please send donations to?' What if I want all the flowers? Every last one of them?"

Patrice shuddered and Bruce added his other hand to the mix, his two great paws wrapped around her long, delicious fingers. When she shivered again, he wrapped an arm around her shoulder, a hand around her arm. She melted more than relaxed into him.

"When I was little, I always dreamed that a man would come along and save me." Patrice said. "Guess I can put that in the fantasy fulfilled column." Patrice blushed crimson before squeezing her hands together as if in prayer. She straightened herself and looked straight ahead at the concrete wall.

Bruce's mind was racing, his emotions colliding so furiously that he was afraid to open his mouth for fear his voice would betray him. He, too, stared straight ahead, looking for patterns in the concrete.

"I'm sorry. I didn't mean to get so personal." She gave him a little smile, picked up her iPod and stood, but the release of all her innermost secrets put her off balance and she faltered. Bruce grabbed an arm to steady her.

"I've known you for two years and in two minutes you quadrupled my database of information." He smiled. "It was my pleasure." He released her arm when she grabbed the banister. "Besides, you're not alone. People in extreme situations always share intimate details of their personal lives with strangers, stuff they wouldn't even tell a lifelong friend under normal circumstances. It relieves some of the stress, a last rites kind of thing. Or maybe it's just a shot at immortality. If even one person knows, then they won't be forgotten. You wouldn't believe some of the stuff people've told me. They go on and on about...." He stopped short, realizing too late that he'd said too much.

Patrice blushed again and compressed her lips. "I guess you can put me in the over-sharers category." She put her earphones back in and turned on the iPod. "Would you open the door for me?" she asked in a professional voice that exceeded conversational tones.

Bruce nodded, hesitating. He didn't want to lose the moment, but not knowing how to prolong it, his mind grasped at the only thing it could under the circumstances.

"What are you listening to?"

"What?" Patrice asked, removing one of the earphones.

"What are you listening to?"

"Andrea Bocelli."

Bruce's smile was so wide he felt like his face was going to crack. Patrice stared at him as if he were loony. When Bruce managed to control all twelve of the muscles his face needed to smile, he said, "Really? You like opera?"

Patrice sighed and looked at her watch. Bruce couldn't discern if it was embarrassment or impatience. Clearly, the moment was over, but he held the only card that would get her out of the stairwell, a card he insisted on playing right now be it ill-fated or a long shot. He'd waited two years and he wasn't going to wait two more. He pulled the access card out of his pocket, holding it in plain view, but making no move toward the door.

"So. Do you? Like opera, I mean."

"My mother loved opera." Patrice looked at the card in his hand and bit her lip. "I think it's good, but it's Bocelli I love. Well, that would be an understatement. I adore him." She blushed at yet another admission. "He'll be performing at Lincoln Center in two weeks. I'd give my right arm to get tickets." A 500-watt smile beamed from Bruce's rugged, tanned face.

"Well, my dear. I guess we're both in luck."

∾

It wasn't enough that he'd kissed her in the stairwell when he thought she was dying, rousing her to life with a ferocity she'd thought only wild animals were capable of, but when he said he had a friend who worked at Lincoln Center that owed him more than a few favors, Patrice felt her knees quake and her pulse race; it was all she could do to remain upright.

She tried to ignore what fate had laid out in full military dress at her feet, shoving thoughts of Bruce's large, warm hands on her heart out the right side to give room enough for Richard's nasal droning to creep in on the left. She did nothing to prep; she was too frightened. Each time the red flags rose like semaphore on a runway she turned them away. She'd figure it all out later.

She made herself so scarce at work that she'd only seen Bruce once in two weeks, on Friday.

"We still on for tomorrow?" So handsome. Warm tone. Ingratiating smile. Patrice smiled back, nodded acquiescence, rubbed her clammy hands on her skirt.

"Still okay to pick you up at five?" he asked, a bit more tentatively.

"Yeah. Sure." The words came out clipped and tinny. *I'm a moron. I'll never get through this.*

"Great," Bruce said. "That'll give us plenty of time to get into the city and have a bite before the performance." As if he'd had to reiterate. Patrice had already been over every inch of highway, the restaurant, the single candle between them illuminating his eyes, yet making it too dim for him to notice her embarrassment.... He was talking again.

"...so wear something a little on the fancy side."

"Hmmm? I'm sorry; I didn't hear the first part."

33

"I said, I have a special surprise for you, so wear something, you know, fancy." He smiled benignly as if he'd just said the most natural thing in the world.

"Well, of course. It's the Metropolitan Opera," she'd replied, but Bruce's little pronouncement sent something akin to microwaves, short little shocks of heat running through Patrice's entire body. She wiped another clammy hand on her linen skirt, necessitating a future trip to the dry cleaner, and watched him walk away.

Patrice racked her brain, but couldn't think of a single fancy item in her closet that would rise to the challenge. She would have gone shopping that very instant if she didn't have a million things to finish up before Richard returned on Saturday and what with the concert and the travel to New York, she knew she wouldn't want to come in on Sunday; she deserved that much. It was Bocelli, and her first date in a kabillion years, all wrapped up in a single evening. The thought made her throat close and she went to the kitchenette to heat water for tea.

When Patrice arrived home Friday night, she spent several hours trying on every available dress in her wardrobe, not counting the three at the dry cleaners, while Danielle sat on the bed and rubbed Vicks on her chest. Danielle had forgiven her and felt the need to give her opinion on each frock: too Plain Jane; too school m'armish; too business-casual; too maternal; too long, "show a little leg for Godsakes,"; too Episcopalian, whatever the hell that meant; too tedious; too uninviting; too Jane Doe; too; too; too, until Patrice couldn't take it anymore and admonished her sister to just shut the heck up, and because Danielle never could, she kicked her out of her room along with the vapors that trailed her like a posse. Patrice flipped on the ceiling fan and waved the door back and forth a few times to circulate the air before closing it. She lay down on the bed surrounded by dozens of dresses, all of them worthless to her at this moment, put a pillow between her legs and one over her head and fell asleep.

When Saturday dawned, so did Patrice, too nervous to sleep another instant, so she proceeded to spend the next two hours walking around the house in tight circles, straightening couch pillows, and transferring the food in the refrigerator to smaller and smaller

Tupperware containers until the fits were just right. By 9 a.m. there was nothing left to rearrange so she turned her attention to something she'd been avoiding for the last thirty-five years: herself.

When Danielle walked into the kitchen, Patrice was all in a dither, hastily downing a scalding cup of coffee so she could get to the mall before it opened.

"When's breakfast?" Danielle asked. Her face had a pillow imprint and she smelled of menthol.

"Whenever you fix it," Patrice replied.

"But I'm hungry," Danielle whined.

"Well, get busy," Patrice said.

"Patrice!"

"What?" The burn on Patrice's tongue left by the steaming coffee focused her anger at her sister and the life she'd been forced to squeeze herself into; it turned Danielle's minor request into a call to action. Patrice set out a sauce pan and a couple eggs, and made for the door like a Muslim on a jihad, leaving Danielle to sift through the rubble.

∾

Patrice's tools for this morning's assault where the only ones she had in her arsenal: a credit card with an obscene credit limit and an obtuse vision of beauty. Four hours later she returned home with a silk Chinese-esque ankle-length dress the color of eggplant, brocaded in shimmery, deeper-hued blossoms and offset intermittently with tiny groups of cascading beads the color of starlight. The traditional mandarin collar with its rolled edging and frog-and-toggle closure accentuated her slender neck, the knee length side-slits her long, shapely legs, the short sleeves her lovely, firm arms. The dress fit her every curve, suggesting there was more where that came from. The sales girl had said it looked stunning on her and having very little experience in such matters, Patrice took the woman's word for it, hoping she hadn't just been trying to make a sale. With the sales girl's help, she bought stockings, not pantyhose, and a pair of black, spaghetti-strap sandals with an understated heel that firmed her calves and still allowed her to walk.

She moved over to cosmetics and bought bunches of other supremely girly beauty products: nail polish, rouge, eye shadow and even a face mask invented by the Aztec Indians over 2,000 years ago, a powdery substance to which you added apple cider vinegar, mixed well, and slathered all over your face. When she got home, she applied the mask and twenty minutes later she looked like a green, plaster of Paris sculpture. Removing the mask proved the more difficult task and Patrice screamed when she half-pulled, half-washed the plaster off her face. Her outburst brought Danielle to Patrice's room, the ever present smell of menthol engulfing Patrice and, in her nervousness, she almost threw up.

She settled down to paint her finger and toe nails. Ultimately she removed the fingernail polish – it seemed totally out of character – but left the painted toes.

"Paint my nails next," Danielle said.

"No," Patrice replied, and would not be budged. When the paint dried, she decided to take a bath, not only to give her very flushed, post-Aztec Indian face a chance to go from pink back to flesh tone, but also to get the smell of Vicks out of her hair. Danielle sat on the toilet while Patrice was in the tub until Patrice couldn't take it anymore.

"Danielle. Could you please leave? I'm trying to relax here."

Danielle pouted, sticking her lip out as far as it would go before saying, "You're not really going to go out, are you?"

"Of course I'm going out. What do you think?"

"Well, who are you going with?"

"A man from work."

"A man?"

"Why do you say it like that? Like it's so alien?"

"Well, because you barely ever go out, and never with a man."

"That's because I'm always home taking care of you. Did you ever maybe once think that I might like to go out and do something on my own without my sister tagging along? Maybe meet some new people? Have some fun?"

Danielle took in a huge lungful of the steamy bathroom air and shook her head: "Actually, I've never even considered it." She put her pinky to her lip and chewed on the nail, then sighed. "You're saying I'm not fun."

Had Danielle noticed the blood rising in Patrice's face, noticed the tightening of the lips, the shallower breath, she might have apologized, or even explained, and the sisters could have put the whole thing behind them, chalking it up, as Patrice always did, to Danielle being Danielle. But Patrice knew that Danielle never noticed such things and no amount of Patrice's fury could have changed her sister's focus, which, like a single beam of light, was aimed only at herself.

"Out."

"But..."

"Out. Now!" Patrice threw an entire cup of bath water at her sister. The droplets missed their mark, but not the floor, where they fell like raindrops, leaving a puddle on the tile.

∾

When the doorbell rang at the preordained time, Danielle rushed to answer it, but Patrice pushed her aside and shuffled her off to the kitchen with the admonition that if she made a single sound Patrice would slit her throat. Danielle put a hand to her neck and sat in a chair to wait. Patrice closed the kitchen door and ran to the foyer. She took a deep breath, smoothed her dress and threw open the arched front door with an unhinged glee. Bruce greeted her with a mixed bouquet of fall colors: chrysanthemums, roses, carnations, alstroemeria, and goldenrod all in such abundance she needed two hands to hold it.

"Oh, they're beautiful," Patrice cooed.

"They're in good company," Bruce said, his eyes bulging. She could tell by the look on his face that the sales girl hadn't lied. They stood gazing at each other, their silence stretching out across the front step like a vast unchartered ocean, until Patrice broke the spell.

"I guess I should put these in water." She was halfway around with Bruce in tow before she realized her predicament. Danielle! She whirled back to face him and stood stone still, gripping the flowers so tightly the paper rattled. "Umm."

Bruce froze in mid-step with one foot on the threshold, the other still on the front step. They stared at each other for several seconds before Bruce said: "Shall I go wait in the..."

"Car. Yes!" Patrice said and ducked inside slamming the door so hard it landed like a slap in its frame. Patrice gasped, put a hand to her heart. She hadn't meant to do that, but the door was so heavy, and he'd been standing so close to it, practically inside the house already. She stuck one eye in the peephole her mother had added to the door soon after her father died and peered into a set of knitted eyebrows which could only mean that his nose was near to scraping the door. She gasped again, uttered a muffled "sorry" and ran off to the kitchen.

Patrice burst in, threw the flowers on the table, pulled the stool over and grabbed a vase down from on the top of the kitchen cabinets. She sprinkled in the miracle preservative pack and filled the vase with water.

"He brought you flowers?" Danielle said, reaching for one of the aromatic blooms. Patrice smacked her hand away. "Don't touch them," she said and began trimming the bottoms.

"Why? It's not like I have cooties or anything."

"'Cause they're mine, is why, and I don't want you wrecking them."

Danielle said nothing, but her hand inched back over to rest lightly on the wrapper. Spotting this, Patrice ripped the entire parcel out from under her and transferred operations to the kitchen counter.

"Soon as I finish with these, I'm leaving. There's pizza in the fridge. Just don't forget to shut the toaster oven off."

"You're not making me dinner?" Danielle looked shocked.

"You can heat up a lousy slice of pizza, Danielle."

"You'll be gone long." It came out flat, not a question.

"At least until midnight, but probably longer depending on traffic. We're going into the city."

"La-de-da."

Patrice placed the trimmed flowers in the vase, arranging them with a precision meant to quell her conflicting emotions.

"Patrice?"

"Hmmm?" Patrice knew what was coming and didn't dare look at her sister. The guilt she felt about leaving her already sat on her chest like a lead weight. Much more and she feared her heart would be crushed.

"Maybe you could stay home tonight. You can go out any old night. I'll even go with you."

Patrice turned to face her sister, a wry, half-smile on her face. "This is a date, Danielle. You know about those, don't you? I can't very well go out with you on a date, now can I?"

"But you're always going. You go off to work all the time. You're always leaving me."

Patrice finished the flowers, threw the paper away and sat down at the table across from Danielle. "To work. I go off to work. That hardly counts as going out." She reached over and squeezed Danielle's hand. "I never go out, Danielle."

"Just this once, please? I promise I won't ever ask you again."

Patrice released Danielle's hand and smacked her own on the table so hard it stung. Danielle jumped. "That's all you do is ask," she snapped. She stood up, grabbed her mother's small evening purse off the counter and tucked it under her arm. "Don't forget to shut the lights before you go to bed. I'll see you in the morning." Patrice grabbed the keys off the wall holder and headed for the door.

"NOOOOOO!" Danielle was up before Patrice made it past the kitchen door. She clawed at her sister's arm, squeezing with long unresolved fury that sent stabs of pain shooting in all directions, then went for Patrice's dress. Patrice's initial panic – my new dress! – turned to hate. She shoved Danielle away with a strength she didn't know she possessed; her sister landed flat on the floor.

Patrice hesitated. In the past, it was at this point that Patrice would have picked Danielle up, smoothed her hair, fixed her shirt and given her a bowl of ice cream. Except that something had snapped, an internal switch had been thrown, and this point was no longer that point.

Patrice bolted for the front door just as Danielle scrambled to her feet. The sisters got to the door at the same time, each struggling for control of the door handle, Patrice pulling it open while Danielle held it shut.

"Don't," Danielle said between labored breaths, "leave. You. . . can't. . . leave. . . me."

"Watch me," Patrice said, struggling to grab hold of the latch.

"I'll kill myself," Danielle said. "While you're away, I'll drink drain cleaner. I won't be here for you anymore."

Patrice stiffened and Danielle snaked her fingers underneath Patrice's to take control of the door handle. Patrice's face contorted with the strain of dozens of emotions retrieved from just as many years; guilt, rage, resentment, fear, all of them in attendance.

"I couldn't stop you the first time."

"I know, but you can now. Just stay with me. Please."

The fight wasn't over. It would never be over, Patrice saw that now. She sighed, and in one long continuous breath, released the past as easily as the body releases carbon dioxide.

"We all make our choices," Patrice whispered, and, sidestepping her sister, threw open the door.

Danielle fell back and landed on the living room carpet. She was crying. "You won't be able to live with yourself. You know you won't. You. . ."

Patrice gently closed the door and stepped into the late afternoon sunlight. She couldn't hear what Danielle was yelling inside and she didn't stop to decipher it. She ran to Bruce's car and climbed in the front seat before he had a chance to get out and open it for her. She slammed the door and buckled herself in.

"I'm ready," she said, staring at the front door as if expecting aliens to emerge.

"Are you all right?" Bruce asked. "You look upset."

Patrice's cheeks were flushed and her eyes wet. "I'm okay. Really. Can we just go?"

"Sure," Bruce said. He started the car and put it in reverse, releasing his foot from the brake.

"WAIT!" Patrice yelled. Bruce jumped. "Umm, I mean, I forgot something," she said, in more subdued tones.

Bruce put the car in park; Patrice bolted and ran inside, slamming the door behind her.

The living room was empty.

"Danielle," Patrice called. Then louder: "Danielle? Where are you?" Patrice half-walked, half-ran to the kitchen, gave it a quick survey. Empty. She moved to the dining room. Empty. She took the stairs two at a time and checked each of the bedrooms, throwing open closet doors and checking under beds. The smell of Vicks that had permeated Danielle's room like a third person was gone. Patrice checked the bathrooms. Empty. She stood in the stairwell and screamed, "DANIELLE!" but no one answered. Patrice began to shake, then crumpled to her knees. She grasped the banister as if it were the last blade of grass, and after a minute, she raised herself up and walked slowly down the stairs.

Patrice stood stock still in the middle of the empty living room. The only sounds she heard were the creaks and groans of her old house. She breathed deeply, her first full breath in thirty-five years. She smiled, a small, concealed thing at first – if she had a fan, she would have hidden behind it – but the smile wouldn't be contained, rather it grew, dragging happiness and relief along with it until a giggle bubbled up, then laughter, followed by a guffaw which turned into what an outside observer might term maniacal. When Patrice was spent, she walked over to the stereo, pulled her favorite Bocelli CD off the rack and headed toward the door.

"Goodbye, Danielle," she said to the empty house and opened the door to her new life.

Finito

List Of 55

~

There are no random events. Every incident, every encounter, no matter how insignificant, absurd, or immense is by design. There are no coincidences.

On the day after her 25th birthday, following a night of hard drinking and little reflection, Belinda decided to change her name from the perky Belinda, a name which inspired thoughts of Spanish Conquistadors, lovely maidens, adventure and high seas, to the more staid Constance, one that evoked a feeling of monks and robes, masses said in Latin, and wooden blocks for pillows. She based this on the assumption that, among other things, a woman's name revealed her destiny and that by changing hers, she might imbue the next quarter century of her life with a stability that had been sorely lacking in the first.

Belinda fell out of bed and hustled – as best as she could given that her brain had been reconfigured to resemble Rotelli – down to

City Hall to do the deed. Had she made it, things might have turned out differently, but fate, that mischievous interloper, saw fit to intervene and a block from City Hall, Belinda ran smack into her future ex-husband, or rather, he drove his bike into her as she was jaywalking on a yellow. It wasn't the most auspicious beginning for the ill-fated lovers, but the serendipity appealed to Belinda, and since she'd not yet tasted life as Constance, she decided to go for it. A few more minutes as Belinda wasn't going to kill her, was it? What she didn't realize was that those few minutes would stretch into a decade and it would be that decade which would almost kill her.

Belinda wasn't a beauty like her sister, Simone, whose natural flaxen hair, fine marble skin and high cheekbones made her the hands down choice for Prom Queen in any high school. What Belinda had that Simone did not were brilliant, watery-blue eyes that suggested an emotional depth both subtle and vulnerable, a vulnerability she'd kept hidden the last dozen years as a self-protective measure. When she collided with Ted of the Two Personalities, it was this particular feature that Ted couldn't help but notice even as he was running her down halfway up 15th Street, just south of Market.

"Oh, Jesus – I'm sorry," were the first words Belinda heard her future ex-husband mutter as the sidewalk became one with her head and the curb ravaged her elbow.

"Uh–ooow," was Belinda's first reply, denoting simultaneous injury and surprise. She held her elbow with her left hand, the back of her head with the right, and, curling into a fetal position, formed her own shell, a living Rodin sculpture. Belinda probed the tender spot on her head and checked her hand for blood. She squinted up into the sun, trying to place a face with the pain, but despite the exceptional beauty of her eyes, Belinda's vision wasn't the best.

"Here, let me see," the second sentence uttered by her future ex. "Oh," her second reply.

Long delicate fingers probed her head while Pain shoved a million tiny pitchforks around inside, forcing tears to the corners of eyes sealed tighter than a jam jar.

43

"No blood. Not on your head, anyway," Ted confirmed, watching the blood drip from her elbow. "So at least there's that." He helped Belinda sit up and wrapped her elbow with his handkerchief. Ted seemed proud of this particular, old-fashioned sensibility, and after he finished he got a good look at her. "Aphrodite," he muttered, and later explained to Belinda that as an architect, he preferred the Greek, Aphrodite, to the Roman, and more common, Venus.

By this time, several passersby had stopped to render their assistance, help which Ted, Belinda would later discover, would have been glad to take on any other morning, predisposed as he was to having other people unravel his messes. The moment he got a glimpse at the ocean blue of Belinda's eyes all was lost, and for the first time in his life Ted thought about someone other than himself. That it happened at all was monumental. That it only lasted a few minutes was simply foreshadowing.

As for her part, it was the first time in Belinda's recent history that someone had lowered a genuine hand to her in assistance. Since first impressions are uniformly the lasting ones, Ted assumed the title of Rescuer, a position for which he was wholly unsuited. For most of the next decade, despite years of disappointments and truckloads of evidence to the contrary, nothing Ted did could dispossess him of his newly acquired station. He had picked her up when she was down, that she knew; the fact that he was directly responsible for her initial downward spiral warranted not even a footnote in their brief, shared history book.

"Are you all right?" Ted asked, wrapping a protective arm around her. "I'm so sorry."

Another monumental moment: Ted VanSant never apologized, mainly because gods didn't have to. His mother had named him Theodore, from the Greek, meaning "divine gift." So far, life had done little to disabuse him of the notion.

They sat side-by-side on the sidewalk, her hands in her lap, his arm around her shoulder.

"What did the magnet say to the paperclip?" Ted asked.

"What?"

"I'm attracted to you." Belinda giggled and Ted was emboldened.

44

"What's the square root of sixty-nine?"

"I don't know," Belinda shrugged.

"Eight something."

Belinda was stunned for a moment, then gave a hearty guffaw before Pain caught her laughter in a choke-hold, forcing her to suck in her breath and drop her chin to her chest.

Ted fell silent and rubbed her back, looking both embarrassed and aroused. Belinda molded herself into the crook of his shoulder and drew a deep, satisfied breath. When the paramedics arrived twenty minutes later, they'd already lived lifetimes in each other's arms.

∽

We are none of us as blameless as we think. Nor are we as guilty. Each of us is born with a tally sheet of our debts, accumulated over lifetimes, both past and present, which we need to make good on before we can move forward. The beauty of life is the choices it presents us. Do we choose to pay our debts with pain and suffering, for this is what the universe will exact from us if we fail to do it consciously? Or do we choose the path of wisdom and transformation, the power of love? We are poised for a spiritual rebirth, but in order to do so, we must first Pay The Piper.

Ted and Belinda were an unlikely pair, but a decent match. He needed an audience, she needed to laugh more; he was always up for fun, she had not had enough; he was irresponsible, she could balance a check book and make sure there were milk and eggs in the fridge; he loved to lounge in bed and snuggle and nurse his hang over, she loved to lounge in bed and snuggle because he would rub her back, and for the first time in her life she felt cherished. They were in the middle of a whirlwind courtship – less than six months since the fated hit and sit – when Belinda discovered she was pregnant. They got married and bought a fixer-upper. Ted was an architect. How hard could it be?

Yet two weeks before the baby was born, the house was still a wreck, and Ted was making daily stops at the local bar. The self-made man that Belinda thought she'd married, the epitome of health, riding his bike to work (his car was in the shop the day he'd run into her and he'd bummed his last ride of the week), running his own firm (he never could work with anyone), spending money generously (he had debt to match), was all a ruse, and as time collapsed, the caricature of the man emerged, stepping out of her dream and into their bedroom.

At 2 a.m., a malodorous vapor, a reeking stench of epic proportions presaged Ted's entrance into the room: stale beer and cigarettes. Belinda's hormonally-enhanced nostrils flared and snorted her to full consciousness. She rarely slept soundly anymore, the baby saw to that, and her eyes flew open as Ted slid across the threshold. He hovered over the bed and through slitted eyes she watched him watching her. He undressed slowly, lacking the equilibrium to stand. His silhouette was bobbing and weaving against the backdrop of the curtain-free window, the man many shades of grey denser than the muted grays of the night sky behind.

He removed the last article of clothing, and flopped naked onto the bed where sleep immediately took him. Belinda tried to loosen the covers beneath him, but he was too heavy. She grabbed the quilt draped over the foot of their sleigh bed and covered him up to his neck. Then she smelled it, the juvenile delinquent of bad smells, snaking its way through the cigarette stink like a flashlight cutting through the dark. It was cheap, like the toilette water Simone used to douse herself in. Damn the hormones that gave a pregnant woman a superhero's sense of smell.

Belinda jabbed Ted in the ribs. He grunted and rolled over. She pulled the quilt off and crawled down to his feet, sniffing every part of him on the way back up, stopping for more than a moment at his privates, a bloodhound on the trail of the enemy's scent. She continued up Ted's torso to the neck and face, the smell was more concentrated here and she wanted to gag, to punch the crap out of him, but resisted the urge and moved on to the top of his head. There was not one inch of her husband where that woman, whoever she was, had not been. Rage propelled her and before she knew it, she was punching Ted's back. That he barely raised an arm in self-defense was a testimony to his level of intoxication. Getting no reaction, she did what any self-respecting woman in her place would have done. She placed both her feet in the small of his back and with all her might, shoved his adulterous butt out of bed. He hit the floor with a hard thud and an "ooph." She sniffed at the quilt, already suffused with the stench, and threw it down after him.

Belinda fell back on her pillow, hugged her belly and stared through watery eyes at the ceiling. She was adrift, holding tight to the tow line of illusion that was dragging her through life's emotionally murky waters, rising to the surface on occasion to gulp a big lung full of air. She searched for a distant shore, but there was none in sight. What would life be like as Constance? Was it too late? After a lengthy internal debate she decided to hold fast, and cling to her preconceived notions, choosing the (relative) safety and security of her marriage to Ted over the fear and uncertainty of a life lived alone which, she didn't realize, was the real definition of a prostitute. For when it came to prostitution, it was not so much any particular act as it was the intent, and it was Belinda's intent to have somebody, anybody, take care of her, even Ted, even if the cost was high and the living conditions were less than stellar. And since bodies in motion stay in motion, their paths were set, their routines begun, and for the next decade, life for Ted and Belinda went on in this linear, yet circuitous fashion.

∽

The negative thoughts of mankind are like airborne diseases. Similar to germs fanning out across an airspace, like a cough from an open mouth to a waiting nose, the negative thoughts disperse, find a random target and lock on, hitting the ill, the defenseless, and in many cases, the self-loathers. No one is immune. Just try watching the news for three continuous hours and see what your body feels like. In this manner, negative thoughts, like germs, assure their proliferation.

Simone sat at the kitchen table reading her horoscope in *Cosmo*. The table was a fourth hand relic that Simone picked up at a flea market. It had a thin plastic veneer painted an unimaginative brown, designed to look like real wood. The corner was peeling and had started to curl and the soft fleshy part of Simone's arm caught on it every time she brought her cigarette to her lips.

"Damn it," she muttered, and took a long, slow drag on her Marlboro Light. She examined the scratch and exhaled every last molecule of smoke in her lungs as if exorcising a demon.

The stream of smoke engulfed Belinda's head where she sat at the table doing her homework. Rather than shrink from the offending vaporous cloud, Belinda inhaled deeply which rendered her a bit lightheaded.

When Simone realized that the cloud had taken a direct flight into Belinda's nasal cavity, she began waving her arms in Belinda's immediate airspace, attempting to disperse the smoky particles.

"What are you doing?" a wide-eyed and woozy Belinda asked.

"Trying to keep you from getting cancer. Don't they teach you anything in 5th grade?" Simone looked incredulous. "Second-hand smoke is even worse than actually smoking."

"I know," Belinda shrugged.

"Then why don't you go outside when I smoke?"

"I think you're the one who's supposed to go outside."

"No way, José. It's too damn cold out," Simone replied, exhaling another toxic cloud.

Belinda took this one in like the first, except this time she held her breath.

Simone punched her in the arm. "Stop that! If you want to smoke I'll give you the damn cigarettes. Just quit it, you little shit." Simone shook a butt out of the pack. "I've seen the commercials and I won't be considered negligent."

"Giving me a cigarette is no different." Belinda took the proffered tobacco, sniffed it, twirled it between her fingers and tested it out in her mouth. She took a fake drag and released the air, blowing imaginary smoke rings, before setting the butt on her notebook.

"I don't want to smoke. I want to watch you smoke." Belinda wanted to explain that breathing in Simone's smoke was like breathing in a piece of her, not the most gratifying one, but a piece of a puzzle that Belinda had found herself on too many occasions putting together alone. She wanted to say these things, but Simone watched her with such disgust that Belinda said nothing, just picked up the cigarette and handed it back.

"You had your mouth all over it." Simone said, pushing it away. "Keep it."

∾

It's the collective hatred of mankind that's the cause of all disasters. And since hatred is so in vogue these days, so are disasters. Simply acknowledging hatred is enough to keep it alive as the tiniest drop may reap exponential amounts in return. Even those rooted in love practice moments, sometimes hours, of hate.

The next day, Simone was in the kitchen making tea when Belinda breezed in, intent on making lunch. Simone blocked her way, standing in the middle where the stove, sink and refrigerator formed a U, seething like a volcano, spewing hunks of molten anger, filling the kitchen with her heat. Belinda watched, externally unfazed, internally on the verge of aggravated assault. Hate raced down Simone's conical sides, a trajectory fueled by ridicule, and headed straight for Belinda. Belinda didn't hate Simone, not like Simone hated her. Belinda just had visions of punching the crap out of her now and then.

Simone was fourteen when Belinda was born to become Nicole's *raison d'être*, the pretty little baby that her mother doted on after Bert took a mistress and banished Nicole from their restaurant. Nicole nursed Belinda, the star of her now limited universe and Nicole's consolation prize, while Simone nursed her anger. Nicole poured her heart into the child, a heart that previously had been unavailable to Simone because of Nicole's demanding work schedule.

After a few initial fights with Nicole, Simone didn't say much, just stock-piled the hurt. When Nicole died, Bert – Belinda never called him dad – remarried that chain-smoking, baby-faced floozy and moved back to France. Bert left Simone, then twenty-two, in charge of nine-year old Belinda with the promise of a generous monthly stipend. But since neither Bert nor Nicole had taught Simone how to handle money, Simone paid the rent and then quickly spent the rest on cosmetics, cigarettes and other non-essentials. At times, there was barely a thing to eat in the house. Simone blamed Belinda for supplanting her. Yet while Belinda was an obligation, she was the only thing that ensured a steady paycheck. So Simone made the best of it, bossing Belinda around, and contenting herself with the errant shove or abusive comment.

Simone glared at Belinda now as she dunked her tea bag, her eyes daring Belinda to speak.

Belinda took the bait. "You know, it doesn't work any faster if you dunk it. You're supposed to let it steep."

Simone smirked. "What are you, the tea expert?"

"Just look at the box. It says steep for three to five minutes, not dunk repeatedly." Belinda tried to hide a smile.

Simone flung the soggy tea bag at Belinda's face, but it missed and skidded to a watery halt on the counter top, splattering the nearby appliances.

Belinda grimaced. "Bitch," she said. "I hate you."

Simone half-choked, half-laughed, and left the room in a huff.

Minutes later, Belinda stood in front of Simone's door, hand poised. Simone had stuffed a towel in the crack below, but she'd been sloppy about it. Through the gaps, pungent whiffs of marijuana smoke escaped. Belinda stood there, frozen with indecision, until, seemingly of its own volition, her knuckles began a steady rap on the door.

"I'm busy," came Simone's muffled reply.

Belinda was persistent; the knocking continued, a monotone, like a funeral dirge.

"Belinda. . . I'm warning you."

Belinda's stomach jumped. Saliva coursed through her mouth. She wanted to turn and go back to her room, but her feet were rooted in place while her hand continued its inexorable knocking. It was hypnotic, and she was lost in the defiance of the moment, her hand behaving as if it had a mind of its own.

Simone threw open the door and her supercilious gaze locked on Belinda like a laser. Belinda soaked it up, a human solar panel. She wasn't aware of time until the legs moved, the ones on top of the mattress. Belinda peeked around Simone's loosely tied robe, but her exposed left boob was nothing compared to the unknown legs attached to a naked torso, lying on the bed. Belinda's throat emitted a shocked, halting protest.

Simone laughed. "Next time, mind your own business," she growled, slamming the door in Belinda's face.

"I wish you were dead!" Belinda shrieked. Simone's breathy cackle reverberated in Belinda's ears long after she'd reached the safety of her own room.

∾

Chaos - uncertainty; pain - fear of failure; suffering - lack of self-worth: flip sides of the same coin; twin daughters of different mothers. Unless and until we believe in what we may not yet be able to see, know that without a doubt that everything really will be okay and feel that we deserve it, darkness will prevail.

Simone sat naked on the edge of the bathtub, tremulous and chain smoking, her brow drenched in perspiration. Thick soupy clouds bullied the oxygen out of the room, a combination of steam from the running shower and the burning of thousands of tobacco leaves. Although running at full bore, the ceiling fan failed to clear even a swath of fresh air.

Simone tossed the cigarette in the toilet and coughed. She put her hand to her mouth, then fell to her knees, draping her head over the bowl. Next came the dry heaves which produced some bile, but little else. She flushed it down along with her last two cigarette butts, and pulled herself to her feet, inching her way to the tiny sink. Everything about this room was tiny, with the exception of Simone's fear which in the last few days had grown enormous and daunting. She turned on the tap, sucking water as it descended, swirled and was gone. Simone would have followed it if she could have contorted her body to squeeze down the drainpipe. After a few more days of living on nothing but cigarettes and water, she soon might. But right now, she couldn't think of anything to do but starve it out, if it could be starved. How did that stuff work? Would she have to die first? Simone had been through it once before and it ruined her life. She couldn't do it again.

She started hacking, unable to catch her breath. The closet of a bathroom had finally gotten too smoky, even for her. Simone opened a window, looking for relief and found no more than a cloudy, half-hearted sky. Lacking the strength to flip it the bird, she coughed in the direction of the sun. Simone examined her stomach, poking and prodding the soft periphery as if it might produce a clue. "Anybody in there," she asked her uterus. She banged the toilet lid shut and dropped herself on it. Someone knocked at the door.

"Are you all right?" Belinda's voice, timid and scared, snaked its way through the molecules comprising the particle board, the waves of sound co-mingling with the stationary matter as if stopping off for cock-tails. By the time they reached Simone's ears, all that remained was a muffled noise, like someone speaking from the bottom of a sock drawer. To Simone it sounded worse than country music at a hundred decibels.

She turned on the tap, dipped her mouth to catch it, checked her reflection in the mirror. *Shit.* Simone smoothed her hair, swallowed some bile and opened the door. Belinda's twelve-year old mouth gaped at her naked sister, but Simone said nothing as she brushed past, a cloud of smoke tailing her like a bloodhound.

"What's wrong with you," Belinda called after her. "Are you sick?"

Simone whirled around with the force of a mid-western tornado. Before Belinda could blink, Simone slapped her face so hard Belinda fell to her knees. "Yeah. Sick of you."

Belinda tried to hit back, but Simone had already cleared an arm's length of Belinda's air space and was heading for her room.

"You jerk," Belinda screamed after her, holding her hand to her face. "I'm telling."

"Who you gonna call?" Simone said, and slammed the door, put-ting the punctuation mark on Belinda's fate.

∞

One of the principle tenets of physics is that like attracts like. If we apply this law to our lives, we see that our thoughts are magnets, pulling to us that which we think about all day long. If your thoughts, words and deeds are harmonious and based on love, then love and harmony is what will be returned to you. Conversely, the mind that dwells on scarcity and lack, on hate and distrust, a mind that worries itself with an endless stream of obsessions, big or small, that mind will draw like flies to honey the disharmonious experiences. It's a universal law – one that can't be altered.

That Belinda married an architect was no surprise. She thought by marrying Ted, she could circumnavigate her rocky beginnings and sail into more stable waters, build a foundation rooted in *terra firma*. She'd been swimming against the current almost her whole life and if she feared her newfound legs might give her a reverse seasickness it was a risk she was willing to take. A few months after Kyle was born, with their respective family roles defined and entrenched, Belinda was feeling particularly out of sorts. It was November of her 26th year, and Ted and Belinda were about to have their first significant fight, the substance of which would set a precedent for years to come, the repetitive pattern acted out into the twilight of their life together.

Ted staggered in, slamming the door behind him. Belinda and Kyle were asleep on the couch, Kyle with his delicate pink baby mouth latched firmly onto his mother's right breast. At the sound of the slamming door, Kyle's little baby dreams scattered like roaches in the glare of a kitchen bulb and he let out a wail that could wake Nostradamus, dead these five hundred years. Too bad, too, that he didn't wake the famed prognosticator, since mother and baby could have taken great advantage of his prowess at this particular crossroads. For had he awoken, Nostradamus probably would have told Belinda to get the hell out, and quick, rather than waste her next nine years replaying the old martyr CDs. Unfortunately, post-baby hormones wreak havoc with a woman's emotional state, not to mention what fear of the unknown will do, so assuming Nostradamus were alive and still had the use of his larynx, it's likely Belinda wouldn't have listened to him anyway.

"Where've you been?" Belinda asked, more sad than angry.

"Out," Ted replied, more drunk than empathetic.

Belinda grimaced, sat up. She'd been looking for love and got attitude. Ted had no clue what she went through, what with hormone fluctuations that would bring Atlas to his knees, and he cared even less about child-rearing. Ted loved his son; he just couldn't handle the responsibility of dealing with an infant.

"I told you I was working late," Ted explained, softening. He sat down next to her and stroked her hair as if she were a Labrador, then sniffed his newborn son's head.

Belinda loved when he did those things. She shrugged and nuzzled into his shoulder, into her safe spot, prepared to forgive him for abandoning her to tedium. But moody manic-depressives who like to drink know no holiday. Like that, Ted's mind snapped and crackled into overdrive.

"All right, let me up. I've got work to do."

"Work? But it's almost ten. Why don't we relax a while and then go to bed?"

"Easy for you to say. You're not paying the bills." He pushed her head from its nesting spot and began to rise. She rested her hand on his thigh to stop him.

"Enough, B. I gotta get up." He rose again.

Days with a colicky baby are long with no one to talk to and Belinda had been feeling the abject loneliness as of late. "Ted," she said with a hint of pleading in her voice. She pulled on his sleeve.

Whether it was the immediacy of the gesture, the tone of her voice, or the fact that he was tanked, Belinda would never know, but it cost him his equilibrium. He fell backwards and banged his head against the wall behind the couch.

Then, as if in slow motion, she saw him sit up, saw his profile turn to her followed by a hand, rising out of a blur of light, a perfect arc, like a rainbow that ends at the pot of gold, but this one ended at her left cheek. She yelped in surprise and a bit from the pain, the open palm inflicting a lot less than a closed fist would have. There was a stinging quality that wasn't on her cheek a moment ago and her eyes grew wide as pomegranates with shock. It was a look she'd lose over the years as she got accustomed to the script, but right now the newness of it was dilating her pupils. Tears gathered, forming support groups in the corners of her eyes. Belinda banished them while her vision took on a refractive quality and her heart followed dutifully. Her mind was preoccupied with its search for the even older tapes, those musty 8-tracks she was sure she'd thrown out the day she'd married Ted and exorcized Simone from her life forever. Simone with her angry eyes and outstretched hand.

He stared at her, befuddled. Perhaps her reticence brought him back. He would lose that too, over time – her failure to react would become all the more reason to strike – but right now he was staring at his hand with a look that could only be interpreted as confusion. He looked so sad and vulnerable that Belinda instinctively reached out and touched him.

"Oh, B, I'm.... What just happened?" His voice had a rough yet soggy quality, full of regret, Scotch, and wet sandpaper. He cleared his throat. His hands were trembling.

Belinda watched them shake, watched him do nothing to stop them. She couldn't stand to see him weak for where did that leave her? It wasn't Simone standing there – just Ted. So rather than walk, she waited. She touched her cheek; the sting was already subsiding.

He put his hand to her face and held it as if it were a piece of fine porcelain. "I don't understand," he said, as he laid his head on her shoulder and squeezed their son to his breast.

And because she had her rose-colored glasses on, the ones with the pre-formed images of Ted the Rescuer, and because her vision hadn't cleared enough for her to see through to the other images of Ted the Manic Depressive and Ted the Alcoholic, she smoothed his hair and uttered the only words she could under the circumstances.

"It's okay. I know you didn't mean it."

∽

Experience is like a mirror to the heart. Even if you are a pacifist by nature, yet do nothing to eradicate the violence in your heart, then violence will persist. If you witness a violent act, it is because on some level your soul believes violence has a rightful place in the world. Ironically, it is self-love, not the ever popular "peace on earth" that is the crucial first step toward eliminating violence.

Belinda dumped the grocery bags and a car seat-laden Kyle down on the counter, then skittered down the hall to the bathroom. The second she sat down, Kyle woke up. She was in mid-pee when he started to cry and wiping when his crescendo reached a full-out wail. Why she had gotten pregnant the very minute her doctor had given her clearance she didn't know. Or rather, she did. Ted wanted another baby. "Just have them and get the baby part over with," he'd said. But it was becoming clearer by the moment that shuffling an infant and a toddler was going to be some kind of Chris Angel *Mind Freak.*

She balanced Kyle on her hip with one hand, put groceries away with her free hand, and wished for the millionth time that Nicole was still alive. Women with babies need their mothers around like a twenty-four hour customer service hotline.

Belinda had stashed everything but a bag of dry goods and the ice cream cake – they were celebrating his first tooth – when Kyle started whining, then crying, then screaming. She stuck a rattle in his hand and a binky in his mouth, enough to buy time to finish unpacking, but Kyle would not be appeased. So they went to his room to nurse and change his diaper and have a lie down.

Two hours later, mother and baby were snoring, intertwined on Belinda and Ted's bed when Belinda was awakened by the shake of a rough hand. She opened one eye and squeezed the other tight, then reversed it in seesaw fashion.

"Hi," she whispered. Ted glared at her.

"What's the matter?"

Ted pointed to the door. A reluctant Belinda covered Kyle and rose to follow her husband, closing the door quietly behind her.

"What the hell's going on?" he snapped.

"Um, it's called a nap. You should try it sometime." She closed the bedroom door and made her way to the stairs, putting distance between them and their sleeping baby.

"I'm talking about this." Ted turned, demonstrating a shoulder, arm and pant leg covered in Vanilla Fudge Ripple.

"Why do you have ice cream all over you?"

Belinda stopped moving the moment realization hit her cerebellum, with one foot on the first step going down. The second step was both shorter and longer: shorter in that it encompassed all the remaining twelve steps to the first floor in one giant arc; longer in that the two seconds it took her to go from the first step to the ground floor seemed like an hour, maybe even a day, the kind one spends in a hospital emergency room, awaiting the fated prognosis of a loved one, the dread and fear bunching up in your gut, your heart, your throat cavity, sitting like a two-by-four wedged in a one-by-three inch space.

She didn't think to raise a hand to stop him. Perhaps she'd seen it coming in that blink before: before the shove, before the bike accident, before the first fist hit her cheekbone. It really was more like a playground shove, rough, but not enough to do any real damage, yet because of her precarious and imbalanced position, one foot on the step, the other foot already in the space between, a well-timed whisper would have sent her spiraling. In that instant, Belinda gave the Flying Gambinis a run for their money and once she had lift, she didn't touch down until she reached the bottom. Unfortunately, someone forget to put up the safety net and she hit, belly first, with a ground-shaking thud. On the bright side, she stuck the landing.

Ted was down the stairs after her in a second, his words sputtering out in a rush and a tumble.

"Jesus, Belinda . . . I'm. . .oh, God . . . sorry. I didn't . . . I just touched you. I mean – oh God, are you all right?" Belinda managed to nod just as Kyle, roused by the noise, started to wail.

"Kyle," she breathed, and nodded her head in that direction. Ted took the stairs, two at a time, pieces of the chocolate crackle filling dripping off his suit jacket and pant leg as he climbed. He returned, whimpering in tandem with his son. Belinda leaned against the wall, holding her sleeve to her bloody nose.

Ted's face was ashen; he looked sick.

"Tissue," Belinda said.

Ted jumped up just as Kyle was reaching for his mother and almost dropped the child. Belinda's shrill cry caused Kyle to jerk and begin a plaintive wail all over again. Ted set the box of tissues next to Belinda.

A squirming Kyle could not be kept from his mother so Belinda set him on her lap while Ted administered to her nose, pinching the bridge to staunch the blood flow, pushing the hair back from her face and making soothing noises. Belinda noticed the tears gathering in the corners of Ted's eyes, and tried to keep her compassion in check, but it was no use. She allowed him to encircle them in his arms; mother, father and baby huddled together.

Belinda was the first to speak: "Do you find it strange that this is what we do best together? Somehow you injure me and we sit around all lovey-dovey while you tend to my wounds."

"B, I didn't mean to . . . It was barely a shove. How was I supposed to know you were going to fall down the stairs?"

Belinda sighed. The 8-tracks again. She had a vague inkling that this was one of those times – times when you could change the course of things if you just said left instead of right, no instead of yes, if you just held on to that single blade of grass and said you weren't walking an inch past. The highway was shutting down, that much was clear, but the alternate routes weren't clearly marked, and she had terrible vision. Kyle was playing with the two days of stubble on his father's face, rubbing it with his chubby little hands and laughing, and suddenly she was so tired.

"I need a drink of water," she said.

"C'mon. Let's get you off the floor." Ted pulled her to her feet and into the kitchen, sweeping around the wide puddle of ebony and ivory melting in harmony on the kitchen floor. Ted handed Belinda a bottle of water from the fridge.

Belinda took a sip, handed Ted the baby, and stood up. "I gotta clean this mess up," she said, before sliding back down to the ground.

"Are you okay?"

"I don't feel so good. My belly."

Ted groaned so soulfully that Belinda was going to ask if his belly hurt. "Okay, off to bed. I'll get this," he said, lifting a chin toward the mess.

"But Kyle needs to be fed and someone's got to make dinner."

"Go, B. I'll take care of it." He picked her up. "I'm worried about you."

Belinda shuffled up the stairs while Ted took to the kitchen with the baby.

The next morning she found the mop standing against the wall, the majority of the ice cream intertwined in its fibers, the rest a dry, sticky mess on the floor, except for what was stuck to the counter and cabinet doors. The remains of Kyle's baby food sat out, the crusty fallen bits solidly adhered to the kitchen table. Three beer bottles and an empty carton of Chinese take-out waved to her from the sink. Belinda threw it all away, tossed the bottles in the recycling, and started in on the counters and floors.

Two days later, while sitting on the toilet, she began a hemorrhage that wouldn't quit. The next day, Belinda was baby free.

ॐ

It isn't enough to cope with our fears. We need to conquer them.

Ted sat at his drafting table in his favorite room, the home office he and Belinda had built as an addition to the house. There was a big bay window and French doors that opened onto a brick patio, housing an outdoor kitchen for entertaining. Several hundred acres of working farm lay beyond their fastidiously maintained lawn, cordoned off by a property boundary consisting of several hundred feet of woods, but for one area directly behind Ted's office, about thirty feet in length, where the farm abutted Ted and Belinda's land in a horseshoe shape. In this space there was nothing to obstruct Ted's bucolic view of the world and the thought of living the entirety of life in this room much appealed to him. Here with his drafting table and pencils, his lithographs of Doric, Ionic and Corinthian columns, his 18th century rendering of the Greek Meander Key, the oldest Greek pattern on the temples, here with symmetry lining the walls next to his back issues of *Architectural Digest*, Ted felt safe inside the millimeters and straight edges of his blueprints with a peephole to the world outside.

Belinda walked in to find Ted hunched over his desk. She gave him a peck on the cheek. He pulled her onto one leg.

"How's Kyle?" Ted asked.

"Still running a fever, but it's going down. He's sleeping again." She brushed back a lock of Ted's sandy brown hair. "Hopefully he'll be better by tomorrow. I don't want him to miss. Kindergarten's tough."

Ted chuckled. "Define tough."

"Homework."

"Yeah, well, we're paying enough to send him." He looked up and gave Belinda a thousand-watt smile before returning his attention to his drawings. "Speaking of which..."

"Which?"

"I think it's time."

"For?"

"You to go back to school."

"And study what? I'm not good at anything other than being a mom."

"Architecture."

"That's a pipe dream."

"You know you want it."

"Yeah and I want to sail around the world, but I'm afraid of the sheer volume of water and besides, I just don't have what it takes."

Ted turned his face to his wife. "You've got an incredible eye. This house, this room," he said, his arm fanning out to take it all in, "it's just as much you as me."

"Are you giving me a compliment?"

"Maybe." Ted laughed and leaned back into his work. "Just don't get used to it."

"Believe me, I won't." Belinda leaned her elbows on the desk, her chin on her cupped hands and sighed.

"B, don't start." He hated when she got all imperial on him. He was feeling good today and nothing was going to blow it.

"It's just like you're two different people. Ted the good husband and father and Ted the raving lunatic."

Ted shrugged. "Blame my parents."

"We can all blame our parents, Ted. Your dad might have beaten you, but at least he came home at night."

Ted stood up so abruptly Belinda was forced to stand or drop to the floor. She turned to her husband, expecting a tirade – they stood inches apart, and for a few moments, simply looked at each other – but instead, he picked her up and carried her to the plush leather arm-chair and sat down with her on top of him. Belinda giggled.

"I know where you can get a job." Ted stroked her arm. "I'm too busy to handle it all. I'm thinking of hiring someone."

"Really, Ted. That's great."

"Be nice to do it together." He smiled his one-dimple smile. The one she could never refuse. "Plus right now I'm flush. So take advantage of me while you can." He kissed her on the nose.

Belinda smiled. "I'll think about it."

"Mommy?" Kyle appeared in the doorway, rubbing one eye. Belinda moved to stand, but Ted pulled her back.

"I got him," Ted said. "Sit here and enjoy the view." He lifted Belinda and set her back down in the chair, kissing her on the lips before turning to scoop up his son.

"Hey buddy. What can we do to get you fixed up?"

"I think ice cream would fix me," Kyle said.

Ted smiled. "Ah, the healing power of ice cream. I think we should test the theory." He poked Kyle in the ribs. "How many kinds do we have?"

"Two. No, three," Kyle said, squirming.

"We should try 'em all. One of them might be more powerful. We want to make sure we're taking the right stuff, eh?" Kyle gave Ted a sincere head nod.

"Let's do it." Ted tossed Belinda a wink and carried Kyle from the room.

∾

Are you stuck in a rut? Do you keep making the same mistakes over and over again? Does everyone take advantage of you? Is your energy running wild, like unharnessed electricity in search of a wire? Perhaps you need a spiritual colonic? Or maybe it's time to listen to your Soul.

At 5:30 a.m., the clock radio sang itself to life, pulsating with the monotone beat of some gangsta rap. Kyle must have been playing with the dial again. Belinda hit the snooze, shutting a bleary eye against the inevitability of the day's events. Ten minutes later, Eminem sang about farting on the dance floor. She nudged Ted in the ribs and chuckled.

"They're playing your song." In response, Ted farted and rolled over, ignoring both Belinda and Eminem.

When Belinda got out of the shower she heard the repetitive beep, beep, beep of Ted's alarm. She stuck her head out the bathroom door.

"Ted!" she whispered. "Kyle." Ted rolled over, shut the alarm, and went back to sleep.

Two hours later, Belinda stood at a drafting table in Ted's office, rendering drawings for a new fitness center. Ted let the previous draftsman go when Belinda came on board "to free up enough money to pay for your salary." She didn't make much, but, technically, she still had another year to go before she got her Masters in Architecture and since working with Ted qualified as an internship, she couldn't really complain. Plus the office was in a rehabbed warehouse with high ceilings, enormous windows and a beautiful view of the city. The drafting tables were scattered randomly, giving the place a feeling of play and ease.

It was her first truly professional job and Belinda approached it with a sense of urgency: her very existence depended on the quality of her work. Do a good job, receive praise. If someone needed her, it followed that they'd have to love her. Of late, though, Belinda began to notice the cracks in her theory.

Ted was thrilled when Belinda joined the firm, bringing his employee total to three architects, a draftsman and a secretary, and, as he told Belinda, allowing him to generate new clients and do the much coveted design work. To her chagrin, Ted now spent five nights a week wining and dining potential clients all in the name of business development.

"Good morning, good morning." Ted blew in the door, drinking a Starbucks coffee and eating a blueberry scone. He tossed his coat on the rack, and strolled over to his wife. "Any calls?"

"Hellman Brothers wanted to see the drawings for the high occupancy condos. I told them they'd be ready by the end of the week."

"Why'd you tell them that, B? I haven't even started them yet. If I don't give them something, they'll drop me, sure as shit."

"Better get busy then," Belinda said, and added as an afterthought, "that's what you get for working with sleazy developers."

Ted slammed his hand on the table. George, one of the architects looked up, caught Ted's eye, then went back to his work.

Ted jumped up and slid his arm around Belinda's waist. "Can you help me?"

"You could've brought me a coffee," Belinda replied.

"I thought you had breakfast with Kyle. You fed him, didn't you? Before dropping him at school?"

"Of course I fed him. But with getting him ready and packing his lunch, I didn't have time for a cup of coffee."

"Well, why didn't you stop and get something on the way?" Ted took the stool next to his wife.

"Because I had to get in here and open the office for George and Marion, remember? It's one of those jobs you added to my list of responsibilities."

Marion, her back to Ted, lifted her arm and waved without looking up.

"Oh, I see how it is." Ted rolled his eyes at her and turned away. "B. It's a five-minute stop. You didn't have five minutes?"

"No, I didn't. I'm not privileged to have your schedule."

"What's that supposed to mean?"

"Forget it. Just next time, it would be nice if you thought of me for a change."

"Oh, for Godsakes." Ted grabbed his half-drunk coffee and scone and theatrically dropped them on Belinda's desk, spilling some of the coffee on to Belinda's drawings. George and Marion exchanged a look.

"Breakfast is served." Ted yanked his coat off the rack – it tee-tered momentarily before righting itself – and tossed a snide glare in Belinda's direction before storming out.

Unraveled and embarrassed, Belinda mopped at the coffee stains on the drawings for a few moments before admitting defeat. She rolled them up and threw them in the trash, beat back the urge to cry, and began anew.

∾

If you start with the premise that everything is intended for your benefit, that inside of everyone is the strength to get from where you are to where you want to be, that no matter what happens, even if it's death, you'll be okay, then there's nothing to fear, is there?

Truth be told, Belinda had caught Ted on the tail end of his reign, an event precipitated by the untimely, yet not completely unexpected, death of his mother. After years of living with an abusive, alcoholic hus-band, Ted's mother had committed suicide. It was questionable whether she meant to do it. The chronically depressed often toy with the idea of suicide and sometimes take steps in that direction, but rarely do they mean to go through with the deed. Ted's father had come home from work one day and found her in the back of their walk-in closet, dangling from the end of a macramé belt she'd made in the '70's when she'd been single and life had been considerably less troublesome. Her hands were at her neck as if trying to pull the belt free. Her face had a puzzled appearance, like she was trying Death on for size and became confused when He snuck up on her and called "no take backs."

Ted cried until his eyes almost swelled shut while his overbearing father sat in the corner, comatose. To find his wife of thirty years, dan-gling and blue-faced next to his neatly pressed pants still in their plas-tic dry cleaners bags, was beyond his reasoning abilities. For all his ver-bal bullying, he was too weak to get her down. Ted's father called Ted instead of 911 – he didn't want the neighbors to know – and insisted they drive her to the hospital themselves. It was the worst job of Ted's

64

life. He carried his mother down the steps from the second floor to the carport, hitting every door jamb in between with either her head or her feet. By the time he laid her in the back seat, Ted was so shaken he ran to the bathroom and threw up.

Two months later, Ted ran Belinda off the road. That she was a rebound for Ted's mom was almost cliché. The woman had adored her son and with her gone, so was Ted's self-confidence. When Belinda looked at him, he felt some of that adoring love again, and so he snatched it up, hoping to replace what was accidentally lost with what had been accidentally found.

∾

The portals aren't open to us every day. We travel along the same road, day after dusty day, decade after decade, sometimes lifetime after lifetime, waiting for an opening, a road crossing, a different track. But we become so routinized that when the fork does appear in the road, we fail to take it because of fear, inertia, tragedy, or past regrets. Yet if we could trust ourselves to just make that move, we might find the unknown to be far sweeter than the stodgy, stuffy, malodorous known that we've been wallowing in. Unfortunately, conditions generally have to completely disintegrate for this to happen.

Belinda stood at the stove stirring a pot of Jambalaya while Kyle sat in the living room hunched over his Legos in front of the TV. Belinda could see his reflection in the window from her spot at the stove when an other-worldly feeling overcame her. She saw, but could not be seen, could hear, but was not heard, a ghost keeping watch on the living. She liked to play voyeur, especially when he had friends over, and listen in on the sound of him growing up. She watched him now, taking note of the small details: the one wavy lock of hair in his eyes, the way he leaned into life, his tongue sticking out the side of his mouth in concentration. He looked so much like Ted it made her heart ache. Belinda could hear the blathering of the TV behind her ear as if it existed both inside and outside herself. She froze, listened more intently. There were two sounds there: the TV's, and

the one inside her, the Drone of Discontent. After years of introspec-
tion, she'd learned to recognize the signs. She couldn't quite put her
finger on it, but something was coming, a test, perhaps a big exam
that would determine her position in class next year.

"Mom?"

Always, when Kyle spoke the droning ceased. He bounced into the
kitchen the way eight-year olds do, all arms, legs and electro-energy,
shooting questions at her in rapid fire, not waiting for her to answer,
and ending with: "Mom, did you know aliens think we're aliens, too?

Belinda chuckled and taste-tested the Jambalaya. "I guess I never
really thought about it, honey. I think you might be right."

Then as if to claim his prize for speaking an ultimate truth: "Can
I play Wii?"

"How about you go outside and get some fresh air? We'll have dinner when your father gets home."

A disgruntled sigh, preceded a reluctant "all right," and then the
dance and shuffle of tying laces and zipping jackets and finally the
door closing.

Belinda drew a deep breath, alone with her as yet unnamed res-
ervations and her pot of Jambalaya. The stove timer beeped and she
pulled a pan of corn muffins from the oven, placing them on the stove
to cool. Ted hadn't said anything about going out tonight to celebrate
her birthday so she hadn't brought it up. It was an inconsequential
birthday, 34, not like 25 or 50, and she didn't feel much like going out
since it meant finding a babysitter for Kyle and getting herself together
to look presentable and all those things that pulled at her energy the
way age was beginning to pull at her body.

She put her face to the muffin pan. Aromatic whiffs tickled her
nose hairs and crept through her sinus cavity. She inhaled and smiled
at one of the few things that brought her pleasure these days. She
grabbed a muffin and slathered it with butter, consuming the whole
buttery mess while standing over the sink. When Ted walked in, she
was washing her hands, her jowls stuffed like a pre-winter chipmunk's.

"You're early," she said through the bulge in her cheeks.

"I can see now why your ass is spreading," he smirked, "but it still doesn't explain why your brain is shrinking."

Belinda held her breath and the cornbread in her mouth simultaneously, a wide-eyed look on her face. Ted laughed.

"Jesus, ease up, B," he said, and tossed a bunch of carnations at her. She reached for it and missed, following its arc to the ground, just out of reach. She squatted there on the floor, hovering over the flowers, but looking up at Ted as if uncertain whether she should retrieve them. But Ted had already turned away and was rummaging around in the refrigerator for a beer.

"You thought I'd forgotten, didn't you?" His voice mingled with the chilled, dry air and spiked its way over the door. He grabbed a beer and leaned back against the counter, sipping it. "So let's go."

"Where?" Belinda asked.

"Out. It's your birthday, girl! Let's go celebrate. Dinner. Drinks. A little dancing."

"What about Kyle?"

"What about him?"

"Is he coming with us?"

"Call the neighbors and see if they'll watch him."

"But it's so last minute."

"It's not last minute," Ted said, stepping toward her. He grabbed her around the waist and dipped her so low her hair touched the floor. But since he failed to put down his beer, half the contents of his bottle did the same.

"Oops," he said. "Ah, well. Shouldn't take long to clean it up." He looked at Belinda when he said this and made no move toward the spreading puddle.

Under normal circumstances, Belinda would have hopped to it, but the Drone of Discontent was playing louder now, louder than she'd ever heard it before. Beyond it, Belinda could see a path, or more like a fork in the road, and on one side a figure beckoning. Its lips were moving, but the words were garbled, inaudible because of the Drone. Belinda was mesmerized, and she stood there, not cleaning up the beer, not paying attention to Ted, not thinking or moving, not even breathing.

"C'mon, B, get moving."

The Drone subsided and Ted's voice blew in on a stream of carbon dioxide. Belinda coughed and sputtered. She hated breathing discarded air. "But you didn't say we were going out. I already made dinner..."

"I already made dinner," he repeated, mimicking her. Ted stepped closer and grabbed her face between his fingers; she braced for the vice that would slowly squeeze her into submission, but he pulled her in for a kiss instead. When he let go, his smile was magnanimous, if not genuine. "It's nine years since we met." He raised his eyebrows and smiled suggestively, lecherous and attractive at the same time. On any other day she would have given over to it, but the Drone was growing in intensity and a disembodied voice raised itself to him.

"Ted, I spent all afternoon making this meal. I want to stay home and eat it. It's my birthday."

"Huh," was all he said. Belinda folded her arms across her chest.

Ted stared hard at her for a few moments before responding. "You know what you can do with your dinner? Do you?" He was across the room in two strides, pulling the expensive Calphalon pot off the stove and turning to shove it at her with such force that it propelled her into the Italian marble counter top. The world went Salvador Dali on her.

"You can shove it up your fat ass, is what you can do," she heard her husband say from some far off distant galaxy.

The Calphalon pot bounced when it hit the ground, sending up a geyser of Jambalaya, splattered the floor, the walls, Belinda's clothes, arms and face. She slumped forward and fell to the ground, but not before her head and the counter exchanged phone numbers. Ted nudged her once in the kidneys and her head made contact with the sticky mess on the floor. His foot tripped over her face before it stomped from the room. The Jambalaya covering her face looked like spicy blood and, but for the bits of parsley and oregano, would have been indistinguishable from that dripping from her nose.

Consciousness was still hers, but she wasn't sure for how much longer. Her first thought was not to let Kyle see her this way, her second, a chiding to herself for her failure to see the truth – again. The bruises and contusions would heal within a few weeks, but the scars she was bound to carry well into the next several lifetimes, unless....

Unless. The word took on epic connotations. The inverted U became the balloon, the N the basket. She boarded it and a series of S's roared into the giant cavern of oxygen, combusting, forcing the chemical reactions to life. She was safe inside the wicker basket, floating higher and higher, looking down on it all from a great height where perspective is always altered.

Yet we can't sleep forever. Kyle came back to find his father gone and his mother passed out on a sea of Jambalaya. His panicked wails – "Mommy, wake up, Mommy, wake up," – finally reached the distant horizon upon which Belinda was floating. She wanted to cover her ears for his shrieking was causing her much discomfort, but she lacked strength for even this most minuscule of tasks. She felt as though she were looking at the world through cheesecloth, one small square at a time; it was all her one good eye could hold. Her other eye was completely swollen shut, her cheek bruised, her jaw maybe off its hinge. She stared at her son while her mind searched its goopy, splattered corners for words of comfort. After all these years of hiding the truth from him, her secret was out. A sorrow, deep and cold as the Black Sea washed over her.

"Call my sister," she breathed. "Call Aunt Simone," before passing out again.

∾

Before birth, the Angel of Allotments gives each person a finite amount of negative words to use over the course of his or her lifetime. This would explain why some people die of a sudden, massive heart attack (perhaps they've used up their last several dozen vituperative phrases like rapid gunfire) while others die a slow, agonizing death over the course of months or years (they've spread their negativity out over time, savoring each hostile utterance). No one knows how many negative, disheartening, vulgar, tasteless, or hateful sentences each of us is allowed – it varies from person to person and many factors are taken into account – but considering the number of negative thoughts that cloud our brains in a single day, we're lucky the Angel of Allotments doesn't read minds.

The room was dark, unlike the cloudless sky behind the curtain. Belinda sat by the window with it drawn just enough for a ray of light to fall upon the book she wasn't reading. The lights were dimmed which was fine by Belinda since the florescent bulbs gave her bruises a sinister glow. The only other light in the room came from the high-tech medical gadgetry, forming a perfect half dome around Simone's bed. The whirring and beeping sounded like Classic Rock on Prozac.

Here lay the woman who had left Belinda at the age of fourteen to fend for herself. That Belinda had gotten through high school was a miracle: always lying to the teachers that her sister was at work, or visiting a sick relative, or simply unavailable to come in for conferences. The truth was, Belinda didn't know where Simone was, at least not for the first six months. Somehow Belinda had managed to survive on the measly amount of money Bert sent from France every month and a little part time job after school. She lived frugally, ate only one meal a day, and by doing so, had enough to cover the rent on her little apartment. Not always the heat or electricity, but at least she had a roof, and then Simone would come crashing back into Belinda's life, dumped by her latest beau and looking for a place to stay.

It was a repeating pattern. Simone, gone for months and then back to make a mess of things: staying out late partying, sleeping on the couch until noon, eating whatever food Belinda had in the house. Belinda knew she'd be better off without Simone, but she couldn't bear the crushing loneliness of her days. Since Simone was her only family, Belinda had a monumental allegiance to her sister despite the Class V rapids under their mutual bridge.

Then Belinda turned eighteen and Bert lost the restaurant and the checks stopped coming. The money had become paltry anyway, but it was something, and now it was nothing. After an audacious and violent fight where Simone blamed Belinda for everything that ever went wrong in her life, Simone split. No "goodbye, it's been real", no "catch you on the flip side", no "screw you if you can't take a joke"; she simply vanished. At first, Belinda thought her sister was dead. But after five years, Simone resurfaced, looking for a handout. Belinda gave her the money as she always had, and agreed to send Simone money when she could with the condition that she stay out of Belinda's life. Simone agreed, and the last time Belinda actually saw Simone she'd made an unscheduled appearance at the hospital where Belinda had been ensconced following Kyle's birth. Simone appeared at the foot of Kyle's hospital bed with her hand out, and Belinda could no longer see past Simone's wretched self-centeredness.

The day of the Jambalaya incident was the first glimpse the sisters had of each other in years, Belinda bruised and battered and broken, Simone just plain broken.

"What the hell happened to you?" Simone had asked before hacking up half a lung. She came inside and cleaned up the mess that was Belinda – Simone had a lot of experience with making messes, but not so much in cleaning them up, so it was a bit of a stretch for her – put Belinda to bed, mopped up the kitchen, fed Kyle, and acted downright motherly. She took up residence in the guest bedroom and tended to Belinda's wounds, those of the body and of the heart. It was very un-Simone-like and Belinda was confused, but extremely grateful.

Three weeks later, Simone passed out in Belinda's living room. Whether Simone was dying now was unclear. Belinda was not surprised to learn Simone had pneumonia, given the sound of her lungs, but shocked to find it was because Simone was HIV positive.

Belinda studied her sister's face, haggard even in sleep. Her beauty was still there, but hidden now in deep crevices, stripped down, blotched up, stretched and thin to the point of translucency. The sneer she'd given to Belinda all these years was now a permanent feature. In the wrong light, which this qualified as, it looked like her skull might pop through her skin. The result was hideous. She tried to imagine what life would be like if Simone were dead and felt a small pang of remorse which quickly dissipated when Simone opened her eyes.

"What are you looking at?" Simone asked.

Belinda returned her sister's gaze with a beatific smile that would rival Jesus. "You."

"Yeah, well, knock it off. And quit smiling at me. You look ridiculous."

Belinda's goodwill from the last three weeks dispersed like dry ice. Resentment flooded into the room, squirting through all the cracks and crevices, trying to breach the levee holding back the old wounds. The susurrus in her head was growing in volume, gaining strength.

"You're a fool who could never do anything. Relying on a child to manage your life."

"You act like you're still a child. Besides, you did fine."

"Compared to you, maybe."

The sisters glared at each other until finally Simone spoke.

"Why did you marry him, anyway? Couldn't you see he was just like me?"

Belinda flopped back in the chair; her lip curled at Simone's admission. "He was the only man I didn't have to hold my stomach in for."

"What's that supposed to mean?"

"It means he liked me for who I was. Liked everything about me. When we first met, anyway. He was totally happy with me."

"That lasted ten minutes."

"Longer than any of your relationships."

"I never let a man raise a hand to me."

"Shut up, Simone. Just shut up! I did what I did to survive. Ted took care of me. Gave me a home. A child. A job. He gave me a life. And yes, he has a short fuse, and you never know which Ted you're going to get, but he had his own problems, too, growing up. And if he raises his hand once in a while, well, he doesn't mean it. He may not be perfect, but at least he comes home at night."

"B, I..."

"And look at you. Dying all alone in a hospital with no one to even spoon some goddamn ice chips into your mouth."

Belinda tossed a grimace her sister's way. After a few seconds and ever so slowly, Simone opened her mouth. She was weak and tired, but her face had a ray of hope, and at that moment, she looked to Belinda like a baby bird whose mother had just returned to the nest. Not meaning to, Belinda laughed, and grabbed the cup with ice chips and a spoon. Simone leaned forward enough to catch a few of the chips in her mouth, then leaned back and sighed, this simple movement exhausting her.

"I'm dying, you know."

"You always say that. That it's a matter of life or death."

"This time it's for real."

"You always say that, too."

"Do I? Well, how about this?" Simone said. "Even in a rainstorm, the sun is shining."

Belinda snorted. "It's awfully late in life to get religion, isn't it?"

"Not for you, it isn't."

Belinda searched Simone's eyes for clues, but Simone had turned away.

"Do my makeup?" Simone said.

Simone – all sugary sweet when she wanted something. Her body was failing, but Charm was still Simone's wing man. If a black-robed boney guy with a long scythe was tracking her, clearly Simone was ignoring him. Belinda removed the makeup case from Simone's drawer and began to apply color to her sister's ashen face in soft, gentle strokes.

"I've not always been kind to you, have I?" Simone asked. Belinda huffed.

"Look. I know I was a crummy role model. But actually, you should thank me 'cause I did my best."

"Your best. Your best! You're dying and you can't even admit how royally you screwed me." The years of being the staid one finally cracked and the sisters' roles reversed. Belinda slammed the makeup down on the cheesy hospital tray table then hurled it across the room. It bounced off the wall and fell to the floor, the cheap plastic fracturing into half a dozen pieces. Belinda kicked at the cluster. "My whole freaking life's a mess thanks to you. You gave me nothing. Nothing! Nothing to stand on or go home to, just a shifting pile of stinking sand. And now I should thank you? Well, Thank You, Simone, for fucking me up." The last bit came out as a hysterical shriek. Compared to Simone's near-death state, Belinda was a woman on the verge.

Simone began an uncontrolled hacking that threatened to flood her lungs from the inside. "Nicole . . . left," was all she managed to say.

"Mom left me, too. And Dad. And everyone, really, except for Ted. And now even he's gone."

Simone sat up, caught her breath. "That little piece . . . of shit? He'll be back."

"You don't know the first thing about it."

Simone shook her head, "I know you're a freakin' doormat," and dropped back onto the pillow. "You gotta make a change, B. While you still can."

"Now you're giving me advice?" Belinda grabbed her coat and purse from the chair and stood before Simone, a mix of defiance and rage: "What do you want from me?"

"What every mother wants for her child. All the best."

Belinda looked at Simone as if her head were on fire.

"You know that song. "Heaven is a Place on Earth?" Simone asked.

"Yeah. So?"

"I named you after her. After Belinda Carlisle."

"How much of a morphine drip do these people have you on?"

"You really didn't know? That I'm your mother?"

Belinda searched her sister's eyes, waiting for the punch line, the trap.

Simone's face softened; regret made an appearance like a shooting star. "I'm sorry, B. I was a terrible mother."

"Simone, you're losing it." Belinda shot a wad of hate in Simone's direction.

"Think about it. You know I'm telling the truth," Simone yelled after her.

Belinda was already halfway down the hall. She didn't want to talk about it anymore.

Nonetheless, since Belinda had always listened to Simone she had no choice, but to do so now. She sat in the cafeteria with a coffee, staring out the window and into her past spread before her like an oil slick across time. She called Kyle's babysitter to say she'd be home late.

She paced the quadrant that comprised the cafeteria. She bought more coffee. She sat at the window and cried. After several hours, she returned to Simone's room, blowing in with a fading fury, coupled with an urgent need to have the missing pieces fitted together for her.

"What about Mom?" Belinda demanded.

"Nicole? She was your grandmother. We were tight, thicker than thieves before you came along. She didn't want me to get an abortion being French and Catholic and everything. I was fourteen, B, I didn't know. I agreed, but then you came along and took my place. You filled the hole Bert made when he took a mistress. Christ, she was barely eighteen. So Nicole claimed you and I was the odd man out. I wanted to love you, I really did, but you made it so damn hard."

For a long time the former sisters just looked past each other. Belinda's throat felt tight. A little of it, maybe a tiny bit, was starting to make sense. She sat down in her chair and stared out the window, straining to keep the sluices sealed. Nothing had changed except that her past wasn't at all what she thought it was and where that left her future she wasn't quite sure.

"Jesus!" Belinda said after what felt like a decade of silence. "Okay, so what if I did believe you. Now what?"

"Whatever. It's wide open."

"Wide open?" Belinda groaned. "So what? I get to be an orphan all over again?"

"You're not an orphan. I'm still alive."

Belinda scrunched up her face and squinted as if it would afford her a better view. "Wait a minute. Is Bert my . . ."

"Jesus, B, give me some credit." Simone closed her eyes and sighed. "No, he's not. He's your grandfather, what did you think?"

Belinda nodded. They sat in silence for a few minutes until Belinda tried it on for size, drawing out the m's, rolling the word around on her tongue, but she still couldn't say the "M" word. "Okay, how about this? My marriage is a wreck. But Kyle needs a father and I'm a year away from getting my Masters in Architecture. I don't know if I have the stamina to finish without Ted, and if I leave him, money will definitely be an issue since all our money's wrapped up in the business. I don't know what to do. Got any parental advice to impart?"

Simone started to cough, stirring up the water in her lungs that threatened to submerge her. She pantomimed to Belinda to bring her the small trash can into which she deposited a lungful of bile. After a few moments of labored breathing, Simone said, "I don't know, but I can tell you this. It's all about choices. That's all we are. So you really gotta think hard about what you're gonna do next."

"I do think hard – about everything I ever do. That's why I never choose anything. I'm adrift on a sea of unmade choices."

"So just choose, and if it's wrong, well, nothin' you can do, but cry about it in the car on the way home." Simone's mouth twitched into a smile. "Just watch what you hand out 'cause Man, does it come back." Simone sighed and lay back, resigned, but not defeated.

Belinda moved closer and touched Simone's hand, a slight gesture with enormous implications.

"Your future's gonna be there. Make sure it's the one you want." She pulled Belinda in and hugged her with the tenacity of one not yet ready to let go of the Silver Cord. Belinda squeezed the rattling lungs and bones that used to be her sister, was suddenly her mother, and for the first time, her friend.

Simone kissed the top of Belinda's head and dismissed her. "You gotta go. Kyle's waiting."

"Kyle...," Belinda sighed, standing up. "He doesn't understand. He knows his father did an awful thing, but he still loves him." Belinda bit the inside of her lip.

"Kids are smart. He'll figure it out."

Belinda shrugged, nodded. "What about Ted?"

"You know how they train elephants in Thailand? They start with a chain, then back it down to a rope, then a string, and at the end of a few weeks, they could keep that elephant under control with a piece of dental floss." Simone's smile was positively evil.

Belinda stared at her sister, eyebrows raised, hands spread open, questioning.

"Discovery channel," Simone replied.

Belinda laughed, hesitating at the door. "I'll bring Kyle back with me."

Simone shook her head. "Tomorrow. I look like shit today." She drew a haggard breath. "Remember, B: stand tall – like an exclamation point, not curved like a question mark." She smiled, and in an uncharacteristic move, put her fingertips to her lips and blew Belinda a kiss. "Good luck out there."

∾

In the beginning, there was a single Original Soul living alone in Eden. Not content to live in paradise, or maybe forgetting the reason for it, the single soul blew itself into billions of tiny pieces, intent on each of its fragments experiencing life in all its conundrums and complexities. When the Original Soul "came to," it found itself living all over the world in such diverse places as Istanbul, Australia, L.A. and Nova Scotia. Each of the fragments had hardwired into their DNA a shard of the Original Soul's Light of Consciousness, but since their hands were empty, they did not know what they carried. Yet as decades turned to millennia, some of the lights began to recognize each other, forming groups, having discussions, asking the hard questions like: Who am I? and Why am I here? A couple thousand years after a huge historical turning point for the earth's inhabitants where parables were taught, sermons on mounts given, loaves and fishes divided, and life after life, along with the date, was transformed, the Lights of Consciousness began to grow dim. Many, it seemed, had reached an impasse and no longer felt like even asking the hard questions. Until someone suggested perhaps if they joined together, became more caring of one another, more interested in each other than in each other's material possessions, more engaging and open and honest about their feelings, and more tolerant of each other's strengths and weaknesses – like one soul with many minds – they just might find the way Home.

Powerful

In her youth, Simone was an absolute beauty, but it wasn't just that. It was beauty combined with a quick wit and a Marilyn Monroe sexuality that made her attractive to every man she met, from the Captain of the football team to the corner grocery store clerk. She didn't try to curry their favor, nor did she turn them away. The more Nicole favored Belinda, the more Simone took love where love was offered. By the age of eighteen, Simone had already had three more lovers, post-Belinda, and was well on her way to filling the List of 55. She would have continued in that vein, growing the list two or three times larger had one thing not occurred: after years of living with HIV, she had contracted AIDS.

At first she pretended that it wasn't happening to her – denial can be a strong elixir – but vulnerability caught her skirts around the same time her immune system crashed around her ankles. She had too many people to make it up to: wives, and girlfriends of boyfriends, not to mention many of the boyfriends themselves. Perhaps making it up with a few of them would be enough to save her the fires, maybe talk her way into an early release program. That her life had been a living hell had to count for something. Going to Hell after the fact seemed redundant. Yet while Simone had squandered more opportunities than some had, each lesson left its own indelible mark on her spirit and, for good or ill, they were hers. Finally, something that no one could take away.

She was smiling at this when Belinda walked in.

"What's up?" Belinda asked, placing a quart of Haagen Dazs White Chocolate Truffle on Simone's tray along with two spoons.

"Nothing," Simone said, reaching for the ice cream. "Taking a walk down memory lane."

"Good stuff?"

"No. Mostly trash." Simone said, struggling with the lid. "But it's my trash."

Belinda opened it and handed Simone a spoon. Simone closed her eyes after a bite, savoring the cool creaminess. Belinda took a seat next to the bed.

"Tell me about my dad."

Simone's eyes fluttered open and her smile reached back into the past where it took a seat at the front of the bus. "Just one more to add to the List of 55, I guess."

"The what?"

"The List of 55.

"He was my first and I loved him huge. He said he loved me, too, but didn't want anything to do with me after I got pregnant." Simone's face took on a pained expression and for a moment she looked fourteen.

"That's terrible."

"Yeah, it sucks, but shit happens."

Belinda shifted in her chair, cleared her throat. "Did you really sleep with fifty-five men?"

"I don't know. Something like that. After fifty-five, I stopped counting. I mean, really, why do I need to keep track of crap like that?"

Belinda eyes grew wide and she ducked her head to conceal her surprise.

"I had a dream I was pregnant," Simone said. "About nine months. Going into the last week of it. My stomach was as round and hard as a bowling ball and I was walking like John Wayne."

"What do you think that means?"

"That I'll be dead within a week."

Belinda smirked. "You're always making death proclamations. Since I was little."

"Odds are in my favor then."

Belinda chuckled. "Well, if that's the case, better eat up. We've got a slew of flavors to get through."

❧

It's hard to see the big picture when you're standing dead center of it.

As promised, Simone died within the week. The funeral was simple given that there were no relatives to speak of just Belinda and Kyle and the funeral director and the few staff on duty that dismal Monday. If there were others who may have seen the announcement in the paper, the icy rain kept them away. By 10:00 a.m., the designated start time, the outside world looked encased in glass, a large, fragile bauble.

One of the male nurses at the hospital that had taken a liking to Simone over the last weeks of her life had come. Simone had worked her charm on this man, and he was there, compelled by an unseen force, the sole representative of Simone's whole sordid List. Kyle held tight to Belinda's hand as he stood beneath a grey, sleet-filled sky and threw dirt atop the coffin, a fitting adieu for an aunt he'd barely known.

The day before the funeral, Belinda called Ted to give him the news. She cried and he came running home to rub her back and make all the appropriate cooing noises. He moved back in that night, promising to be at the funeral for support. He never showed. After ten long years of abuse, it was this single act of neglect, of dispirit, that forced Belinda's hand. As the coffin was lowered, Belinda made the sign of the cross over them both, Simone and Ted, one a blessing, the other a curse. She could do this one thing for her mother.

Three weeks later, Belinda began the Great Purge.

Wary, she climbed the steps to the attic where the Akashic record of her life lay side-by-side with Ted's and Simone's. Belinda's thoughts on living were governed by the dictates of architecture: clean lines and solid forms against the balance of empty space. Clutter unnerved her. Since she and Simone had moved so much, Belinda had whittled down her possessions to a precious few boxes. All that changed when she got married. She may not have come to the marriage with much baggage, but she'd certainly accumulated it over the last ten years.

The day after the funeral, a moving truck arrived with Simone's belongings pulled from storage. Boxes of childhood memories sat piled in the living room. Belinda took one look at it all and threw up. Ted, sensing his wife's imminent breakdown and trying to make amends for his no-show at the funeral, took charge for once and schlepped everything off to the attic. Belinda sat down on a crate now, and scanned the four corners where the clutter of their collective lives, boxed and bagged, was making her woozy.

She observed the accumulated items with distrust, then pulled on a pair of Ted's old waders, long-forgotten in the corner, and dove into the fray, prepared to dispense sentences on her past like Lady

Justice holding tight to the scales only she wasn't wearin' no stinking blindfold!

She started slowly at first, handling boxes and bags with reverence as if they were relics, reviewing the contents, making life's tougher decisions: what to keep; what to let go. In the end she'd have to let it all go, but The End might be thirty or sixty years away, and this wasn't Kyle's gig it was hers. She determined to do it with alacrity.

Belinda had barely gotten through the first box – one of Simone's that held a few comic books, a battered stuffed lamb, a yellowed blanket whose silk edge had long since frayed, when she started to cry, long buried tears – tears of pain and exhaustion, betrayal and lovelessness. Why me? She got no answer, so she dried her eyes on her sleeve and blew her nose in a slightly damp tissue. Then she heard it – a small voice, not her own, not timid, just small, yet full of wonder and promise and potential. "Why not?" it said.

Outside, snow had started to fall, swirling around the Blue Spruce and Hemlock and she watched, transfixed by the whiteness, the lightness, the impossibility that any two flakes shared the same crystalline structure. She opened the small window to release the heavy attic air, redolent with the ghosts of memory, and drew a deep breath of the harsh winter into her lungs. Cat-like, she curled herself on to the battered blanket, hoping to stem the wave of dizziness that threatened to overtake her. In a moment, she was asleep.

After twenty minutes, long enough to catch her balance and recharge her battery, Belinda woke up. She caught the tail-end of a dream, stretched for it with her conscious mind. But dreams are fragile things, chimeras locked between the worlds, to be analyzed in the dim light of dawn, and brought out into the day with an abundance of caution lest the thin veil enveloping them burst in the sun and the messages they contain scatter before their meaning be taken.

Belinda sat up. The dream was gone.

She rubbed her eyes and yawned. The air in the room felt less dense. She shivered, pulled the tattered blanket around her and closed the window. She remembered now: the blanket was Simone's and Belinda had taken it over just as she did with most things that were originally her sister's. Simone who never met a grudge she didn't like. Belinda was beginning to see why. She sighed, laid back down on the floor.

"Why don't you help me then?" The air around her stirred. "I'll take that as a yes."

She started with the things closest to her: Simone's Victorian lamp that sat on her bedroom night stand when she was a child; the binoculars that Bert and Nicole used at the racetrack on Saturday nights; Nicole's lovely Venetian glass perfume bottle with a chip in the dropper; an orange neo-deco, crystal bowl that had been a wedding present to Bert and Nicole. She felt the specific shape that each thing had given her, and now, sitting alone in the attic she shared with a husband who'd left his own indelible stamp on her soul, she used these things to reshape herself.

"By the time I'm done with the attic, maybe I'll be back to a size eight." She pulled on the elastic waist band of her chintzy, easy-fitting house pants, letting it go with a small pop each time something loosed its hold on her. She'd keep the orange fruit bowl. Its asymmetrical design and lack of concentricity appealed to her, speaking to the way she suspected her life was about to go – in undulating, quirky directions. She'd travel light, relegating the rest to the recycle bin. It was the ecologically-minded thing to do.

That night, as she swam in the vernal pools where tadpoles got their starts, Belinda dreamed she could breathe underwater. There her thoughts breathed, too, taking on shape and clarity, and she heard her own small voice say: *time to leave the pond.*

∾

It's like training an Elephant....

The next day, Belinda and Kyle were lying on the couch, Simone's ratty blanket wrapped around both their shoulders. Belinda studied

Kyle's face as he slept. He was a few months away from his tenth birthday where the changes from youngster to adolescent lay hidden, yet evident, like tracks in freshly fallen snow. She stroked his head, putting herself in a trance. The clocks chimed eleven and Ted still wasn't home. She roused Kyle and walked him up to his bed, covering him with Simone's blanket.

She lay on her own bed, listening to the roaring sound of nothingness. It was louder these last few days, screaming in her ears, and it hit her nervous system harder than any fist or flight of stairs ever could. She no longer cared when or if he came home. Even if she had to hold a tin cup and stand on the corner collecting money from strangers so she and Kyle could eat, it had to be preferable to this.

The night before, Belinda had made love to Ted with the ferocity of one who knows something is about to die.

"You're going to give me a heart attack," he gasped.

Belinda wouldn't stop and swept him up in her urgent passion. Afterwards, they lay side-by-side.

"God, B. That was just like when we were first married. Where's that hellcat been all these years?"

"You used up her nine lives with your drinking."

Ted stopped rubbing her arm and rolled over to face her. "Can't we just enjoy the moment for once?"

"Post-coital truce?" Belinda sat up, breaking free of his embrace. "Why can't we ever call a post-work truce? Or a post-Kyle truce? Or a post-dinner truce? It's always on your terms?"

"Awww, B, knock it off. I'm tired."

"Yeah, well, I've been tired for years. Tired of folding your laundry, tired of cooking your meals, tired of raising your child and running your office, all without help from you. I'm tired of running your whole life when all I get in return are snide comments and rude remarks.

"All right, I'm sorry."

"Yeah, until tomorrow." Belinda stood, pulled the comforter off the bed and wrapped it around herself. "I'm through with living in the Victim-Hood. As of this moment, I no longer feel sorry for me."

"Where are you going?" Ted asked.

"To sleep on the couch. Alone, and in peace."

She closed the door, leaving her husband lying naked on the bed without a blanket.

∾

Every action of every individual is creating our collective reality. To transform the world, we must transform ourselves. It's simple: lay down your arms.

The next day, Belinda pulled half a dozen large plastic storage boxes from the basement and brought them up to the bedroom. They'd sell the house. It had tripled in value since they'd bought it ten years ago with appreciation plus all the work they'd done. She could use the money to finish school, buy a little house for herself and Kyle. Ted could use his share to drink himself to death. She'd start with her things, and then pack Kyle's. If Ted refused, she'd hire a mover. She'd even pack for him. Belinda draped a load of her business suits across the bed. She'd find bags for them later. It was all progressing at a fast clip until the civility of her actions hit her. Ten years with this man and what did she have to show for it? A lump sum payment? She sank to the floor and rubbed her eyes while a plan formed in the periphery. *What have I got to lose?*

She started slowly at first, pulling things out of Ted's drawers and closets, his side of the bathroom, and picked up speed as she went. When his drawers were completely empty, she ran downstairs for the sewing kit. Next came the brooms and the mops and the rakes and the shovels, pulled from divergent corners of the house, thirteen being called to service. Belinda trudged back and forth, cackling, while she carried them all to the bedroom. If only Ted could see her at this moment: Belinda the Tried and True, Belinda the Dependable. Belinda the Protector of Strays and Misfits, now morphed into Belinda the Wife from Hell, one fine thread at a time.

She sewed them all together: the boxers to the briefs, the calf-length socks, leg-hole to toe – Belinda hated when socks didn't stay together – the silk tie to the cuff of a freshly laundered shirt. She didn't exempt the suits, stitching them to each other and then to Ted's undershirts. She formed trains, twelve, thirteen feet long, suturing them like patients in the E.R. *Pull the needle, pull the thread, pull the needle, pull the thread...* Belinda worked for hours, squinting and hunched over her work. She couldn't sew for crap. Her knots were a laborious and intensive use of thread which would, like her tangled life, take years to unravel.

Hours passed and still she worked. After a decade of longing for the love and security she never had, Belinda decided it was time to change the game plan, one that foreclosed the possibility of retreat. Once Ted got a look at this, there'd be no turning back.

Belinda threw open the window and sucked in some icy midnight air. There was a hint of spring lurking just beyond the bitter cold, she could smell it. She blessed the full moon for its bountiful light, and one by one, she shoved them out, her ambassadors of hope, holding aloft her dreams for the future. She wedged the poles between the window and the sill: her brooms and mops and rakes, all sporting long expensive tails. They floated on the wind like Tibetan prayer flags, the Haines and the Fruit of the Looms, running the length of the house, poking out of every second story window. Some just flapped while the longer ones lay strewn across the magnolia and the Japanese maple, the box bushes lining the house, the crocuses just poking up from the ground. With each mounting she felt lighter, and the lightness enveloped her like the spirits of the two mothers she'd lost. It carried her up on the breeze and from this vantage point, life's problems looked approachable.

Belinda peered out the window, but her less than stellar vision put her at a disadvantage so she slipped on her fuzzy slippers and traipsed outside to get a better look. The house looked like a feudal castle under siege.

"Surrender!" Belinda yelled to the night air. A light wind ruffled the oak leaves and Ted's underwear in response. Satisfied with her accomplishments, she went to bed. The question was not whether Ted would notice this flagrant assault on his wardrobe, but which one of them would survive the revelation.

Belinda awoke at 5 a.m., drool leaking from the side of her mouth. Simone's face floated to the edge of her consciousness, and like a drunkard recalling the events of the previous evening, Belinda had a sudden clarity followed by a full blown panic attack which redoubled its efforts, nearly stopping her heart when she looked out the window: the yard was a mess.

When Ted staggered up the driveway, half an hour later, and half in the bag, fractured rays of sunlight were streaking northward, up and above the horizon, piercing their way through the grey cloud cover that lay tight across the sky, all puckered and drawn like a disapproving headmistress. Still, the light was sufficient for Ted to get a good look at his silk chili pepper underwear, risqué and sprawled wide across the rhododendron. To say he snapped seeing his Italian silk ties, Ralph Lauren polos, and Banana Republic linen pants scattered like refuse in a windstorm would have been like saying Hurricane Katrina caused a bit of property damage.

"Belinda!" he roared, and plowed through the front door like a linebacker at the Rose Bowl.

Belinda was ready for him. She sat on the couch with Ted's handgun – the one he kept in the night stand drawer in case of intruders – pointed directly at his crotch. Ted froze. Belinda squinted. An icy silence enveloped them. Beads of sweat formed on his upper lip.

"What? No pithy comment? No quick retort? No astute observation regarding the size of my ass?" *Pull the needle...* Belinda cocked the gun.

Ted ran a hand through his wavy hair. He furrowed his brow and cocked his head at his wife. Realization, along with a smile, spread across his face. "B," he said quietly – the Wife Whisperer. He took a step toward her, hands outstretched like Jesus. "You don't even know how to work it."

Pull the thread... Belinda fired off a shot. It whizzed by Ted's head, close enough to graze his ear, and continued on, lodging in the wall.

"Aaaaaaa!" Ted cupped his ear, feeling for the blood. A great stickiness oozed forth. "Belinda!" he squealed. Ted's breathing was quick and rhythmic like an injured animal who would choose flight if the option were available to him.

"Did I get you? I don't have my glasses on." Belinda smiled sweetly, holding Ted's gaze with her squint, although she couldn't be sure, until he was forced to look away. Ted began to whimper.

"Now, now, don't start that. What is it you always say? If I could just save up your tears I wouldn't have to go to the car wash." Belinda reached over to the coffee table and put on her glasses. "Ah, that's better." She flopped back against the couch and watched Ted who stood, sifting and rolling in his own imaginary breeze.

"Mom? You all right?" Kyle, called from his room.

"Go back to bed, honey. It's just the TV." After a beat, Belinda heard the door close. She strained to listen and, hearing no more questions, turned her attention back to her husband.

"Are you okay? You look like you're going to pass out."

Ted's pleading eyes looked about to drown in their sockets, but he said nothing.

"Poor Teddy. My tears never meant anything to you. And now, here you are, asking me to consider yours." Belinda rubbed her eyes behind her glasses. "Feeding your vanity. Nursing your wounds. Covering your tracks. It was me that kept you afloat. And what do I have to show for it other than the scars from a case of cervical warts and a C-Section?" She raised the gun again, pointing it in Ted's general direction. *Pull the needle...*

"Kyle!" Panic was creeping in. "You have Kyle."

"Kyle," Belinda repeated, her voice taking on a dream-like quality. She sighed. "But I already have him and so there are parts of you that are no longer of use to me."

Belinda lowered the gun to Ted's crotch. *Pull the thread...* Ted sank to his knees, sobbing. "Please, B. No."

"Go ahead and beg, Ted." *Pull the needle...* "It suits you."

"I'm sorry."

"You're full of it." She released, then cocked the gun again. In the utter silence surrounding them, the clicking noises may as well have been a jackhammer. *Pull the thread...*

"B, I didn't mean to hurt you."

At the sound of those words, ephemeral pools formed in Belinda's eyes and her throat became solidifying concrete. She hated those words. Ted tossed them out like candy. He never meant it. It would be so easy to kill him. *Pull the needle...* She could claim self-defense. *Pull the thread...* She had half a dozen bruises as witnesses. *Pull the trigger...* She'd get Kyle . . . the architecture practice . . . the life insurance money . . . . *Now he's dead....*

She cleared her throat, raising the gun to his mid-section. Ted dropped his elbows to the floor and sat on his haunches, a repentant sinner. Had he been practicing yoga, this position would be called, "Child's Pose." At the moment Belinda took aim, she heard it: Simone's voice, just above a whisper.

"Belinda."

She turned to look, but her sister/mother wasn't there. If Ted heard it, he didn't move. She squeezed her eyes shut. She could practically feel the brush of angel wings. The ephemeral pools gave way to rays of summer sun. Belinda screamed, a closed mouthed thing that came out garbled, then fired into the floor, inches from Ted's outstretched hands. Ted screamed back, a retaliatory anthem of fear, rolled onto his side, covering his head and balls simultaneously. Belinda threw the gun down. It skidded across the floor, clattering to a halt in front of her cowering husband.

"Just remember this day. The day I could have. We'll call it your brush burn with death." Belinda turned and walked from the room.

Well, that decade was over.

∽

When choosing a partner in life we have two choices: Darkness or Light. Darkness will walk the walk with you. He'll keep your secrets and harbor your delusions. He'll tell you to go out and grab what you can out of life, seize it, before someone else does, horde it, or life will horde back and you'll have nothing. Darkness stands by and applauds your self-loathing and self-destructive behavior. And in the end, you are left with only Darkness – the place where Light goes to die.

Belinda walked in and dropped her bags in the foyer. She took off her coat, replaced her shoes with her house slippers, and padded to the kitchen to pour herself a glass of wine. If recent history was any indication, she'd finish the bottle before the night was out. Ten minutes later she was propped up in bed, a glass of wine in hand, ensconced in a sea of pillows. She flipped open the romance novel she'd been reading, *Skin Deep*, by Cynthia Gregory. Romance novels were balm for her addled brain; she liked the feel of the words as they flung themselves against the empty chamber walls of her heart.

She drained her glass, tossed the book aside, and headed to the kitchen for a refill. Kyle was at Ted's, and although she didn't like this arrangement – every other weekend with his dad – she'd live with it because Kyle really wanted to see his father. She filled her glass, a California Cab, and gulped it down, shunting a fresh batch of tears off toward the living room while she went back to her bed, her book, and her solo life.

Her drinking schedule made getting up in the morning a killer, but since the separation, Ted had taken some of Belinda's more menial work responsibilities from her. Perhaps it was his attempt at helping the divorce in proceeding smoothly, perhaps it was to appease her since she did have a large stake in the business – it had grown while they were married – or perhaps Ted had grown emotionally, and this was simply the result. Whatever the reason, he treated her with the respect accorded an architect which she almost was. It seemed that since his *brush burn with death,* Ted was taking all of life's responsibilities a little more seriously. He'd even become a decent parent. Too bad for Belinda, too, because both Ted and Kyle, and sometimes even Belinda herself, were starting to forget what all the hubbub had been about.

ॐ

After all that, could it have been an addiction?

The sun inched upward in the late winter sky, moving into the landscape with all the speed and purpose of a tortoise. Its rays filtered through the trees and window and came to rest on the wall, leaving its mutable pastiche in broad, soft strokes. Across this landscape, a spider moved in shadow, barely touching the periphery, like a fleeting thought or a whisper. Belinda lay there watching the spectacle for several minutes until the spider became bored of having his shadow on display and scurried off to a corner to hide. Belinda threw back the covers and drew a rattled breath. "Gym or bust," she said to Chester. The stray cat had found her a month ago and refused to relinquish the degree of pampering to which he'd become accustomed. Belinda scratched his head and he pawed the comforter contentedly. She thought to learn some things from him, like how to be coolly confident and detached, how to ignore the world until it suited you, how to let others do your bidding. She ignored the clichés about single women and cats. Chester had allowed her to take down the Vacancy sign that had been blinking on and off in her heart.

Breakfast consisted of a cup of coffee – black – the preferred drink of the habitually hung over, Bert used to say. He would know. So would Nicole, for that matter, at least until she stopped hanging with Bert at the restaurant after hours. Belinda threw on a tee shirt, sweat pants and a hoody, grabbed an old Woolrich shirt of Ted's from the hall closet, and headed out to the gym. The thirty-two degree weather had left a coating of frost on the windshield, but she couldn't find the ice scraper. That was Ted's job. He may not have been much of a husband, but he'd always shoveled her out, changed the oil regularly, kept the tires balanced, and the alignment just right, his one glimpse into a well-ordered universe.

No time to get the defroster up to speed; Belinda was on a mission. She squirted windshield washer fluid, cleared the frost with a few wipes of the blades, and put it in reverse. She had to lean her head out the window because of the frost on the back windshield and by the time she'd put it in drive, her front windshield had fogged up again. She hit it with the fluid. It bought her another ten seconds. Squirt, swipe, see, squirt, swipe, and see. She managed to make it the two miles to the gym without a head-on collision.

Ten months without Ted and sometimes the crush of loneliness was palpable, threatening to dismantle what little bits of equilibrium remained to Belinda after their split. She found herself running faster, trying to out sweat it, outsmart it, outdistance it, and most days she did, but loneliness had a long reach and some nights it pulled her back down to its level.

This is why Dale was a wonderful distraction. Tall and thin, he had a bicyclist's body and a fine head of hair with just a touch of grey at the temples. He was running along with a client, both were on treadmills, when Belinda walked into the circuit room. She knew his name was Dale, not because he'd told her, but because of the little name tag he wore. She punched in her vital statistics and made tracks on the elliptical machine, pretending to read a People magazine while she studied his gorgeous face in the mirror. He could have been Viggo Mortensen's brother. She watched him slow his pace to match the middle-aged man he was coaching, watched him surreptitiously until his training session ended.

When Belinda finished, she wiped down the equipment, pulled her hood up and her wool jacket on, and headed out, taking the steps two at a time. Dale was at the snack bar, drinking a bottle of water. Because of her hood, she didn't see him until they were practically face-to-face.

"Uh," a quick intake of breath. Her heart thumped so loudly, the people in the next circuit room could keep time to it. She clutched her magazine tightly to her chest, hoping to smother the sound.

"Hey, how's it going?"

"Good."

"You know, I notice you always use the same machine. Has anyone ever showed you how to use the rest of the equipment?"

Belinda shook her head no, adjusted her glasses, clutched the magazine tighter.

"Well, if you ever want a lesson, break out of your rut, maybe do some cross-training, just let the front desk know." He grinned. "I have very reasonable rates."

"Okay," was all Belinda could manage.

"Have a good weekend," Dale said. He even sounded like Viggo with that languid voice, as if it just rolled over and rubbed its sleepy eyes. Her heart jumped up into her throat with such force it knocked the magazine from her hands. Dale bent down to pick it up, their fingers touching as he handed it back. He smiled again.

"Thank you," Belinda croaked, lowering her eyes as she scurried past. By the time she got to the car, she was sweating again.

∾

There is no such thing as predestination. We create our universe, one moment to the next, based upon our choices, and our reactions to those choices. A brunette today can be a blond tomorrow. A widow can be happily married. A childless couple can adopt or conceive. Once we learn to accept parallel universes as the norm, and our innate ability to have an impact on them, in fact, to create them, one tiny decision or attitude at a time, life becomes infinitely less complicated and more enjoyable.

Belinda was on week four of her early morning gym routine. She'd started with every other day and was contemplating a move to five days a week. The energy it gave her was incredible now that she no longer felt so winded. She'd all but given up her nightly glass of wine – by the end she'd been drinking from tumblers the size of Big Gulps – and suddenly it wasn't so hard to get up in the morning. Her world was changing again, not in the earthquake, flood or fire kind of way. It wasn't that kind of shift at all. More like a tilt of half a degree, enough to see the world refracting on the surface of the water, or maybe like rearranging the furniture and looking out the window at the right side of the Japanese maple instead of the left. Belinda suspected that an attribute to being human was the way things usually happened in stages, rather than all at once. It gave you time to adjust.

Maybe enlightenment was like that, a moment of absolute brilliant clarity followed by a face splat in a mud puddle. Recently, especially since she put the bottle away, her life seemed to come to her in scenes and dreams that she then proceeded to build her movie around. She liked the scenes at the gym. She'd already lost a congratulatory seven or eight pounds for her effort. Not that she was fat. Ted's deprecating remarks notwithstanding, there was nothing wrong with being a size 10. So she reshaped and reformed while traces of the old Belinda, like sunspots on the eyes, slowly dissipated. It was a question of mind over matter. Of manifesting. Of bringing into form that which was still formless.

Sometimes she thought about her old desire to change her name to Constance, and the shape her life would have taken had she followed through. She still believed in semantics, that what we call ourselves is what we are, but whether it was an emotional or intellectual argument made no difference. Belinda was desperate to leave her past behind, to draw afresh on the chalkboard of a brilliant new day, but in failing to shape the present, she had no clear idea for the future. Her days were rumbling under the weight of that future as it galloped toward her, but because of the stampede, she couldn't see more than an oncoming dust cloud. Had she stopped for a moment to take a GPS reading, pinpoint a location, set a dream in reality, maybe it would be different. Instead she sat waiting, and missing the point of power which was always the present.

Then something happened. She was on her way out of the gym, all sweaty and disheveled, when she saw Dale coming in the front door. With the angle of the sun low in the morning sky, silhouetting his athletic, firm figure, he looked like Jesus might have a millisecond before he became waterborne. She gasped. Dale looked up.

"Hey, how's it going?" He held his fists out in front of him, thumbs out and almost touching, and rattled them up and down, opposite each other. "We're almost there."

"Almost where?"

"The weekend. Got any plans?"

Belinda wasn't a dimwit, but in that moment she suffered from dull tack syndrome. "Um, kayaking. With my son."

"Oh yeah? Whereabouts?"

"Down the Little Rosemont."

"Really? I live down there. Last house before the confluence opens up into the bay. There are some really sweet little rapids right around there."

Only then did Belinda realize – Dale was fishing. She smiled, feeling a need to redeem herself, but not quite sure how. "What...what are you doing this weekend?"

"Teaching. I got three group fitness classes. Hey, there's a Saturday morning RPM class you should come to. Awesome workout."

"Too hard," Belinda shook her head. "Too many people."

Dale laughed. "You work as hard as you want. Group fitness is actually a misnomer. It's only ever about you. Besides, you're on a stationary bike. You afraid you won't keep up?" The lopsided Viggo-grin again.

Belinda giggled. She felt fifteen.

"Maybe another time then," he said.

"Um, yeah. Well...bye." Belinda nodded and sprinted off before she could do further damage.

∾

Need advice? Are you sad and alone? Do you wish you could talk to someone whose opinion you revere, but who's already crossed over? Well, close your eyes and call them up. Kind of like talking to God, but less amorphous since you already know what your loved one looks like. Death is a ruse, the biggest con of all. The veil between the worlds is thinner than a spider's web. You just have to want to see through it.

On the morning of the one-year anniversary of Simone's death, Belinda noticed a wrinkle. It started as a laugh line around her mouth and continued down halfway to her jaw. It hadn't been there when she went to bed and now here it was, a shout-out from her future self, screaming up at her from the bottom of a deep gully. She slathered it with creams and oils, trying to fill the crevice that had opened while she slept, but the gully remained. Age was yucking it up, having the first of many good belly laughs at her expense.

She made coffee and sat down with the mail: circulars, advertisements, charities, and a single envelope from Domestic Court. She tore it open. It was official. Belinda was divorced. She should have been relieved to have her singularity back, to be rid of all those heaping spoonfuls of emotional detachment, or worse, derision, but instead she cried. She missed Ted in a weird, now you see him, now you don't, David Copperfield sort of way. At the root was one of Belinda's major truths: she wanted a family no matter how dysfunctional and had always been willing to give up personal safety to have one. She poured a second cup of black, steaming coffee and booted up her laptop. "I'll call him after I read my email. He should be up by then," she said to the room at large. The computer hummed and whirred, finally announcing its readiness to scan cyberspace with its trademark, "Good morning, Belinda" greeting.

As always, the Spam in her inbox runneth over. She deleted these emails unopened, but one which said simply, "Belinda" caught her eye. She clicked on it. It read:

B: Don't idolize the past or yearn for the future. The present has a certain trippy-ness about it that only those who stick with it realize. Besides, all yearning's gonna give you is a hernia. Don't die with the music still inside you . . . and forget that loser! Love, S

Belinda reread the message. A chill ran the length of her spine. She shivered and closed the laptop without shutting it off.

∾

When Jesus admonished his followers to turn the other cheek it wasn't because he liked being slapped. Nor was he lording a holier than thou attitude over anybody. Being God, Jesus could see all sides – everyone's perspective. He knew that people could have the most divergent views yet still all be at least partially right. Because rarely is it black or white, right or left, up or down, but usually some version of them all. Jesus's message was simple: tolerance for the other guy's point of view. Without tolerance there could be no harmony, no unity, no lasting happiness. Jesus also knew that the highest truth, the brightest light, comes not from being right, but from being at peace. And if he were alive today, he'd probably say that reacting with intolerance to life's various injustices no matter how right you might be guarantees only one thing: you aren't gonna sleep well tonight.

Belinda sat on the porch of her little bungalow watching the rise of the night sky, those brief iridescent, other-worldly moments when it changed like an artist's color wheel – first pale blue, then dusky, then cobalt, and finally, midnight. She longed to be under a big open expanse of it where she could see all the hues with their lingering intensities at once. Spring was a tardy student this year and she was grateful it had finally arrived. This past winter in all its unpredictability had bent her more than all the snows of her previous winters combined. Yet she'd arrived, sitting firmly on the doorstep of another new beginning, bedraggled, but not beaten. She drew a big breath of the chilly night air – it made her giddy like a good stiff drink – and resolved to do something to mark the occasion.

On Saturday morning, Belinda stood at the kitchen counter sorting through two days of mail, at least a hectare of trees by her estimation, what with all the junk mail, catalogues and solicitations. As was her custom, she looked once, ripped twice, and sent the whole lot into the circular file, sentencing wrapping paper, birthday cards, even free money – dimes, pennies, and the infamous check rebates – to landfill heaven. Through all this, Kyle stood by, still in his PJs, eating his cereal. She knew he was waiting until she left the room so he could sail in like a modern day Magellan, looking to discover a new world, sifting through the coffee grounds, banana peels, and bagel bits to get to the discarded circulars, pulling things out piece-meal in search of the spare nickel, the errant pen, the free note cards. She guessed this behavior had something to do with the dissolution of her marriage and Kyle's need to hang on to even the most inconsequential of things – the empty box from a gift his father had given him for his birthday was still under his bed – but there was nothing she could do about it other than pay for therapy later. At least that's what her psychologist had advised.

Kyle was in mid-resurrection when the phone rang and Belinda returned to the kitchen to answer it.

"Hello." She paused, and then, "But it's not your weekend." Another pause. "Fine." She hung up the phone, stared out the window for several moments before turning to Kyle.

"Your father wants to take you to a ball game," Belinda sighed; Kyle's eyes lit up, a question. "Go get ready then."

"Yessss!" He hesitated at the door. "What about kayaking?

"I waited thirty-six years. I can wait another weekend," Belinda said. She smiled to prove she wasn't angry, which she was, and Kyle bounded out of the room, guilt-free.

Twenty-minutes later, Ted arrived.

"Hey."

"Hey."

"Kyle ready?"

"I don't know. Go see."

"B..."

"Anything to mess me up, right?

"I'm not trying to mess you up. It's just that I got box seats and he loves baseball. What were you going to do today?

"Kayaking."

"Since when do you kayak?"

"Since today. And I wanted to go with my son." Belinda stared at her former husband, her anger threatening to split her like an overripe melon.

Ted studied his cuticles for a moment before giving Belinda his best Ted the Sincere face. "Look, I know I made a few errors – more than a few." He took a step toward her. "I know I hurt you, but maybe it's not too late, maybe pull the rabbit out of the hat in the bottom of the ninth?" He smiled, a tentative gesture. "We make a good team, Belinda."

Belinda felt her world tilt. Mixed metaphors swirled in her grey matter. She'd waited nights and weekends and holidays for just such an admission, of guilt, of repentance, of the fact that he needed her. And now that it had arrived, dripping wet and shaking from the cold, she wasn't sure whether she should let it in.

"What are you talking about?" she asked, even though she knew damn well. In their decade-long marriage, Belinda had never put him down so succinctly, yet so pointedly.

It was Ted's turn to stare. Belinda heard the word reconciliation clearly, though Ted's lips hadn't moved. He smiled his award-winning, Mick Jagger smile, capturing the insouciant boyishness of Ted of the Early Years. Something stirred inside Belinda. She stood on that stupid slope of many slips, peeking over the edge. She dared not take a single step more as those lips and that smile, big and saucy and full of insecurity disguised as love, came floating toward her. She squeezed her eyes shut and opened them again. His lips were gaining ground. In a moment, her lips would be surrounded like the Lakota at Wounded Knee.

Had it gone on just a nanosecond longer, had Belinda contained herself for even a millisecond more, the moment would have ended – to quote a bad 70's pop song – with a kiss. Maybe it was the Diet Coke she had for breakfast, maybe the butterflies in her stomach, or maybe an avoidance tactic, but just as Ted was about to plant one, and just as Belinda's mouth parted slightly to receive it – she burped. Not one of those loud, rude, roof-shaking burps, rather something small and petite, something you could take out to dinner, something more like a hiccup. She covered her mouth in apology and giggled. Ted looked chagrined. By the time Kyle walked into the room Belinda was hysterical and Ted was mortified.

"What's up, Mom?

"Uh," Belinda lurched forward, brushed his cheek with a kiss. "Everything," she giggled.

Kyle shrugged, planted a kiss on her cheek, grabbed his father's hand and pulled him to the door.

"Don't be home late," Belinda said as they got in the car.

"You still going?" Ted asked.

"Yep."

"I don't know if it's such a good idea for you to be out on the water by yourself. You know how you get lost," Ted said, half accusation, half observation. "Plus your vision's for shit."

Belinda stared at him, trying to gauge his level of concern versus sarcasm, but he was already backing out of the driveway. She waved after them as they pulled away, smiling like June Cleaver.

The minute Ted's tail lights were out of sight, Belinda began a blubber that lasted all the way to her car. On the way to the sporting goods store, she stopped at the entrance to the cemetery where they fenced in the dead. The juxtaposition of things that she'd formerly taken for granted confused her: her mother now her grandmother; her sister now her mother; her husband now her ex. She had a cat for comfort and a single love, her son, even though she was smart enough to know that putting all her love eggs in one basket left her prone and vulnerable to breakage. Still, the worst sin of all was her sheer, unremarkable life. Belinda stared at the ancient, fading gravestones with an affinity she hadn't felt for herself or another human being in a thousand lifetimes. She sighed, wiped her eyes, blew her nose on a scrap of tissue that Kyle had left wadded up in the console, and headed to the mall where they fenced in the living.

∾

Suppose we could "see it coming." How clear would our vision be? And would knowledge of the consequences whether ill or beneficent be sufficient for us to choose the right path?

At the sporting goods store, Belinda picked out a mid-range kayak, a Pongo, and a few bungee cords, and had the clerk, a young muscular boy, strap it on her Honda Pilot. She got a glimpse of her future again, swimming toward her like spawning salmon, using themselves up in their last great effort. Belinda headed for the river before she had a chance to think twice.

She drove by a cleared, open expanse of nothingness, what used to be a forest land. The earth had been turned, as if in preparation for farming, and sprayed with a lethal mist, a pesticide cocktail that knocked out everything in sight, leaving nothing moving, or growing. They sat in rows, the mechanical beasts, with their many arms – long, lean, impenetrable – arms that dug and stabbed and grabbed, leaving a flat, arid moonscape primed for development, arms that wanted more than they could hold, all arms and not a heart among them.

Belinda felt the weight of this on her chest, mounted on a shelf below her own heart. The temperature dropped a good ten degrees in this hallowed ground, devoid of its life force, haunted by the ghosts of the grove. She shivered and hit the accelerator.

The afternoon sun was still high in the sky when she unloaded the Pongo. She turned her face up to the blue ceiling; not a cloud for decades. It helped her shed the funk that Kyle's absence had created. She could have stayed home and sulked, or maybe banged her head against the wall, an activity, she read, which burned approximately 150 calories/hour. Kissing burned a mere 6 calories an hour, kissing Ted probably about 3 or 4, given that her heart didn't even race anymore. Kayaking had to be good for 200 to 300. Time to burn some calories.

∾

Water is the nectar of the gods, the juice of immortality. Water is the source of all life. At its base, the primordial ooze from which we've all evolved was water. Water is an integral part of our humanness, the source of our emotions, from the beginning when we floated in our mother's womb in a glorious, warm water sac, until the end when the last thing our bodies do is release their water. We cook with it, bathe with it, play in it, horde it, pollute it, steal it, hold sacred rites with it, and couldn't last more than four days without it. We drink the same water that's been on this planet since the days of the dinosaur, yet behave as if it will never run out. Water washes away our sins, provides us with a new start and a sense of renewal. So why are we so nonchalant about it?

By the time Belinda put the boat in the water the sun's trajectory was more diagonal than she'd expected, yet she wasn't deterred. She wasn't planning on being gone that long and if she stuck to the banks, she'd be okay. In theory it sounded fine, but in actuality, she knew she was in deep ten minutes after she launched. This was no way as easy as the rowing machine at the gym, plus the mosquitos were out in full battle gear, the temperature was a dozen degrees cooler on the water, and the sun's four o'clock rays were casting long lazy shadows along the shoreline. Ted was right. Belinda hated being alone. What else was he right about? She paddled harder, determined to meet her demons head on, and after half an hour, still nervous, but getting the hang of it, she squinted into the sun, and offered a silent supplication that the water might carry her safely.

So it wasn't the idyllic first-time out she'd envisioned, but Kyle had been part of that picture. Adjustments needed to be made. The nagging thought that she'd be better off with Ted refused to leave her. After all, Kyle did nothing to deserve a fractured family. He wanted to live in the same house as both his parents, yet despite her son's desires, and lonely as she was, another ten years with Ted would be torturous. There were a thousand reasons why she couldn't: her arms were weary from pulling him up all those hills; her throat was raw from screaming out instructions; her knees were weak from carrying his weight for so long; her heart heavy from having to feel for two. Worst of all, Belinda was a moon to his shining star and more and more she felt the need to shine in her own light. That was it, the whole enchilada. She took off her glasses, leaned back and let the kayak drift down river, forgetting everything. One of the positive things about nearsightedness is if you can't see it, you didn't have to deal with it. Toward the end of her time with Ted, that inward, narcissistic reflection had almost killed her. But today, floating down the river, it was an asset. Belinda felt serene, and for the umpteenth and hopefully final time, decided she was better off without him. It was time for her own happiness to matter.

She let the weight of it settle on her breastbone and a warmth spread, soft and slow, out through all her extremities. Belinda pulled the paddle across her lap and held her hands aloft. Bits of light emanated from her fingertips. She was completely engrossed, studying her fingers like a toddler plays with its toes, when the last gilded rays shot from her fingers and around a tree, dropping like an anchor below the horizon, leaving only a dense, smoky quality behind.

No! Belinda thrust herself forward and made a grab for that last bit of light, but the Pongo didn't take kindly to sudden changes in equilibrium. The sun with all its masculine bravado had split the scene, and Belinda, her gear, and most importantly, her glasses, had left the boat.

It takes twenty seconds for a red blood cell to circulate throughout the entire body, but panic made it through Belinda's in ten, sweeping up her leg, racing through her abdomen, and settling in the thymus gland, the place where decisions are made and judgments rendered. Her internal auditor swung into action. "What an idiot. What was I thinking? That I could actually do this alone?"

She could call Ted to come get her. With one hand she clung to the kayak. With the other, she flailed the water in search of the dry bag with her cell phone. After a couple crazed minutes, she stopped flailing and treaded water. Another heroic rescue effort by her ex-husband would lock her in for a lifetime. Besides, he couldn't find her if he wanted to. Not then and not now. Belinda stopped and drew a deep breath. She was at large and the freedom that came with this thought was both terrifying and exhilarating.

The water wasn't deep and Belinda could touch bottom if she stood on her toes. After a few tries, she flipped the boat and clambered back in. Her gear and glasses were gone and there were a couple gallons of water left in the bottom of the kayak. She'd have to wing it. She turned the boat around and started paddling. After a few ridiculous minutes of fighting the current, Belinda realized she was going nowhere. She was wet and shivering, there was no spit left in her mouth, and the idea of finding the dock, let alone pulling the boat out, all without her glasses, felt just like the day she and Simone left Bert and Nicole's house that last time: extraordinarily sad and hopeless. She sighed, pulled her paddle out of the water and let the swollen and cranky river carry her to parts unknown – backwards. *Oh God.* There had to be another way to go through life rather than to sit there like a lummox, waiting for it to dictate its desires. She thought of all those self-help books she'd devoured like dark chocolate over the course of her post-Ted internment and the apt metaphor for rebirth that was wailing in her face. What if God was a neutral third-party observer that had no desire other than to see life through my eyes? Her baptism would be here on the river where she would take hold of her life, even if only for the few minutes left of it.

She'd meant that in the metaphorical sense, of course, and was surprised to hear the amplified sound of gushing water. She turned in her seat, then turned the kayak around to get a better look. She couldn't see it, but she could hear it, as she rushed forward along with it. *Shit!* She wanted to vomit and sucked in the cool air to keep the nausea down. Could this be it? Her whole life boiled down to this one hydrated and random event. Simone was right. The present did have a certain trippyness about it. She looked about frantically for an escape route, began paddling toward the shore, riding the coattails of adrenaline, but the current was stronger here in the center of the river and she made little progress.

Even with the potential for death, it was soothing and hypnotic, like Niagara Falls. She floated into a lull in her consciousness where the space/time continuum was spilling out possibilities like a risk/management analyst. She took a sip. Her thoughts, crystalline with the full light of Death shining on them were of a much clearer nature here. Her whole life had been reduced to drops of water: blood, sweat and tears, mostly tears. She didn't remember hearing that the final moments before death were quite this lucid, but then how many people actually came back to discuss details.

In her mind's eye she was four again, swimming the breaststroke, holding her breath as long as she could, pushing herself, each time further without air. With every gulp, she'd catch a small glimpse, a photo in a mutable frame: the glorious, sunny day; the other kids splashing around; Simone, sunbathing and reading a magazine; Nicole's adoring face as she watched Belinda swim toward them. It may have taken a dozen of those breaths to get her across the pool. Some she struggled for, others not. She didn't remember any individual breath, just the overall feel of the swim, the strength of her arms and legs and determination. And no matter how hard she'd struggled en route, she always felt powerful upon arrival.

She pushed forward now, propelled by that thought. She kicked Fear with its sinister little grin to the bottom of the boat. It never did anything for her. Maybe it was better this way. She wouldn't see the end until she was literally going over the edge. It would be a fitting finale, one for the Queen of Hearts, like in the tarot cards, the woman who'd achieved mastery over her own soul.

She squinted in the direction of the shoreline. A light was glowing, swaying in the breeze. "Am I already dead?" She didn't remember going over the falls, didn't remember any pain whatsoever, but....

The light was growing closer and a real terror gripped her. She was dead, and any minute Nicole and Simone were going to walk through that light, grab her hand and bring her home. *Kyle!* She wasn't ready, not one bit. After thirty-six years, it was only in the last forty-five minutes that she'd finally figured out how to walk on her own. "Is this what I get for trying?"

"Belinda."

Belinda yelped. "Dammit, Simone. Not yet!" She clutched at the paddle, ready to fight for her life if need be. The voice did sound familiar, but it wasn't Simone. *Bert? Was he dead, too?* It had been a few years since she'd spoken to him, but . . .

"Belinda." the voice again, something familiar.... She felt a rush of energy in her solar plexus; warmth permeated her fifty trillion cells.

"Belinda!"

"Who is it?" She squinted hard, but her heart already knew the answer.

"Paddle harder. You're almost here," the voice replied. The light grew brighter.

"Is that you?" Belinda asked.

"Keep coming. You got this."

All she could see was the light, a ghostly, luminous thing, swaying in the night, embracing her in its sheen. Belinda took a deep breath and gave it one last push. She paddled straight into the dock. It hit with a thud. She grabbed the dock and yanked herself and the boat alongside it. A hand reached down and pulled her to the ladder, threw a rope around the handle of the kayak. As Belinda stepped out, she looked into the face of a man to whom she'd never uttered a complete sentence, at least not one that didn't include a stammer.

"How'd you find me?"

"You found me," Dale said. "I live here." He indicated a form loom- ing in the shadowy background, only the outline of which Belinda could see. Dale stepped aside to allow Belinda onto the dock.

"But how did you know I was out here?"

"Saw you coming. I was out watching the sunset. I was kinda hopin' you'd stop." Dale reached down and grabbed the rope handle on the tip of the kayak.

"Didn't have much choice, did I?" Belinda said, indicating the noise downriver.

"Sure you did. The rapids sound a lot worse than they are. But you've got to be able to see them to navigate." Dale chuckled. "Lost your glasses, eh?" He nodded toward the kayak. "Wanna get the other end?"

"Oh. Sure." Belinda reached down and together they brought the boat up onto the dock. "Still, what are the odds? That you'd be out here, I mean?"

"Well, you did say you might be going kayaking down here."

"That was three weeks ago."

"About how long I've been out here. Just at night and on the week- ends, though. I gotta job, you know."

Belinda managed an "oh," while contemplating that no one had ever waited on her that long.

"C'mon, have a seat. You just missed the sunset."

"Oh, I saw it."

Dale laughed again, a beautiful, light-hearted melody, and led her to a chair on the dock. He offered her a bottled water which she gulped gratefully and threw a towel around her shoulders.

"Three weeks? So no chance of this being a spontaneous encoun- ter? My last one ended in a ten-year detour."

"No, this was definitely planned. It almost rises to the level of stalk- ing, except I never left my back deck."

Belinda giggled.

"We've never been formally introduced. I'm Dale. I'll be your tour guide for this evening." He bowed at the waist in an exaggerated fash- ion and took a seat next to her. "I don't know what you know about me, but in the interest of honesty, I know everything that our computer knows about you." The Viggo-grin again. "One of the perks of the job." He held out his hand.

Belinda smiled, and this time, with the utmost of care and forethought and precision, she extended her hand. Dale took it. His grip was firm and warm.

"Actually, the computer probably didn't tell you that I prefer Constance. But you can call me Connie," Belinda replied, extending in addition to her hand, a more robust, more mature version of her formerly wide-open heart, this new version boasting a sturdy fissure and friendly lions at the gate.

"My pleasure, Connie."

So on this day, Belinda changed her destiny and finally became Constance, the immovable mountain that the clouds caressed, but could not cajole; that the water flooded, but could not drown; that the sun beat upon, but could not scorch; and she made peace with who she was, giving it a fresh face for the new Who she was becoming. But as with all things that shed one skin and grew another, traces of the old remained, little shiny bits, and some scaly ones, too, and so did bits of Belinda remain, sometimes muddy, sometimes murky, often bubbling and beautiful, like a river, like the name her mother gave her.

THE END

LEGEND:
Doc: ☼☼☼
Ellie: ☆ ☆ ☆
Celia: ❤ ❦ ♥
Harley: ✿ ❀ ❁

The Quality Of Light

☼☼☼

They climbed, suspended between worlds. Ellie set the pace, her agile legs scampering over pebbles and boulders alike. Doc had no trouble keeping up; he was accustomed to his wife's rhythm. He watched her, maneuvering around brush and rock, yielding nothing to the steep grade, meeting her formidable opponent at an erect, forty-five degree angle. Her posture spoke volumes, yet Doc knew it was just overcompensation for the pudgy girl who never really recognized the firm and sculpted woman she'd become.

When they reached the mesa, Doc pulled a bottle of water from his pack and handed it to Ellie. They shared long drafts until the bottle was empty then sat down on a boulder to catch their breaths. Doc tossed the bottle to the ground and fished around in his backpack.

"Recycling fourteen of those bottles can make one extra-large polyester t-shirt."

"So you've said."

"You're not going to leave it there, are you?"

"Yes, Ellie, I hiked miles into the sky to look at this magnificent view and leave a plastic water bottle."

They exchanged grins, his sardonic, hers sheepish. She held a hand out for the binoculars and Doc placed them there without taking his eyes from her face. She surveyed the valley like a general in enemy territory, squinting against the glare of the early morning sun inches above the horizon and already broadcasting the tenor of the day. Doc used a handkerchief to wipe the sweat from his wife's brow then applied it to his own forehead. She leaned back against him despite the heat.

"It's got to be ninety already," Doc said.

Ellie nodded. "Look. Right there . . . and there. Not more than a quarter mile between them, I'd say. That's just too damn close."

He agreed, but Doc was more interested in watching Ellie watch the miles of valley below, the slight breeze, ruffling her sun-kissed auburn hair; her unique and captivating eyes – one brown, one green; the sleek curve of her neck; and her long, delicate fingers as they held the binoculars. At forty-one, Ellie retained the athleticism of a thirty-year old. She was a handsome woman with a classic beauty that might not have been appealing to everyone in the age of supermodels and skinny jeans. To Doc, she was the most beautiful woman he'd ever seen, even with the fine lines that had begun to form around her eyes, lines that could etch into deep crevices and still not change his appraisal.

Ellie handed Doc the glasses; Doc swiveled his gaze. He could see them, minuscule specs against the expanse of land and sky, the sunlight glinting off their shiny little heads. Move even a decimeter in any direction and they disappeared. He could see the noxious fumes emanating, rising in a fine mist and dispersing particulate matter into the atmosphere. Of course, he was making the latter part up. It was only his knowledge of alchemical processes along with an engineering degree that now accessed a diagram from the computer-like recesses of his brain. Ellie would say instead that he was accessing the Zero Point Field, the web of life where all possibility resides, but Doc didn't buy into such nonsense.

Still, he thought he could see something rising up, and not just the blazing heat of the morning that slowed and twisted the atmosphere until you could almost touch each molecule as it shimmied in the sun. No, it was something else. Maybe it would account for the headache that was gaining momentum at the base of his skull. Even looking at those wells felt toxic. Something should be done, he knew, but he wasn't the man for the job.

Celia stood in the center of an open field, her arms raised, her face to the sky.

"Thank you for coming to our village. We hope you will stay with us," she said to the few wispy clouds dotting the sky, not in a booming voice, but with an unrivaled sense of commanding, of certainty, less asking than demanding. She paused, brought her hands together in prayer at her heart center, and proceeded through a series of three sun salutations in each of the four directions. When she finished, Celia repeated her mantra while walking in circles. The air was redolent of the sage that stretched for acres, each connected to the other like family. A gentle wind blew, suggesting that Celia's prayers had already been answered and now it was simply a matter of manifestation. She circled and chanted and sometimes shook her rain stick. After twenty-five minutes, she sat down, cross-legged in the middle of the great open expanse, toning her vibration to that of the earth, using her body as a musical instrument. Celia was named for the patron saint of music, St. Cecelia, and as a result, toning was second nature to her. So she sat, humming and breathing her energy into the earth and taking the earth's energy back in again, a reciprocal arrangement. Twenty minutes later Celia got back in her car and drove to a local diner. She was starving so she ate a full breakfast of eggs, turkey bacon, toast and coffee. Two days later, the drought that had plagued Santa Fe for most of the spring and all of the summer ended.

Unfortunately, the rain brought the thunder and lightning which inadvertently accelerated a change that Celia would never have consciously invoked in a single one of the parallel universes she sometimes found herself living. If she was upset by the role her actions played in the fate of those she loved, however, she didn't say.

✧✧✧

One week after the rains abated, on the last ride of their married life together, Doc gave Ellie the silent treatment. What was different today was that Ellie wasn't talking either.

Doc had showered, shaved and eaten a bowl of yogurt and granola with bits of dried mango and cranberry. He chewed and swallowed and watched CNN, followed by the local news that gave the weather every eight minutes. It was going to be chilly so he chose a brown plaid sports jacket and Dockers. He polished his black leather shoes to an oily slick sheen; he owned no other color, and having never been possessed of a discerning eye for fashion, found black to be the hands-down universal favorite. He read the paper until Harley was ready to go.

The first noticeable divergence, proof that something was different about today, came when he stepped into the hearse. At precisely 8:00 a.m. – God, these people were nothing if not punctual – the limo pulled into the driveway, its windows reflecting the clouds hovering above his head, menacing puffs of vapor that seemed to surround and intimidate him. He was keenly aware of how ridiculous he looked, batting at the air as he slid into the back after Harley. "Get," he said, slamming the door before the clouds swallowed him. Perhaps he was being inane, but considering the havoc a cumulonimbus could wreak, Doc couldn't be too careful.

The hearse should have been the epitome of comfort, but felt like central lock down, and Doc found himself gasping for air as he unfolded his six foot three-inch frame into the plush leather. He fiddled with the electronic windows – up, down, up, down, up, down – hoping for an air stream of relief. The hearse driver glanced at him in the rear view mirror and asked, pertly, if everything was to his satisfaction. Doc managed a weak nod before proceeding with his internal wrestling match, fighting his mind for control of his body. Harley sat next to him, her thirteen-year old inquisitiveness eerily silent for a change. Doc skirted her eye, opting for the window where an early morning azure with an air of immense promise was on the fast track.

Ellie lay snuggled in the back, he presumed, in her lacquered wooden eternity bed. He and Celia had decided on a closed casket for the obvious reason – what now passed for Ellie wasn't too much to look at. He hadn't seen his wife since she took off for work seven days ago. Instead he had to rely on the veracity of strangers: that she'd been struck by lightning; that what remained lay inside the coffin; that the singed and half-eaten body – he couldn't stop thinking of it as wolf barbecue – that he used to call his wife was completely, wholly, and inexorably dead. He had the sudden urge to lift the lid and get one more look meant to last him his remaining lifetime, but didn't want to diminish the random and beautiful visions he retained of her. Had Doc been the one to find Ellie where she lay, smoldering in the rain, or worse, baking in the sun – he likely wouldn't have slept ever again. He looked at Ellie's daughter with a mixture of sadness, regret, and utter confusion. Now only they two remained.

What was it Harley always said? OMG?

The weeks that followed the funeral stretched and finally settled into oblivion. Every day, Doc got up, showered, shaved and ate a bowl of yogurt and granola. When he came home he gave Harley dinner, asked her if she needed help with her homework – sometimes she needed help with math – or watched a movie with her on TV until she'd announce, "I'm going to bed," and Doc would nod, accept the proffered kiss, and they'd get up the next day and do it all again. It wasn't hard, so much as singular. Even sitting in the same room together, they were each alone. Nothing had changed between them except that the central focus of their lives had been removed from the equation, leaving them to see more clearly who they'd been all along – free neutrons, unstable and in search of a nucleus.

He started talking to himself. He dreamed of resting for days on end, to get his bearings and catch up on some long-neglected restorative sleep. It might ease the dull ache at his temples to dream some of his heartache away, but there was Harley and work, so he plodded along, the good soldier, despite that his very existence had been riven by fate.

Doc's first indication that something was wrong came the day Harley shook him awake. He never slept late, but the bed was cushy as he lay there, sleep within his grasp, falling into the fibers of the sheets, the defining line between his body and the mattress blurred and sketchy and imperceptible. He was sharing space with a dust mote, careening erratically through a robust shaft of light, but Harley's grip on Doc's shoulder seemed determined to rip him from his narcoleptic state. Just as he and the dust mote landed on the down comforter, Doc looked up and noted two things: the digital alarm clock read 5:55 a.m.; and Harley had tears in her eyes.

Had he been a good sign reader, he would have concluded that something was amiss. But reading signs had never been his forte so he mumbled a phlegmatic "thank you" and closed his eyes to regroup. Harley shook his shoulder again, hard.

Doc cleared his throat. "I'm late," was all he could manage as he pulled himself up on one elbow and threw his feet over the edge of the bed. A scream rose from his penis, got stuck there. The pain doubled him over until he caught his breath along with a glimpse of the catheter. Something in the mirror above the dresser caught his eye, something primal and unsettling. A man with a wild, bristly beard and a big shock of white hair, approximately two-inches in diameter, sticking straight out from the right side of his head like a single antler. The face was sallow, almost jaundiced, indicating a liver condition or perhaps not enough sun. Or maybe it was a heart that couldn't muster the energy to pump blood to all the extraneous parts of the body.

Stranger. In the room. Doc gasped. *Harley!*

Doc tried to pull himself up, but couldn't stand.

"Aunt Celia!"

Harley. Running. Go. Quick. Scary stranger. Doc tried to yell after her, but something was wrong with his vocal cords, the muscles irresolute. He touched his Adam's apple, pushed it from side to side. It made him cough. Panic ensued, wreaking chaos along the inside track of his esophagus, like dust at the feet of a race horse. Doc made small inane movements with his lips for several seconds, but no air passed between them. He couldn't breathe, couldn't speak. He fell over onto the bed in slow motion. His descent ended with a final drum beat when his right eyebrow hit the night stand and his shoulder hit the floor.

Then Celia was there, drawn by the thundering floor boards, grunting and pulling along with Harley, whose lithe, ninety-two pound frame was giving all she had to the task. He wanted to say something, to explain to them the danger. *Take Harley and go...*but his tongue had fused with the roof of his mouth and he couldn't pull it free. Then they were covering him with a sheet and smoothing his hair and pushing him down and muttering soothingly, standing there, both of them, looking queerly at him, and there was no stranger, just them, at the foot of his bed, and....

He felt the shift when realization hit his cerebellum. Something deep was rising, filling him up, forcing his mouth wide. It started low, and guttural, shifted, grew louder, needier, and then the sound of his own voice, pouring into his ears until he rode the wave of it back into present time where a sob burst through that would not be stopped.

☼☼☼

He would've never guessed it. Nobody in his position could have. From his vantage point it had all been very normal. He'd gone to work, taken care of Harley, answered his email every day, or so he thought. Granted it was all in the spirit of a functioning alcoholic – there, but not quite – still he'd managed by telling himself that if he could just get through the first year he'd be all right. He'd not contemplated how difficult the living would be, or that time only works as a healing tool if you're taking up space inside of it. Time had misplaced him. Or perhaps, he had misplaced time.

How long?

Doc heard a rustle in the doorway. He didn't have to turn to know it was her. The smell of lavender and cedar announced her arrival. A barefoot Celia wore faded jeans and a light blue hoody. She took a chair next to the bed while Doc laid there in an unblinking posture of foreboding. Celia sat down; her steady breathing sat with her. After a few minutes, she lit a smudge stick and began to chant, waving the smudge stick above the lintel and surrounding door frame, her silver bracelets clinking, soothing, like water dripping over rocks. Doc knew what she was up to. She was reciting the blessings, cleansing the space of his negative energy, asking the white spirits to fill it up. She circled the windows, billowing whiffs of burning sage and cedar, permeating a room already filled with their fragrance. What chance did his negativity have against such odiferous and purposeful clouds of smoke? The incense diffused, joined with air molecules, and suffused his alveoli, those millions of tiny air sacs housed in his lungs which shared responsibility for exchanging oxygen for carbon dioxide. *Stop!* He wanted to scream, but the onslaught of cedar had left him weak and heady and breathless.

When Celia finished working the room she began working Doc, smudging him from head to toe, using her hand to sweep something toward the window with each movement. Doc followed *something's* trajectory, but saw nothing. Celia placed a hand on his heart and he twitched as if electrocuted. She placed both hands there and a warmth spread through his body. The warmth grew into serious heat and he squirmed, but Celia formed an imaginary pair of scissors with her index and middle fingers and began to cut away at the space above his heart, circling the perimeter. There was something dark and hard and impenetrable in the center, protecting him from an invasion of hostile forces. *If she cuts that bit away, what will she see?*

Doc strained his eyes, saw nothing but a smoky haze. Celia pushed the refuse into a small trash can, opened the blinds and corralled in the sunlight, making scooping motions with her hands. More hocus pocus. She pointed three fingers at Doc's chest prompting a sharp intake of breath. Celia coughed several times as Doc experienced a now familiar emotion, welling in his throat and stinging his eyes. He swallowed it before it could rise any higher, but Celia coughed again and Doc's throat popped and his mouth felt full. He opened it and he, too, coughed, expecting a swarm of moths to emerge, but there was nothing but air, at least to the naked eye. Doc's mind reached back to touch the precipitating factor in this schematic, but a deep, black chasm lay before him and he didn't have the strength to jump it. His heart felt like someone had soldered the valves shut. He closed his eyes and watched as a long thin bridge of ice two feet across began to sprout, spanning the diameter of the chasm.

"Put your hands on it," he heard a voice say. He touched it with his foot. It was solid. As he began to cross, the bridge misted over until Doc could no longer see his feet buried beneath the fog. He took a tentative step, slipped and dropped to his knees, grabbing the icy surface with both hands. More comfortable with this navigation process, he began anew. Just when he thought he could see the edge of the land mass on the other side, when he could almost reach out and touch it, the bridge abruptly ended. No blinking lights. No yellow caution signs. Just emptiness. Doc was so engrossed in his forward progress, he didn't realize it until he started to fall. He tried to scream, but his voice failed him so he buried his head and prepared to take a seat in the front row of oblivion.

"I can't help you if you won't stay with me."

Doc rolled over and looked at the clock. 5:55 p.m.. *Damn numbers.* The last rays of the day nudged their way into the room, making love to the Levolor blinds. Celia was there again, this time in black slacks and a shawl with flowing, vivid colors, her jewelry tinkling, the slimmest of smiles on her face. Ellie's twin. He watched her watching him, saw a shadow cross striking blue eyes. Her eyebrows twitched upward. She tilted her head, a question. Doc nodded, barely perceptible.

"Three weeks."

Her words floated toward him like reconnaissance ships, testing the waters. Doc cleared his throat and tried to bend his rusty vocal chords to his will, but they barely budged.

"Three," he croaked, his voice catching on emotion and mucus.

Three weeks? A spasm shot through his solar plexus. He looked down at his once muscular body now loose with its flaccid skin and gelatinous muscles. He'd seen a face in the mirror, a stranger's face, and recoiled. He cleared his throat again.

"How do you always know – what I'm about to ask?" The words lurched out hoarse and gnarled.

"Process of elimination."

"Where's my wife? Where's Ellie?"

Doc braced for an answer he already knew, but Celia didn't deliver, just shook her head and smiled through watery eyes. She rose, her musical adornments rising with her.

"I'll give you some time to digest this," she said, leaving Doc alone with a haze of cedar and fragments of his former life.

He emerged an hour later, wearing sweats and a T-shirt, his hair in all directions, the one shock of white sticking out in a northeasterly direction. He tugged at it. It felt thicker than the rest of his hair as if each individual strand was made of fibrous wood. It hadn't been there when he went to bed three weeks ago. He shuffled from one piece of furniture to the next until he found Harley in the living room, reading a book, the page inches from her face. She looked unhappy and he suspected, wore her crabbiness to hide a bruised and battered heart. He noted the title as he turtled his way past, *A Series of Unfortunate Events*, considered its origins for a moment, fell over. Harley was at his side in a second, pulling him up as he pulled down. He didn't want to get up, didn't want to be helped to his feet by a thirteen-year old, but then relented, rolled onto his knees, and between the two of them, he got off the ground. She helped him into a chair opposite the couch where she'd been sitting, then retreated to her own corner and waited for him to speak. She smiled, but it looked like she'd just been poked with a sharp object and was trying not to scream.

"Hello," he said.

"Hello," she replied, nothing genuine, but in that halfhearted way that told Doc she was using his face as a mirror by which she could gauge her performance. She studied him for a moment, smiled again, lifted her chin to him. He flushed, unaccustomed to being under the microscope, usually the observer, but now the observed. When he didn't speak she went back to reading. He wished for one of those "Sham-Wow" cloths they advertised on late-night infomercials. But instead of soaking up water or spills, he could soak up Harley's anger and enmity and distrust. She glanced over the top of her book periodically, but said nothing. About three minutes went by before he spoke:

"Harley!" a bit too sharp, considering. She flinched, dropped the book to her lap. He noted she didn't lose the page.

"How's it going?"

"Good."

The monosyllabic answer. He hated that. *Would it kill her to elaborate?*

"What have you been doing?"

Harley shrugged. The zero-syllabic answer. Worse. He felt his ire rise.

"Do you think you could help me out a little bit here, Lee? I've been out of it for three weeks. What do you want me to do? Apologize? Okay. I'm sorry, all right?"

She tilted her head to the side and shrugged a shoulder up to meet it, then looked down at her lap. He thought he saw a tear let loose, followed by a second, a coconspirator.

Shit. Did she need to do this right now? He rose to go. "Tell you what. I'm going to leave you alone until we've both had time to get used to..." Doc struggled for the words, "me being awake. I'll be in the kitchen, making tea, maybe staring at my toe jam, maybe driving a nail into my temple. Stop by when you get a chance." He turned and shuffled, with unbalanced, painful steps, to the kitchen.

What he wouldn't have given to be able to sprint away, maybe even slam a door.

I knew the minute I conceived her. I didn't want to tell him so I watched him drive away with a promise to send for me when he got set up in the next city. He couldn't take me on his cycle, he said, but I was no fool, and as he waved goodbye, I knew exactly what he was taking and what I was keeping. I was fine with it. It was probably selfish of me not to tell him: that his baby was only a minute old, and growing in my belly, and that I needed it as no leverage, or tether, or hook. I needed nothing other than what he'd already given me. I loved him, but I knew now we were free, baby and me, to live the life we wanted.

I hadn't known how much I'd wanted a child until presented with the option. My body closed around her like a Venus Fly Trap, and for the first time in my life I felt whole, like all my parts were accounted for. It's funny how you can carry your brain around for a lifetime and never feel the weight, but just try ignoring your heart. In that moment, my heart swelled with love and grief and hope and loss and promise which were way too many emotions to dissect while standing on a street corner with my hand in the air. The weight of my decision felt like being buried alive, but I knew we'd be all right. I named the baby Harley while watching his tail lights fade, as much for practicality as anything. Boy or girl, I'd be covered. Harley's father beeped once as he rounded the corner, and my hand responded whether in farewell or benediction, even I don't know. At that exact moment the baby that would become Harley waved, too.

She had an inauspicious beginning, and but for the intervention of medical science, it would have ended differently, perhaps with a death or even two. Harley led with her elbow, ripping and tearing like a front-end tackle. When she emerged she looked like pulled taffy, all arms and legs and neck, practically a mutation, but with the right luck and lighting, maybe a supermodel.

"Better to have people flocking for an autograph than chasing you out of town with a pitch fork," Celia said. Celia was full of that kind of sarcasm.

"Just another one of the free services I offer," she'd quipped. I alternated between fierce love and sheer frustration when it came to my sister, but after Harley was born it was all love all the time. We were an Eastern Bloc: Celia, Harley and me. We three.

My father is a liar. My father is an emotional cripple. My father is a worthless sack of shit. My father isn't even my father, but he's all I've got right now, so I'm trying, a bit desperately, to make things work.

My real father was a musician, classically trained as a violinist. He did a teaching gig at my mother's college so he could spend a summer in the states, giving violin lessons to would-be prodigies, of which my mother was definitely not, but she needed to fill her elective. She described him as tall and handsome, with a small cleft in his squarish, strong chin. Classic, right? My mother was a biology major with no personal or familial musical abilities to draw upon. She said that when she met my father she was, to use her cliché, swept off her feet, but she was only twenty-one, just a baby-adult, barely legal to drink alcohol and so what could she possibly know about anything?

Anyway, my mom fell in love with the wimpy violin guy – I mean, at least play the cello bass or something with a little heft to it. They had a summer of love, and then he was gone, back on the road, playing in the orchestra in cities all over the world, gone before he even knew I was a probability. My mother could have tracked him down. He played for the Vancouver Symphony, and it's not like they're not in the phone book. Heck, she could have just called the office and left a message: "Baby on the way. Give me a call," but she had some crazy notions about the lasting nature of love. She said that by letting it go she could preserve it in perpetuity, whatever that means. She said that the summer of love they had shared would always be there for her, unaffected by time or age or ennui, and I know that means boredom because I looked it up.

"That's the only kind of love that lasts, Harley," Mom said. "The kind that's under glass."

She always added that she was only talking about romantic love. "Different than the love I have for you, Lee, which is unquantifiable and positively outside of time or space."

She said stuff like that a lot. I'm not sure I understood what she was talking about at the time, but I do know now at least this much: for the first six years of my life I had the starring role in mom's daytime soap, the undivided center of her universe. Then He came along and busted the whole thing up. What Mom didn't understand was that you can't just glue random parts together and expect it to form a perfect circle. She thought it would make our lives better, but the truth is, when he showed up, all the walks in the park and swinging on the swings, the bedtime stories and dancing around the living room until I thought I would puke, all those points of light in a near perfect bubble of light became tainted, and some even disappeared, leaving just their shadows behind, because he was always there, getting in the way and ruining it for me.

Imagine the sun at the end of the day just before dusk comes to walk it home. Imagine the color, the quality of light. The rays are deep and rich and filled with the memory of everything that happened during the day like the world could go on forever. There they are, all those memories, locked up in those few last moments of light. It's not rocket science to see why people are always praying to the sun. It makes you feel warm and safe and loved all at the same time. That's the bubble we lived in, me and Mom. Then Doc came along and Mom tried to attach him to our bubble, but instead of floating we sagged and hovered near the ground like helium balloons the day after the party. She tried to show him, to pull him in along the edges, but he ended up sitting right in the middle, taking up space, and after that it was never the same for me and Mom. Our bubble had sharp edges and squiggly lines sticking out in weird places. There was no smoothing it out, either. It's hard to know how it would have turned out if Doc never came along. If it would have just been me and Mom, two single girls, living our lives, and Aunt Celia, too, of course. It would have been great, I think, but maybe that's selfish and maybe I'm wrong. Maybe Mom would have turned sour from missing out. Who knows? No one can ever say what the path not taken looks like because they didn't take it, right? We did do a lot of cool stuff with Doc. Fun stuff that me and Mom wouldn't have done without him. Plus, he could make her laugh. But not like I could. Never like that.

★ ☆ ☆

"I want you to have this."

He pulled a small red box out of his sock and slid it across the table toward me. My eyes were riveted.

"That's not a ring, is it? Because if it's a ring…. I mean, it's only been a few months, right? Tell me it's not a ring."

He laughed, but didn't reply. It was a four-star restaurant and my thirty-fifth birthday. Doc was determined to make it a five-star night. A woman knows, after all, when a man wants her.

"You're enjoying watching me squirm, aren't you?"

"Immensely," he said.

"Why did you have this in your sock?"

"Well, if you remember, a bit earlier we were rolling around on the bed. I didn't want you to find it before dinner."

I cocked one eyebrow and presented him with my most skeptical look.

"Open it."

I know my hands shook as I opened it, removing the spongy white cotton to get to the prize: a gleaming skeleton key. I took it out of the box carefully, like it was a precious archeological remnant.

"What's it to?"

He smiled, took my hand, and placed it over his heart without any sense of restraint or embarrassment. He was only half-serious when he started, but by the time he finished, I could tell he meant it.

"It's the key to my heart. Something I've never given away." He looked at Ellie. "Do you accept?"

In response, I kissed him.

He hadn't asked for her. Rather, she'd asked for him directly and in earnest, walked him down a red-carpeted path strewn with paper roses. Gave him a crown to wear made of foil flowers. So eager was she to fit in, that at six, she sold her soul without care, just to have a father in her life. She knew nothing of him, just that she wanted him, or a reasonable facsimile of him, wanted what he could represent, what the totality of We Three could become – a nuclear family to round out the life that she'd imagined, the one that lives on repeatedly in the princess books she was so fond of. Harley didn't even have words for what she wanted, or if she did, they were six-year old words.

"You look like husband and wife," she'd said on Doc's first date with her mother. Ellie blushed; Harley beamed. "I need a father and you're as good a choice as any," she may as well have said.

As reluctant as Doc was to take on such a daunting task, the moment he decided on Ellie, he decided on Harley, too. There wasn't a choice, really. Harley was just part of the bargain, like, buy this set of Encyclopedia Britannica and we'll throw in a free bookcase. Overnight, Doc became a husband and a father, and it took him years to catch up to the decision. Whereas most people have the fecund space of nine months, followed by a couple years of goo-goo-ga-ga-ing to get used to the fraternal requirements, Doc had about three hours. The first time they sat down to dinner in their new house Doc felt like screaming. Suddenly he was hurtling down the highway at warp speed with a blind bend ahead. He knocked over a water glass and made a great escape.

Harley started to cry as Doc bolted for the door.

"I'll be back," he'd said, but hadn't meant it. What he had meant was to turn tail and run and never look back. If Ellie was concerned, she didn't let on, just watched him run out on her.

☼☼☼

When Doc got back from the bar a few hours later, Harley was asleep. Ellie was in bed, reading, waiting for him. It was his first meeting with something he'd not known before – selflessness. She didn't need him, yet she waited for him and what he had to offer: the gestalt of them as a family, something greater than their discreet parts as individuals. So Doc climbed into bed while Fear clutched at his solar plexus and Love managed to pull the covers over them both.

It was tough in the beginning, eased up, got tough again. Their problems, Doc and Harley's, revolved around the fact that he wasn't her dad, that she had no memories about her real dad, and that she now had to share her mom. The most overarching problem, though, was that they didn't share the same DNA. Communication issues abounded. They may as well have been speaking different languages because neither had a clue what the other was saying. Problems shifted like beach sand, sometimes heading out to sea, always returning to the shore that was Ellie. Ellie was the cushy down comforter, the bringer of joy, the ultimate mediator, but when the mediator quits, you're left with angry factions, staring out of separate windows.

Which was where they found themselves now: Doc looking north, Harley looking east. It was unfortunate, but every word he spoke to her came out as a rebuke. He could hand her a $100 bill and it would appear condescending. He didn't mean it that way, honestly he didn't, but there was something about her that at worst grated on his last nerve and at best invoked a feeling of avuncular indulgence, not the fatherly pride that he was so longing to feel. He wasn't sure if this was a result of something either one of them did. Rather, it was this feeling of *deja vu*, that they'd been down this long and rocky path before, that something abominably unforgivable had transpired between them and there was little that could be done to replace that kind of past with feelings of genuine affection. Perhaps they'd been arch enemies in another lifetime where her knights had vanquished his knights and burnt his castle to the ground. It would have made sense if Doc believed in such things. He knew his ill feelings caused an imperceptible rift between him and

Ellie, yet every time he vowed to make it right all his tenderness withered in the sweltering sun of Harley's provocative gaze.

Doc walked to the doorway and peered through squinting eyes at Harley still reading her book. He calculated the steps that it would take to walk from here to the couch. The distance was too great to walk alone. He imagined sitting next to her, his arm wrapped around her, listening to whatever it was she cared to talk about the way fathers are supposed to do. Maybe this time....

He cleared his throat and took a step across the threshold, a tentative olive branch. Harley started to turn, caught herself, tensed up instead. She resumed reading with hyper-vigilance while every muscle in her body remained rigid. That's all it took. Doc's own body responded in a transference of negative energy, and there they were again, back at their pitiful start.

Had Doc allowed himself to break free of these constrictions, there's no telling to what level his Soul may have risen, but he was a practical man, not prone to exaltations. To even dip a toe in the river of ecstasy would have been way beyond his comfort zone. However disagreeable, friction was much more manageable than ecstasy. Where he'd always defined himself and his body by certain parameters – intelligent, muscular, pensive, prudent, energetic, to name a few – he found that since the non-weeks, during which his profound depression over his wife's death had rendered him useless and incoherent, the rules he'd followed no longer applied. Doc wished there was a pill to take, something to make the *acida*, the heartburn, go away. It wasn't a physical burn, more of a heat ache. Ellie had maintained all manner of feng shui remedies to balance their home, their garden and their lives, but without her, Doc was incapable of balancing his heart. Defeated, he went and sat back down.

"How'd you sleep?"

Doc jumped, spilling coffee on his pajama pants. She'd come into the kitchen on cat-feet, startling him with *The Question*. She couldn't stop asking and he couldn't stop being irritated by it. In the three days he'd been awake, he'd barely slept more than a few hours a night, and now here she was with *The Question*. She'd always asked it of him, and even with a good eight-hours under his belt, her asking it of him had always chapped his ass. When anyone else asked, it was just a question. When Harley asked, it was an icebreaker, like chatting up a stranger about the weather. Weather was neutral. Weather was safe. Weather didn't mean shit. After seven years they hadn't gotten past The Question. In response, his spirit retreated, took cover inside the long spindly tentacles of inertia and exhaustion. It took energy to have a breakdown and he was flat out. He'd failed Ellie. Not only did he not understand her daughter; he didn't care to try. Everything she said had an air of plasticity, of unctuousness about it. He would take a bilious, naked confrontation rather than the smarmy weak chatter that passed for their dialogue. At least that would be genuine. Doc blinked. Harley cleared her throat...

"Why are you sitting in the dark?" she asked, flipping on the light.

A logical question. Doc wasn't sure how to answer except to say that light, in general, peeled away at the details of his life until it reached the core and exposed the rotting parts. Given Doc's tremulous physical state he wasn't ready for any groundbreaking discoveries.

"Please turn off the light." He buried his head in the newspaper, but the sun hadn't reached the kitchen window yet and he could barely see the print. He watched Harley peripherally, pouring her cereal, then the milk. Even with her mouth closed, she sounded like a cow chewing its cud as it sloshed and smacked and slurped against her teeth. He wanted to scream, to reach across the table and smack the food out of her mouth, make the noise stop, but he just sat there, frozen, assembling and reassembling the same sentence in his brain, trying to make sense of the words as he read them, but they were drowned out by the incessant chomping of Apple Cinnamon Cheerios.

He sighed, a harsh, audible statement, and abruptly rose, knocking the chair over. Harley jumped.

"Bathroom," he mumbled, set the chair upright, and limped from the room.

☼☼☼

The weather forecast called for rain, but the sky to the East was cerulean without a speck of white. Not so with the sky to the North. The horizon held back an angry menace, water molecules, swollen and overcrowded, thumping and crashing against their neighbors, inciting revolution. Doc watched Ellie, lying on the blanket where minutes earlier they'd made love, transfixed as distant rain drops danced, whirling dervishes in the sky. Thunder, moisture, air and light embraced and dispersed, locked in a terrifying energetic battle, congealing to form a vaporous nightmare.

"We gotta go," Doc said, and put on his backpack.

"The show's just getting started." Ellie wasn't afraid, simply captivated.

"We'll be French Toast if we stay here until intermission."

Ellie laughed her deep belly laugh and Doc laughed in tandem, swept up in its effervescence. He reached out a hand and pulled her to her feet, planted a kiss on her lips. Ellie picked up the blanket, stowed it under her arm, and grabbed Doc's hand. She was lit from within.

"I love you, too," he said.

A crack of thunder sent them scrambling. Even though it was still a mile away, storms in this valley were erratic. They could take an hour, or three minutes to arrive and Doc didn't want to find out which it would be. He took one last look at the valley. Storm scouts were already dulling the sun. Without the light to provide the identifying markers, he could no longer make out the wells which was fine, because somehow they were going to change his life and the less he knew the better. Doc closed his eyes against the wind and by instinct guided Ellie home.

❦ ❦ ❦

"Hello!" Celia blew in the door like a gale force wind. Harley was sitting on the couch, hunkered down, pretending to read. Celia wasn't fooled.

"What's the matter, baby?"

Harley shrugged, buried her face in her book. Celia felt Harley's forehead. For Harley's first twelve years, she looked like a mutant: arms too boney, legs too long for her torso, swan-like neck — before the swan acquired grace and beauty — feet the size of a longshoreman. The girls made fun of her while the boys ignored even the thought of ignoring her. Of course, Ellie and Celia adored her and saw only the most beautiful girl in the world every time they looked at the child. Now, in her thirteenth year, all but traces of the ugly duckling remained. The swan was ready to make her debut.

"Lee...?"

Harley cleared her throat, threw herself back on the couch. Celia brushed Harley's hair back. Water droplets crested the bridge of her nose sideways and fell away, sucked into the fibers of the pillow.

Celia wiped Harley's eyes. "Awww, honey."

"I just feel like crying all the time." She buried her face into the pillow. "I miss Mommy so much."

"That's okay. That's what you're supposed to do when someone dies."

"For like, ever?" she sputtered. "'Cause it doesn't feel like it's ever gonna stop and I don't know if I have the stamina."

"No. Not forever, but for a while."

"I'm trying really hard to be happy because I know that's what Mom would want, but sometimes I just want to die, too, you know? I don't want to live my life when Mommy isn't in it."

Celia sat down on the couch at Harley's waist and wrapped an arm around her.

"I know, honey. You guys had a really special bond. Would it help if I told you you'll see her again? That you'll have more lifetimes together?" Harley shrugged.

"Picture this: a bleak winter sky, a small town, the houses all built close together. A place where snow falls from September to May. The weather's harsh, but there's always a nice fire going and water for tea and neighbors who pull together because that is the only way everyone survives. You might like this lifetime more than one lived in, say, Hawaii, because of the people who live with you, and what if in that lifetime you were the mom and Ellie was the daughter."

"That's crazy."

"Yes, and possible. We can only guess where we've been. It doesn't matter because time isn't really linear. We just choose to see it that way. Right this very minute, you and your mom are also somewhere else, doing something else. Maybe you're her brother, or her best friend."

"Maybe." Harley grimaced. "And I get your point, but that doesn't really help me right now, Aunt Celia." She wrapped her bottom lip around the top and frowned. "It's like there's these feelings all standing in front of my heart with their arms crossed."

"That's what the heart does to get your attention." Celia brushed back several strands of Harley's hair, and presented her with a sad smile.

"Well, how do I make them go away?"

"Talk to them. Once they've had their turn to speak, they'll go. They don't really want to hang around either."

"I don't want to talk to them. Can't they just go?"

"Emotions are like magnets. It's your sadness that's pulling in those yucky thoughts. Some might not even be yours. They're just trying to get you to pay attention." Celia pulled Harley to a sitting position. "If not, they'll just be back stronger." She pulled Harley up onto her feet. "Come with me. I've got something to show you that might help."

Celia pulled a reluctant Harley into the kitchen and stood her before the sink. She turned on the tap. "Okay, so you place your left hand at the base of your spine and with your right, you start at the first chakra." She pushed Harley's first two fingers into the small stream issuing from the faucet. "Imagine your body is the face of a dirty clock,

130

I mean gobs of dirt. So with your two fingers, you go counterclockwise in the space in front of each chakra and collect the gunk. After a couple swipes, you rinse your fingers in the water. Don't forget to thank the water for taking your gunk, by the way."

Harley smiled for the first time in weeks. "Feels like bubbles going up my spine." She moved her fingers up to the second chakra then rinsed them under the faucet.

"You do this for all seven chakras. It eliminates the sludge you carry around in your energetic field."

"I feel kind of stupid doing this. I can't even see anything going down the drain.

"Maybe not now, but you will with practice. Everything is energy," Celia said, "electrical impulses that our eyes convert into images for our brain. Kind of like a TV cable. The energy goes into the visual cortex in the back of the head where the electrical impulses are translated into images sent from the optic nerve and Voila! Pictures."

"How do you know so much?" Harley asked, washing her hand for the final time.

"Books." Celia grinned and took Harley's hand. "You're not done. Now you have to go back up and spin clockwise. Just like winding a clock, you're winding your chakras up. It's not enough to clean them. You have to polish, too."

"C'mon, Aunt Celia, this is taking forever."

"True, but you're not crying anymore, are you?" Celia shook her head and smiled.

"No."

"Good. Now get busy. Three or four times around each one. By the end of it, you'll be positively luminous."

Celia left Harley to her energetic housecleaning and went in search of a cure.

✧✧✧

He had turned the bench around, his back to the house and the garden, his view now centered on the driveway. He found it easier this way. Macadam evoked none of his reminiscent and uncontrollable emotions. Doc felt her standing behind him before she'd said a word.

"Why are you such a smacked ass?"

Doc groaned, shifted his weight, turned his face to his lap. He stared at his long neglected cuticles, meticulously chewed at a piece of dead skin, and imagined Celia vaporizing.

"I know you hear me. I can smell your fear," Celia said to his back.

He made no move to face his sister-in-law. In the dusky light where perceptions dimmed and all things became possible she sounded just like Ellie. He held fast, pushing down the urge to turn, greet her face, Ellie's face, to take in the heat of her.

Doc closed his eyes while his thoughts scattered like refugees after a coup, landing on his body temperature. He felt as though he was in the midst of his own personal summer. *So this is what a hot flash feels like.*

"The hypothalamus reacts to a particular trigger – it could be a day at the beach, gardening, a car wreck, whatever passes by your visual cortex – and assesses the situation. The hypothalamus exchanges its information with the part of your brain where Divinity resides." Celia stood beside him. "The heart then synthesizes the lower vibrations of the first three chakras with the vibrations of the upper three. Translation: Heaven and Earth, blending, together right there in your heart." She popped Doc in the center of his chest. "That's when it releases a hormone." Celia inhaled a deep, full breath. "Fear smells different then love."

The one hundred billion neurons in Doc's brain along with the fifty-trillion cells in his body collectively shivered. "Is that the kind of crap they feed you in that school of yours," Doc asked. He did not turn to face her. "What is it? The Institute for Shamanic Studies? Can you take correspondence courses?"

Celia flashed a lopsided smiled and walked over to pull a few weeds from the flower bed.

"If so, maybe I could do a little studying on the side. Try and understand just what the hell it is you're always talking about." Having waded into the waters of sarcasm, Doc was loathe to dry off.

"What are you afraid of?" Celia asked.

"Truthfully?" Doc replied with mock drama followed by perfect timing: "you."

Celia laughed. "I'd say a particular adolescent was closer to the truth."

"Jesus, Celia, stop trying to convert me, would ya'?"

Celia tossed the weeds on the grass and looked him square in both eyes. How she managed that, Doc wasn't sure since the human eyes operate in tandem, only possessing the capacity to focus on one spot at a time. Yet each time he switched his gaze from her right to her left eye, both eyes were always looking at him. He tried to figure it out, but she hadn't moved a millimeter. The woman was freaky.

"Your daughter needs a father."

"She's not my daughter," Doc said, before developing a keen interest in his knees. He watched them as one would a bad hand of cards, straining to appear confident, realizing the strategic need for a good bluff, but with full knowledge that at any moment he might be forced to fold.

Celia took a seat. The sun settled itself over the horizon. Azure turned to cobalt then to deep blue and finally to navy. Night took the sky hostage. Stars popped, taking their familiar places, putting their mega-watt smiles on display. Neither of them bothered to turn on the outside light. Finally she spoke, but it was from a remote location, somewhere far distant from the bench in the backyard now facing the driveway, somewhere beyond generations.

"A Native American boy was talking with his grandfather. He said, 'Grandfather, what do you think about the world. Is there any hope for us?' The grandfather replied, 'I feel like wolves are fighting in my heart. One is full of anger and hatred and the other is full of love, forgiveness and peace.' 'But which one will win?' the boy asked. The grandfather replied: 'The one that I feed.'"

Doc smirked. "You're not even a full-blooded Native American."

"And you're not even dead, although you're acting like it."

She was quick, he'd give her that. Always casting pithy statements like shadows on the sidewalk. Maybe even quicker than Ellie. Celia stretched her legs; Doc exhaled loudly through his nose.

"I don't need to be a full-blooded Native American to invoke their philosophy. The difference between the Native Americans and the current day shamans is that we operate on the assumption that God is within us. Otherwise, how could we make it rain?"

There was another long pause, enough for a generation of mayflies to hatch, reproduce and die, and still Doc gave no response.

"Harley needs you."

"Harley needs her mother. And since I'm not her mother, it stands to reason it's not me she needs. You, on the other hand, are almost a replica." He rose unsteadily, grabbed the shillelagh, the one Ellie's grandfather had made, and steered a course for the back door, not just yards, but miles away.

"Tell her for me, will you?" he called over his shoulder. Had Celia done anything to stop him, he may have hit her with his stick even if it meant falling over himself. Instead, he left her sitting on the bench, Celia and her judgments, both facing the driveway.

✧✧✧

Doc woke from a dead sleep, choking.

In his dream, the bottom half of his face was covered in white scaly, wiggly things. His lips were blue and the left side of his face swollen. The shock of white hair that he'd taken to calling, "the Antler," danced and swayed of its own accord to some silent rhythm. He shivered, horrified by his reflection, and brushed away the scales. They dropped, en masse, one mind, falling back. He stared at the last remaining squiggle, waiting for it to fall. It did, but sideways, right into his mouth.

Which is exactly when he began choking.

In the bathroom, Doc splashed water on his face then stuck his mouth under the spigot and swallowed fast, trying to flush out the fear. It was Celia who planted that dream, he was sure of it. Celia and her energetic manipulations. Probably trying to get back at him for how he spoke to her earlier. He dried his face and shuffled down the hall to Harley's room to see if her nighttime meanderings were faring any better.

Harley slept with a piece of cheese cloth taped over her mouth, which gave her the appearance of being in constant shock. Even though this extreme behavior predated Ellie's death, Doc still felt responsible. He'd made the mistake of relaying to Harley the unbelievable, yet supposedly true fact that over 70,000 people a year swallowed a spider while sleeping. Every year, 70,000 spiders were sucked into 70,000 tracheas. Maybe they crawled out and took a stroll down the esophagus – assuming they made it that far without causing a gag reflex – maybe they ended in a flourish with a wallop of digestive juices. It was difficult to know for sure without conducting a controlled experiment. But upon hearing the news, Harley refused to become a statistic and took to covering her mouth. Originally, it was a piece of tulle from her grandmother's wedding veil, frayed after all the years in the attic, and causing its own health hazards. When Ellie saw it, she made Harley switch to cheese cloth.

Celia relayed the Native American myth of the spider who first brought language to the world when it gave man the alphabet, but it didn't allay Harley's fears. Watching the rise and fall of white mesh on her face now, Doc concluded that it wasn't his dream that caused him to choke, but his very own spider. It made perfect sense: if anyone needed a language tutorial, it was Doc.

He was wide awake so he headed to the living room where, shillelagh in hand, he paced in a three-legged fit of pique until his legs gave out and he tumbled into the armchair. The padded arm poked at his midsection until he found the breath to maneuver himself into an upright position. He stared out the window into the ink-black night, conjuring Ellie's ghost, but all he got for his effort was a gnawing pain behind his occipital lobes. He pushed his eyelids down hard, hoping to counterbalance the pressure behind them, but the dream came back in all its maggoty glory.

Doc tried to remember when his body didn't feel so encumbered. Emotions used to be something he could ignore as needed. Except for this last bit with Ellie dying and him having a massive, depressive freak-out episode in response, he'd always successfully segregated his emotions. Compartmentalization, he'd found, was a quality indigenous to the male species. Women couldn't do it to save their lives, yet Doc would take a flat-lined view of the world over the onus of emotions any day.

Outside, the sky remained black and unchanged. Doc leaned over and pulled a random magazine from the rack. It was a high gloss twenty-page brochure for his company, Harburnette Oil and Gas, which, until recently, was the yardstick against which he measured his life. Yet let a little lightning strike hit and it's funny how juxtapositions begin occurring at warp speed. To Doc, Harburnette had become the equivalent of Darth Vader and the Evil Empire.

The brochure set out Harburnette's services generally then went on to describe such services in detail. He flipped to the section on hydrofracturing gas wells. Doc knew the facts: that the shale wells required fracturing the limestone formations to reach the gas trapped within it; that in order to fracture the limestone you had to inject copious amounts of water and sand, and a mixture of hazardous chemicals into the vertical drilling hole under extremely high pressure; that the injected water forced the fracturing of the limestone horizontally and resulted in the oil and gas, and now sullied water, being forced to the surface. There was a likelihood, although Harburnette denied it, that this process water could breach the cement casing and invade the ground water aquifers that serviced households and communities with drinking water; and that many of the chemicals added to the sand and water were listed hazardous substances which the government regulated under any number of laws, but which the company deftly outmaneuvered reporting by claiming a business confidential exemption, whining that even listing them would harm their profit margin and competitive edge. Corporate interests and greed trumped human interest and need again.

It took about a million gallons of fresh water to frack a well and each well was fracked a dozen or more times. That's a lot of water to dispose of, especially now that it was a confidentially hazardous cocktail that needed to be treated before it was released. New Mexico, like many states, hadn't been prepared for the Big Gas Rush and so the treated water went back into the river, sans chemicals perhaps, but with loads of brine and suspended solids intact. Fish kills occurred at alarming rates and Harburnette was making money like the world was going to end tomorrow, which, if they kept this pace, it just might.

Doc had known all these things, but the most disturbing fact was that until three and a half weeks ago, and because of his ability to compartmentalize, none of these facts really bothered him. Now, like the hazardous substances Harburnette was pumping into the ground, the facts were boring a hole in his grey matter and fracturing his peace of mind.

Doc rose from his bed where he'd thrashed his way through the last few hours. Celia lived only a mile away. Harley could stay with her and still go to the same school, have the same friends, live the same life. Then there was the added benefit of Celia being Ellie's twin. Harley might find herself in a parallel universe of sorts, her mother gone, but not really. Meanwhile, he could get his strength back, plot next steps. With Ellie gone, he may not even stay in New Mexico. California could be nice. A new start, maybe? But not with Harley. It would be too disruptive for her and Celia. He sighed, expelling old air, but retaining older, decrepit thoughts.

He found Harley out back, talking to the stones. At least that's what it looked like. She hunkered over the palm-sized rock she'd extracted from its cozy spot in the flowerbed edging where it kept watch over the pansies and bachelor buttons, making sure they didn't escape.

Doc hobbled outside, shillelagh in hand. "Hey," he said, peering over her shoulder and blocking her sun, a partial eclipse in the making.

"Hey," she said holding tight to the stone as if to conceal its secrets between her haunches.

Doc rested his weight on the shillelagh. He felt ludicrous using it, but circumstances controlled. Ellie's grandfather, a bow and arrow maker in the Lakota-Sioux tradition had carved it for Ellie when she was born. The old man had long since died, yet the stick lived on. Doc and Ellie had taken it with them a few times on their hikes though mostly it stood in a corner by Ellie's side of the bed. Ellie put it there, "in case the bad guys got in," but given that Doc slept closest to the door, the place Ellie assigned to him, he suspected she just wanted to be near the spirit of her grandfather. The stick had stood there until this week when Doc found he was greatly in need of its assistance.

The doctors had checked and rechecked Doc's musculoskeletal system, bone alignment, the ligaments, the tendons, even the tiny bones in his feet and found nothing, yet his inability to move forward unassisted continued. He could move right, left, and back, no problem. But ask him to take a step into the future and his brain put on the brakes. It was not until he started using that stick – his third leg, or more appropriately, the probe, sent out like a scout to test the terrain – that the forward motion had begun. At least he didn't end up in a heap on the floor.

"Give yourself time to heal. You'll move on," Celia had said.

A quaint concept, but how does one move on at forty-four years old? He was right smack in the center of middle age, holding fast to a dead wife and hiding from a thirteen-year old kid who expected answers from a man who couldn't get out of bed in the morning without the help of a piece of oak, cut, sanded and polished by a thirty-year-dead Lakota-Sioux.

Doc cleared his throat. "I packed you a little bag."

Harley said nothing.

"It's only for a few months, Lee."

Harley wouldn't look at him.

"Once I get my act together, maybe lose this ridiculous stick, then you can come back. Aunt Celia will take you to school in the meantime. Pack your lunch and stuff." He knew she knew. He could tell by the way she hunched her shoulders and held her breath, poised to run. He waited for the levy to break. When it did give, it sounded like a tire going flat, a long slow hiss. He doubted the strength of her poison although he wished she would strike anyway and assuage his guilt. She grazed him with a look, turned back to her stones.

"Aunt Celia said the stones told the first stories."

"Oh, yeah? I can see that," Doc replied with more sarcasm than intended.

Harley rocked on her haunches. "I thought if I hung out long enough, they'd tell me a story about Mom. Why she went away."

"Harley, when are you going to stop listening to your aunt? She's a nice enough person, but she's got a skewed view of things. Sometimes it borders on delusional." Harley flinched as if struck.

"You're never going to lose that crutch. You're going to hang on to it for the rest of your life."

"What?" Doc said.

"Nothing." She started to hum, but it wasn't joyful, more of a lament, a Lakota funeral dirge.

"Who taught you that song?"

"Aunt Celia."

"It's sad...kind of pretty."

Harley moved a few more rocks, strategically laid them down. "Mom's here."

"Hmmm?"

"She's here. In the rocks and stones and trees. She's not at Aunt Celia's. I want to stay here with Mommy." She turned to look at him, her head bent unnaturally from her crouched position. Her welling eyes threatened to unravel him, to burn a hole in his resolve like sun through a magnifying glass. Had she kept her eyes trained on him he would have cracked, but instead she turned back to her stones, and severed the connection.

"We gotta go," Doc said. He leaned over for a glimpse of what was so fascinating.

"Okay," Harley said, hunkering down.

"Lee, the rocks aren't going to talk to you."

"I know."

"Well, what are you doing?"

She raised her palm without turning back to look. Doc's visual inspection revealed a tiny orange and brown salamander, resting on the rock. He placed the stone on his palm and watched it for a bit, growing inpatient. Harley stared at the ground where a sliver of light sat, penetrating the edge of Doc's enormous shadow.

"Why isn't it moving?" Doc asked.

"Because it's dead. I'm just keeping it company."

"Well..." he said, trailing off. A vision of Ellie's face, resting within the outline of the back of Harley's head stole the breath he'd intended to use to finish his sentence. She held out her hand and he placed the rock into her palm. She squeezed her delicate fingers around it, laid it back on the earth.

"I'll be inside when you're ready," he said, turned and limped toward the backdoor.

He turned to look just before he went inside. He knew it was The Time of The Ending for them, but as he watched Harley crouched over her dead salamander and her living rocks, watched the space, the very air around her dancing and swirling, shining as if charged with the light of Creation itself, he knew that for her – without him – it would be The Time of the Beginning.

I watched him from the corner of my eye until the screen door banged shut and all that was left of Doc was three pin pricks of yellow light. Aunt Celia would have said he left some of his energy behind. Just like him, too. He was always leaving stuff behind.

He kept looking out the window. Every 30 seconds or so he'd peek out, then slip behind the curtain. I examined my orange-striped salamander while Doc examined me like the millions of bugs I'd looked at under the microscope he and Mommy gave me for Christmas two years ago. Now I know what the bugs felt like.

He was kicking me out of my own house and there was nothing I could do about it. I wanted to be mad at him. I wanted to hate him with every hate bone I had, but he looked so pathetic that I decided to let him off the lousy parent hook he'd hung himself from and open the door of conversation. He jumped when I banged the screen door shut.

"I just thought of how moths can die."

He was sitting at the kitchen table. He bumped his chin up a notch, the universal symbol for "go on."

"You know how they have to get to the light? Well, maybe they fly too close to the sun and burn up."

"Maybe," Doc said. "It's a theory."

"A good theory," I said. "Can you see the planets in the daytime?"

"No."

"I mean if you took a spaceship."

"Yeah. The planets are always visible. It just depends on where you are."

"I want to see the aliens, but I don't want to burn up. You know, because I got too close to the sun."

Doc looked out the window, nodded in assent, but had no idea what I'd said. *Classic.*

"Do you think it might be the same for Mom? Like if we just took a spaceship maybe we could see her."

He cleared his throat and studied his fingernails. I could see a small pool forming in the corner of the one eye still visible.

"Mr. Pathetic."

"What?"

"I said...," I coughed. I was trying not to cry, trying not to yell, trying not to stomp my feet and blame him for everything that ever went wrong in my life. "I said, I lost somebody, too. Somebody more important to me than you could ever know. Somebody who I'll never see again ever and all you can do is sit there and feel sorry for yourself. Well, I knew her first. She was mine, not yours." I dashed from the room and threw myself on the couch. I know it was dumb. I know it was high drama. I just couldn't help it. I'd jump off a bridge if one were close.

Doc came into the living room five minutes later. You know when he's coming because you can hear the step, step, step, like bad salsa dancing, his feet and the shillelagh, stepping out for the night.

"Hey. I'm sorry. I..."

I got up before he could finish. I didn't need his half-baked regrets.

"Harley, I..."

"I've got to pee and then I'm ready." I dashed from the room, went to the bathroom and washed my face. He so didn't get it. At least Aunt Celia would.

On the ride there, I couldn't shut up. I wanted to, but I was nervous, and still mad, but trying not to be, and my brain couldn't control my mouth.

"Did you know that Neptune is the name of the Roman God of the ocean? Did you also know that Neptune may contain substantial amounts of water? And considering that they didn't discover Neptune until 1846 – that is, if you don't count Galileo who first spotted it in 1612, but he thought it was a star so for some reason it didn't count – it's pretty wild that they named it Neptune, especially if it turns out to have, like, a beach and stuff on it."

Doc nodded, ignoring me. He was good at that. I wanted to beat him on the chest, to pummel him in the face, but he'd just sit there like a stuffed bear so what was the point? So I kept talking, and when we got to Aunt Celia's, I grabbed my bag, gave him a kiss on the cheek, nodded when he said he'd see me in a couple days, and stood on the step, waving as he pulled out of the driveway – probably my new driveway – fixed his hair in the rearview mirror and didn't look back.

✿✿✿

Doc drove away, leaving Ellie's little girl, standing in the driveway, waving like an immigrant leaving the Old Country. He checked the rearview mirror once, pretending to smooth down The Antler, but couldn't bring himself to look again. Then he turned the corner and she was gone.

"Aunt Celia," Harley whispered as she stood above her aunt. She poked her once in the arm. "Aunt Celia."

Celia opened her eyes to find Harley, her mouth covered in cheese-cloth, staring at her with wild eyes. "Hi, baby. What's up?" Celia rubbed her eyes awake and smiled. "Bad dream?"

Harley nodded and Celia held the covers up. Harley snuggled in beside her aunt who wrapped her own body around Harley's like a slip cover. Within moments, Harley's tense, angular frame relaxed. "Tell me about it."

"Well, I'm sleeping and I feel something crawling on my cheek. I flick it off, but it takes a couple flicks and I think, eeewww, yuck, stupid spiders, but I'm too tired to get up and turn on the light so I go back to sleep which takes a while because now I'm on alert for other creepy crawly things, but I adjust my cheesecloth and soon, it's morning. So I sweep the crystals out from under my pillow – I always have at least one, like you, but lately two because I've been feeling sad and I really want to talk to Mommy – and when I do I feel something hard, not like the feather I know you put under there the other day, and I think it's probably the carapace of some yucky dead beetle bug ..."

"Nice use of the word carapace..."

"Thanks, I just learned it. Anyway, I shift it to my other hand and almost drop it, but somehow it bounces into my palm. I walk to the bathroom and toss it in the trash can and I hear a pop. The thing hits the floor! Now I know for sure it's not a feather. I turn on the light and see a dark bug wearing, like, armor. It's a beetle and it JUMPS, and I JUMP, and I pick up a tissue and throw it in the toilet where it starts marching up and down the tissue looking for a way to escape. I hate creepy crawly things, but I don't like to kill anything either. I did the only thing I could think of which was to flush it down the toilet. Then I was so upset I couldn't go back to sleep." Celia laughed and stroked Harley's hair.

"Do you think God will be mad because I killed it?" asked Harley.

"I think he'll be relieved that you took out some of your psychic trash."

"What's that mean?"

"It means the beetle was just a manifestation of one of your demons. You went ahead and vanquished it. A little bitty demon, but a demon all the same." Celia pulled the covers up higher. "The sun's not even up yet. Why don't we go back to sleep for a while and when it crests we'll greet it with sun salutations and eggs and toast. I promise that they'll be no more beetles – or spiders – tonight. So you can lose the cheesecloth."

Harley removed the cheesecloth, placed it on the night stand. Celia kissed her on the back of the head. So cocooned, they drifted off to sleep.

☼☼☼

Doc dropped Harley at Celia's, and in an effort to restock the empty shelves of his heart, went straight to the grocery store. Of all the jobs he'd inherited since Ellie died, shopping was his least favorite. The choices overwhelmed him so he figured he'd wait until he came down to the end: the last square of toilet paper, a single remaining bite of cheese, a curdled drop of milk. When famine and stinking to death were his hardcore reality, only then could he gather Ellie's reusable grocery sacks and head north, to the Food Giant, the land of twenty-four hour, fluorescent-lighted shopping. Two a.m. would have been his favorite time to go – he wasn't asleep then anyway – but today it was 1:30 p.m., and the place was crowded as hell. The whole ordeal was giving him the shakes. He'd left his shillelagh in the car and felt off-kilter so he grabbed a head of lettuce, a bunch of broccoli and some carrots, and quickly moved on to the processed meats. It was here and only here, in the meat department, that a man could feel at home in a grocery store. He ordered a pound each of smoked turkey, provolone, and prosciutto, and a quarter pound of olive loaf, the latter for him because Harley thought it was gross. He scooped up his bundles and pushed on past the fish, stopping to admire the sheer girth of the Atlantic salmon. There was an old woman with a little cart in front of the fish counter, cooking the daily special and serving it up in small portions. He ambled by, watching her work, her fingers deftly maneuvering bite-sized pieces into little plastic cups.

"Swordfish," she said in a voice so husky it could have been a man's, "in bourbon sauce." She handed him one of the little cups, a plastic fork handle sticking out jauntily to one side. He hesitated, accepted it with a wan smile, and walked on.

"It's to eat, not to adopt," she called after him. He turned to see her pantomime the act of spooning food into her mouth.

Doc blushed. He wasn't used to people verbally accosting him in the grocery. Her admonition was meant to be in jest; he saw that in her grandmother-eyes when she smiled up at him, so he downed it in one bite. The rich, multilayered flavors dissolved on his tongue in harmony. It was delicious.

"Can I have more?" he asked, and she laughed as she handed him another cup. Doc bought two pounds because she had fed him, because he felt the need to reciprocate, because in buying the fish he was buying some of her buoyancy, her longevity, perhaps some of her wisdom. It was a time-tested method, the sampling of wares, and it had worked; there would be no offering otherwise. Still he felt the purchase had enriched him. By taking this piece of fish home, he was taking home a moment of connection.

❦ ❦ ❦

Celia poured milk into Harley's glass, dropped a spoonful of honey down the side and took a seat at the counter. The child hadn't stopped talking since her eyes popped open that morning and now at the dinner table, the one-sided dialogue continued.

"It was a weird scary thing, Aunt Celia. It had really red eyes and it looked like a big cat in its body, but its head and neck looked like a snake. What do you think it means?"

"Well, it could mean you're in touch with your animal totem, or it could mean that you're just like your mother who never stops asking questions," Celia offered. Ellie sat at the counter, marking up her will. At the mention of her name, she looked at Harley and rolled her eyes.

"Are you okay with this?" Ellie asked Celia.

"I got your back."

"You mean Harley's back."

"Yes, Harley's back. And yours."

Celia turned her attention to her niece. "Well, a dream like that can only mean you're nervous about being in first grade," Celia said. "It's called an anxiety dream. Has anybody been bothering you?"

"Yeah," Ellie piped up. "That kid Matthew says he's the smartest kid in school. Harley's intimidated by him."

"He says I'm dumb."

"In an advanced class?" Celia asked.

Harley nodded, somber. Celia burst out laughing.

"Lee, even if it's true, to be at the bottom of the top is not something to stress about," Celia said. "Besides, you're six."

"That's what I told her," Ellie said. Harley looked from mother to aunt, seemed satisfied.

"What kind of dreams did you have last night, Mommy?"

"Gosh, that was so long ago, I don't remember."

"It wasn't even a day ago." Harley scrunched up her nose.

"Where would you live?" Ellie asked Celia. "If something happened, I mean."

"My house, of course. Or here. It doesn't matter."

Ellie nodded, made a note on the will. Harley took a bite.

"Can you at least try?" Harley asked, pushing her plate toward Celia, but talking to her mother. "Can I have some more green beans?" she said to her aunt.

"Well, I had some really weird dreams," Ellie said, "like flying without a plane dreams." Celia scooped a small helping of beans onto Harley's plate, but Harley signaled for more. Celia put a heaping spoonful on, then felt Harley's forehead.

"Are you sick?"

"No, I'm hungry."

Half an hour later Harley was pushing a dish of half-finished pudding away. "I'm done."

Celia raised an eyebrow. "Is something wrong, Lee?"

Harley smiled, shook her head. "I don't know. Maybe my mouth is changing."

"Maybe something big is about to happen," Ellie said. "Could change your whole life."

"Nobody likes change," Celia said, "but when there's a tsunami, you may as well run outside and hang ten."

Harley smiled, but Celia knew Harley had no idea what she was talking about.

A week later, Ellie met Doc. The tsunami had hit.

☼☼☼

Doc had been holed up inside for hours, pacing a well-worn route from the bedroom to the kitchen to the living room and round again. The light rain the weather man predicted had turned into a full-blown monsoon. Two weeks had passed since he'd moved Harley and a few bags of her clothes over to Celia's. Ostensibly, Harley still lived here with him, but practically, she may as well have been living in the stratosphere. The days had flown by, interwoven, as they were, in gossamer and Prozac – airy and burden free now that Harley was gone. Since he didn't have to get her on the bus, Doc rose late every day. Since he didn't have to go to work, Doc read the morning paper while he ate breakfast, lingering over a second and sometimes third cup of coffee. Since he didn't have to do any housework – Celia had hired a woman when Doc was in La-La-Land and Doc had kept her on – he took slow morning walks, and afternoon naps. He stretched, made dinner, watched the news – every day – then went to bed. It was like being retired without the complications of old age. It would have been a beautiful existence but for one cruel fact that defined his days: he missed Ellie in a bone-crushing, asphyxiating way. Celia told him to meet Ellie on the astral plane, the place where dreams lived and life was previewed. Doc thought, as usual, that Celia was full of it.

He saw Harley on weekends and one night during the week for dinner, as if he were sharing custody. He'd never taken full ownership, never legally adopted her, never crossed over the "what if something happened to Ellie" bridge that would have made him sole caretaker of Ellie's daughter.

Ellie seemed okay with that, knowing that these things take time – years, sometimes decades – and never suspecting for a moment that she wouldn't be there to shepherd Harley through the tenuous middle school years, the high school dramas, the separation anxiety of college leaving. No. Leaving was something Ellie had definitely not banked on. If she did, she would have relayed in greater detail her expectations for Harley's future. Besides, Ellie always held a trump card: Celia.

So sharing Harley, or actually, borrowing Harley from Celia seemed prudent. Still Doc worried. Although Celia would do anything for her niece, she had no children of her own and to have a thirteen-year old shoved upon her seemed cruel.

Doc took another lap around the living room. Damn rain. New Mexico was dry by nature and the earth could use a good stiff drink, but being cooped up in this house where Ellie hovered in every corner was getting to him. Now he knew how chickens felt, traveling cross-country in those pint-sized crates, squawking and pecking and poking each other's beaks off – literally – with no space of their own.

That's it. Doc spun on his heel toward the closet, dug his boots out, grabbed a rain coat and stumbled from the front porch. A block later, he stepped in a monstrous puddle, lost his footing and got soaked to mid-thigh. He cursed, suppressing the urge to bang his head against the sidewalk. Defeated, he trudged home.

He took a bath to clean off the sludge, but the contaminated feeling remained. Decisions needed to be made. Lives reassembled. He'd been out of work for weeks and was going to have to go back, but back to what? The very place that was leaving a cancerous trail all over the county? Ellie told him that one out of three homes in Garfield County had some form of cancer. The evidence was clear: stillborn goats, cattle mutations; and in humans, rashes, headaches, lung disease, joint aches and pains. Should he go to his CEO and demand that Harburnette cease the work that was making them millions? And if they said no? Quit?

Quitting seemed like the neon-light option, but given his recent bout with ill-health, he didn't want to lose his health benefits, plus Harley was on his ticket and if he quit, she'd be quit, too. The choices were making him dizzy so he lay down on the couch for a moment and closed his eyes.

"They have plenty to work with," Ellie said. She stood at the kitchen sink meticulously washing recyclables and placing them in bags, separated by density. Doc watched, amused by her relentless chatter.

"A law. One little law making recycling mandatory. With universal coding. If you don't know what it was, you can't say what it will become, right? Coding could solve all that. Did you know that recycling a one-gallon milk jug saves enough energy to light a 100-watt bulb for eleven hours? A glass bottle's only good for four. Aluminum can? Twenty."

"I think you should go to D.C. and wring a few necks."

"Don't make fun of me. When the planet is completely wrapped in plastic and there's nowhere to put all those millions of spring water bottles we use every year – when you're choking on dioxin residue because it's seeped into your ground water supply, then you'll care."

Doc rose and wrapped his arms around his wife's waist, nestled his face in her neck. "I care now," he said, kissing her in the soft, fleshy part. "Watching you get riled up is just so much fun."

"If spending a little time putting things in their places will help, maybe buy the planet a few more years, then I'll have succeeded at something." She tipped her head back onto his shoulder. "Do you know that the energy burned by a hybrid car on a trip from San Francisco to L.A. and back would be enough to feed a person for a year?"

"What's that mean? They eat gas and electricity?"

"I don't know what it means. Probably that they could use the energy to cook something."

"Where'd you hear that?"

"I read it somewhere."

"Oh, well, I'm sold."

Ellie pulled away, forcing Doc to release his grip. She gave him the single raised eyebrow and grabbed the recyclables and her car keys.

"Someday you'll thank me." With that, she was gone.

Doc rubbed his eyes and shook his brain awake as the memory retreated. He was a holy mess, not like God holy, more like a strainer full of holes. He wanted out, wanted to stop the hurting and the heartache. If he could focus on something else – people push on through the pain for their children all the time – but Doc couldn't do it, not with the competition. Jealousy is a vicious and cunning ally and right now, to muster even a micron of emotion for Harley seemed more difficult than transatlantic air flight without a plane. Ridiculous, feeling threatened by a child, yet the feeling had grown and festered even now that Ellie was gone. Doc knew his behavior had periodically driven a wedge between him and Ellie, but like a pack-a-day smoker, he was powerless to quit. So the animosity lingered, systematically destroying the rooms of their affection. He knew she had come close to kicking him out a couple times, and, knowing her devotion, worried that one day she would choose Harley and say to hell with him. He just needed to hang in there until Harley left the nest and left them in peace. Because of her, their relationship had been a tidal river, undulating on familiar banks, ebbing and flowing with the moon, the tides, and Harley's whims and possessiveness. Now the only thing undulating was his mind. He sighed, threw on his shoes and went out to retrieve the mail.

Doc surveyed the front yard. A few tentative blooms were holding fast to the branches of the crepe myrtle. The chrysanthemums were in full throttle as befits fall, and the hardier of the Impatiens still smiled up at him. It was a day in flux. Rain drops spread their glistening, overripe bodies across the Impatiens and Begonias, the last bit of contentment those drops would feel today by the time the sun got through with them. Ellie had planted the flowers next to the mailbox. "Good feng shui," she'd said. "It'll bring us abundance." Doc smiled just as the sun, held hostage by a unified cluster of stratus clouds, poked a tentative ray, first here, then there, until it finally found the break it was looking for and popped through. The sky was a magnificent study in contrast as storm clouds receded and light burst forth. The raindrops that had been lounging at poolside gave themselves up for the greater twin causes of transpiration and evaporation, but not before grabbing some of the sun's grace, taking that small gift with them as they left.

For the first time in a while, Doc took a solid breath. Here was the essence of nature in all its luminous glory, the quality of light played upon the earth like an ephemeral pool that disappears in the dry season, allowing memory alone to sustain its vibration. Doc drew another breath, this one deeper, filling his lungs with the infinite consciousness of all things. For three seconds he felt the pure bliss that comes with innocent perception. For three magical seconds he looked at the world in wonder, possessed of only love and gratitude. The yard was a tangled weed-fest in serious need of attention, but even the weeds were beautiful in this light. *Never has there been a moment as incredibly beautiful as this.* Then, as if on cue, Doc's analytical mind interrupted: "Ahem. The mail?" Cliché as it was, Doc was an engineer, and any brilliance born of a resting mind must be channeled into usable goods and services. The moment passed; bliss abandoned him.

Doc tugged on the mailbox door. There was the usual crush of catalogues, the familiar bills and solicitations, a card-sized letter, and a plain brown envelope from a lab whose name he didn't recognize. The latter caught his attention because he hadn't sent any water samples in for testing. Their house had a well and it was good practice to get it tested every six months. He knew he was a few months late, but since it was only him in the house these days, it hadn't mattered. Maybe Celia had sent it in for him. He shrugged and schlepped the whole pile into the house, leaving the last few rain drops to their cruel, beautiful fate.

Doc dropped the mail in a heap on the table then put the kettle on for tea. He couldn't concentrate on a task for too long, preferring always to return to the singular driving task of every day: finding traces of Ellie. Other than the pictures of her lining the walls, she'd left barely a whisper.

Doc chaffed at the unfairness of Fate, denying them their last date together. Instead of dinner with Doc, Ellie had lunch with Harley.

"I pulled her out of school on a whim. We ate pizza and giggled like we were playing hooky. Well, Harley kind of was."

Ellie's joy in describing such a simultaneously mundane and miraculous event as mother and daughter having lunch on a school day agitated Doc. He felt a pinch in his heart, recalling their conversation, and the sadness settled upon him like dust. It was Harley, not Doc, who was the last person to see Ellie alive. Soon after she'd hiked up to the mesa with her survey equipment, intent on putting the finishing touches on her report to City Council regarding the wells. Instead, her spirit vanished in a flash of light.

He glanced at the plethora of mail spread before him, an insurmountable task. Celia had already separated a week's worth, and with a sweep of his arm, Doc shifted the catalogues straight into a double-strength trash bag for recycling, and chuckled. *Oh, the irony.* After years of ignoring Ellie's recycling habits, he'd given in, but now that she was dead, she couldn't claim her victory. Doc's laughter gave up ground, fell to bafflement, then rage – silvers to blacks to reds in minutes.

His lungs felt like solidifying concrete, not the elastic, life-giving balloons they were. Anger tore at the catalogues, ripping them apart with greater ease than any commercial shredder, until all that was left was a pile of confetti and a singular sadness. Back to blacks.

Doc blinked at the window and regulated the water level in his eyes. The grumpy weather had all but retreated. Too bad his mood didn't match it. He watched the sky unfold when an odd phenomena occurred; the tightness in his chest eased. Other rays joined the group, pledging allegiance to their common father, the sun. The remaining holdouts hung like stretched taffy in the sky before disbanding from within, leaving behind what promised to be a brilliant day.

Doc had separated everything, retaining only the bills, the "get-well-soons" from friends and colleagues, and the unidentified envelopes that would require further investigation. One envelope had already been opened and taped shut. Inside was a bill for lab analysis. He was about to set it aside and deal with bills later when the caption caught his eye. Ellie Sandberg. Huh? The bill was for Ellie, not him. He studied the contents more closely.

It was a lab analysis for tissue samples taken eight weeks earlier. Doc flipped through to the conclusion. Positive for carcinoma; it was in the lymph nodes and had spread to the organs. Doc rubbed his eyes. His mind flooding with small details previously overlooked: Ellie's sudden desire to update their wills, her fanatical shopping sprees, buying clothes and gifts for the future; her sudden zeal for cooking and freezing several months' worth of meals.

Cancer!

Ellie had cancer. Bad cancer. As in months, maybe weeks to live. He dropped the papers. They fell like notes in a descending scale. He watched their inert shapes, lying upon the carpet, gathering strength, for surely insurrection was at hand. He waited for them to jump up, declare a mutiny. Thought trajectories formed on the periphery of his consciousness. No words as yet, just a semi-dark mass, swirling and bumping and coalescing upon itself in the corner of his brain. He slumped down amidst the reticent sheets of paper. A memory of the sound of her voice reached his inner ear, washing over him like an ancient truth. Ruffles of energy followed in the truth's wake. *She knew and she kept it from me.* He shivered as this new knowledge transferred to each of the 50 trillion cells in his body. Pain constricted his chest, put him down for a moment, but rage, his new best friend, propped him up. He cleared the table with a sweep of his arm, the remaining unopened pieces of mail scattering like marbles on a waxy floor. *Did the last six years mean nothing to her?* Doc kicked at the closest pile of mail on the floor. One of the envelopes went flying and smacked against the wooden leg of the table with a muffled clink. Doc picked up the letter. He hadn't noticed it before. It was Ellie's handwriting and said: "Doc." He tore it open and a small skeleton key fell to the ground.

Doc,

> *By now you will have learned the truth of my own personal state of the union. The degeneration of my cells, giving over to cancer, their ultimate betrayal of me as they ravage my mind and spirit is an unspeakable hardship. I'm sorry I didn't have the courage to share it with you. If you could only have known my dreams of late, you would understand why. I had so wanted to grow old with you. Next to my dearest doll, you were the only one for me. Take care of her. I'm asking you in death where there are no take-backs. Do it for her, but more, do it for you. You love each other. You just don't realize it yet. For now, I give you back your key. You're too young to bury your love with me. We would have had a beautiful future together.*
> *All my love,*
> *Ellie*

"NO!" Doc fell over in a heap while his eviscerated breath leaked out with his life force. The skeleton key lay in his line of vision, winking at

☼☼☼

Doc heaved, hoping to relieve some of the pressure on his lungs and when that didn't work he rolled down the window. The local church had a sign out that said: "Jesus Saves." *And Mary manages to put away a few pennies, too.* He chuckled at his blasphemy, then choked on his own saliva. He'd never understood God. It wasn't dislike, but mistrust of the false prophets and fundamentalist-extremist bible-thumpers who condoned hate in the name of love and used God's name to cover their tracks. He put that aside for Ellie and learned, perhaps if not to love God, at least to live in an amiable silence. With Ellie gone, the terrain was altered and mistrust had transmogrified into loathing. Without her to guide him he found the old prejudices creeping in like Kudzu, the vine that strangles everything it embraces. Had he been at home, Doc would sit alone in the dankness, revisiting old memories like a stray cat revisits old smells. Instead, he let them drift out the open window into the freezing night air.

"Aaaaaaachoooooo!" Celia's sneeze shook the house so that Doc heard the reverberation through the window panes. As he stepped across the threshold, Celia greeted him with a second, more powerful one. Doc found her in the living room, stoking the fire. Dressed in a t-shirt, jeans and a tie-dye hoodie, she looked half her forty-four years. It was a welcome sight against the early dark of fall, but he hadn't come to socialize. He threw the lab results on the coffee table.

"You knew about this, didn't you?"

Celia sneezed a third time. "God bless you, too," she said, grabbing a tissue. "It's good, sneezing. It wakes up your whole body; every one of your cells goes, 'Danger! Danger!' wondering if this time the heart stops for good. Sneeze a bunch of times in a row and you can almost hear sirens going off in your head. It's as close as you can get to a near death experience, without really losing consciousness, that is." Celia put the poker down, brushed her hands on the sides of her jeans and rose to her feet. Celia had a way of soothing even the most chronically imbalanced situation simply by her presence and, even though Doc hated to admit it, he loved being around her for that reason. She leveled her gaze at him, then cast her eyes down at the large brown envelope on the table. She picked it up, turned it over in her hands, ran a light touch along the broken seal, placed it back on the table. Celia looked at Doc with so much love that he felt his heart would pop. Rather than the vituperative tirade he came to deliver, Doc slumped into a chair, sullen and brooding, while Celia stood before him and placed her hands on him.

He felt himself splitting in two: half of him full of anger and resentment and hate toward God for not saving Ellie, at Celia for not telling him, and even toward Ellie, the woman he'd lie on hot coals for, especially her, for leaving him; the other half was grateful to have a warm fire to gaze upon and Celia's warm hands to heal him. So he let Anger drop to the floor in a bloody heap while Contentment sat straight up in the chair, closed its eyes and wagged its tail in joy. He could feel the energy Celia was pumping through his heart, almost see the twin arcs it made from her third eye and heart as it welded together in his own heart. It wasn't a figment of his imagination. He could feel himself filling from his toes to his scalp, 1,000 volts of direct current, waves of love and gratitude washing over him. He blinked at his empty hands as if surprised to find them there.

"Thank you," he said, remembering his manners. Celia smiled in response. They sat in silence for a bit.

"Why didn't she tell me?"

"She tried."

"She never even brought it up." Anger rapped lightly at the window; Doc pulled the shade for now.

"I know she tried at least once. I was there. It was difficult for her to focus on it, but she did. You didn't want to hear it."

"When?"

"We were sitting on the back porch, watching the sunset. She was trying to ease her own fears and alert you to the problem. You shut her down before she even got three words out."

"I remember the night, Celia, but honest-to-God I don't remember the conversation."

"She was talking about dying. About how she hoped her soul would treat it as a personal challenge and not a need to despair. You know – about getting lost being half the fun."

Doc expelled air in a long resigned breath, his hope of higher alignments dashed by the inevitability of past failures. Now he recalled the conversation.

"Then you said, 'It's never fun to be alone on the island, especially if you don't have provisions like food and drinking water or any other kind of infrastructure.' Ellie looked sick and changed the subject."

"That conversation cannot possibly qualify for trying to tell me. It's an incomprehensible metaphor. I was speaking literally."

"I admit it was a bit obtuse, but it was the best she could do considering the time she had left."

"What about you? Couldn't you save her? She was your sister."

"I loved her to pieces, yes, but healers only facilitate. Ultimately, everyone is responsible for themselves. Otherwise, other people, God, or life itself will take control for them." Celia shrugged. "God will work with you, but he won't do it for you."

"So, if you're to be believed, Ellie had a choice, and she chose to check out."

"It's hard to know what she was thinking that day and what agreements were made before she even incarnated. It may surprise you if you knew."

"A few months...." Doc coughed and sputtered on a fresh wave of emotion. He glared at his sister-in-law with all the anger he'd have given his wife had he been offered the chance. "Wasn't I worth the last few months?" Doc roared.

Celia took a seat on the couch across from Doc as if she were about to conduct an interview. "Today I saw a woman cross the taxi area in front of the train station. As she did, a cab had to slow down to avoid hitting her. The woman raised her hand and pointed at the cab. He beeped his horn. He was angry. She gesticulated again; he gave her the finger then sped away. The woman shook her head at the driver. The cabby shook his head at the woman. They both added a little negativity to the world and to everyone they encountered."

"The woman started it."

"It was dusk and the cabby's car lights were off. She was trying to tell him is all." Celia rubbed her eyes and rested her head on her hand. "Ellie didn't fan the fires of negativity. If you remember, that night was really fun."

Doc stared sullenly at a mosquito on the ceiling. Celia leaned over and tapped his heart. The simple gesture sent a wave of energy shooting straight through to the top of his head and the hair on his scalp, particularly The Antler, prickled as if he'd stuck his finger in an electrical socket.

"What are you doing anyway? It's very intense."

"Sending Reiki energy through your body. Your heart needs a lift. I can see it leaking all over the place."

Doc looked down at himself, blinked hard, trying to spot the leaking bodily fluids, running in rivulets onto the floor, but he saw nothing, only Celia's beautiful and firm hand.

"Around every body is a field, like a big doughnut radiating around you. Some people can see it. It's called an aura, like a protective bubble of light we all live in. The heart has its own special bubble. It's even bigger, but the equipment they use to measure it is only so precise, so they're not sure how big."

"Who's they?"

"The Institute of HeartMath."

"Sounds like a cult."

"No, they're real scientists."

"So you're saying you can see my bubble leaking?"

Celia nodded. "Yeah."

"By putting your hand over my heart you're repairing the leak with what, some kind of cosmic duct tape?"

"Kind of like an oil change for your body." Doc chuckled, but didn't protest.

"Any shift you ever make has to come through the heart first."

"Celia, sometimes..." Doc began, but let it drop. He closed his eyes. Waves, palpable and heat-infused, radiated from her hands, steadily rippling out, pulsating like a star in every cell. A bond stretched, hooked and locked into place, a connection he'd never felt with Celia before, followed by a stirring in his loins. Then Celia was talking and she smiled, just like Ellie, and he could. . . .

The energy made him do it – pleasant and soothing one moment – raw and unbridled the next, and he grabbed Celia's arm, a little more roughly than he'd intended if intention were even a factor, and pulled her down to him, smothering her mouth with his own. His heart wasn't leaking now, but alive and throbbing with the force of creation itself. He wanted this woman, this virtual reality of his wife, with every ounce of energy she'd just unleashed in him. Had he stopped to take a vote, he was sure every one of the individual parts of his anatomy would have said "ay". In the split second it took him to make the move from sitting in a chair to lying on top of her, no votes were cast, no ballots counted, not a single hanging chad to raise the slightest hint of dissension among the trillions of cells, just Doc and his one little head to rule them all. He was panting now in his excitement and yes, even Grief had a spot at this table, but he pushed on, not in a domineering, take-no-prisoners kind of way, but in a Labrador Retriever way, in a six-year-old-on-Christmas-morning way, and since Celia was showing no signs of resistance, then he guessed it was okay...but...why wasn't Celia...?

He stopped when he got the buckle off. Then he saw her looking at him with nothing but love and he understood. She was gifting him this one more time with his wife.

"You'd do that for me?" Doc asked, his voice husky and cracked and raw.

Celia shook her head; Doc sighed, relieved. He couldn't go through with it anyway.

"Well, Celia wouldn't, but I would. Actually, Celia would, considering she's the only way I can."

Doc's heart stopped; he sat up and took stock. "Ellie?"

A whisper: "Hi, Jonathan."

He searched the face – Ellie's. Here was his wife. Here was her hip, and her breast, and her thigh. Here was her smile. There was no mistaking it! The circumstances presenting themselves to him were indeed strange, but his senses, acute and heightened, were undoubtedly right. And although he was not proud of it, animal instinct took over, and just as he was about to get on with it, Clarity invaded Doc's frontal lobe and raised its hand to ask a question. Doc caught his breath to answer, and still panting, rolled over onto his side, pushing himself up with the agility of an eighty-year old. He scanned the terrain, looking for clues while his balls cried out in frustration at the sound of retreat. His dick, however, refused to give up hope and stood steadfastly at attention.

Doc leaned back against the couch and rubbed his outraged appendages. The wood crackled in response. Across from him sat someone who looked like Celia, but who possessed the very real aura of his wife.

"Why did you stop?"

Doc eyed her with suspicion. "Either you're doing a really good job of throwing your voice or you're pulling some shaman shape-shifter crap on me." In response, the woman cocked one eyebrow, Ellie's trademark response, something Celia couldn't do. The alien life form chuckled – just like Ellie.

"Sometimes you just have to trust the process, Jonathan."

Her voiced reached him over the barren desert of the last five weeks, over the bitterness and rejection, over his cowardice and trepidation, over his abandonment and failure.

"Is it really you?" His throat, thick with accumulated loss, spasmed.

"Yeah, hon."

Doc coughed. How many people ever got a second chance like this? Yet here it was being offered to him, offered without his even asking, that is, if you didn't count the three weeks in the ethers deciding whether to follow her, or the two weeks after spent walking into walls. But technically, he hadn't asked. At least not outright.

"It's okay. Celia says it's okay. Consider it the wedding present she never gave us."

It was true. Celia hadn't wanted Ellie to marry Doc. "Too cerebral," she'd said, and she didn't give them a wedding present in protest. Yet here she was offering her body to be used as a pawn just so they could do it one more time. There was something to be said for these shamans and their ability to move crap around.

"She'll be watching."

"Who?"

"Celia."

"No. She's temporarily out of the office. It's just you and me."

"Well, where is she?"

"It's complicated. She's where I should be...." Ellie ran a hand through Celia's wavy hair, another classic Ellie move. "It's just...it'll just be the once."

Grateful to know this, Doc took his time, navigating around every road and byway, every nook and cranny, every up and downhill slope they'd traveled together, and when neither his nor Celia's body could hold on any longer, when he and Ellie were aching from the pleasure, and what would surely later be the pain of another separation, Doc rode the wave of gratitude and sorrow, of desire and joy, straight into her and didn't stop once to ask for directions.

☼☼☼

That night, Harley burst through the door of Celia's house. Celia greeted her with a broad smile that stiffened like meringue the minute she saw Doc. Doc had expected it to be weird, but he wasn't prepared for the level of comfort he now felt in her house so when Harley plopped down on the couch, he followed. From the looks of her, Celia hadn't had the same kind of warm and fuzzy day. When Harley went off to the kitchen, Celia lit into him.

"What the hell did you do this afternoon?"

"You know."

"No, I don't. I mean, I suspect, and it's really none of my business, but Jesus, I couldn't be any more sore."

Doc tried not to smile, but couldn't help it.

"Oh, I should have figured. All right, whatever. It's over. It's not going to happen again though, got it?"

She glared at him and he knew that whatever secret hopes he may have harbored, like the chance of spending another surreal afternoon in paradise, those options were no longer on the table.

Celia's mother was a full-blooded Lakota-Sioux, her father of Pennsylvanian Dutch descent, and as children, Celia and Ellie were exposed to all the indecipherable truths that a half-ethnicity afforded. They were equal and opposite, her parents: their father, stubborn and stoic like clay soil; her mother, fluid and fungible like the nomad tribe from which she descended. Her father had come west to experience life and find his fortune, leaving his large, extended family behind. There he met Celia's mother, and to support his bride, worked the land like his people had taught him, hoping to dominate the earth with his digging and tilling and excavating. But the land was not so forgiving as the fertile farmlands of Central Pennsylvania and so the family's income languished.

Meanwhile, Celia's mother whispered to the winds, hummed as she gathered berries, and wrote love songs to babbling brooks. Her parents spoke no more a common language than people from Venus and Mars, leaving Celia and Ellie to cull bits and pieces of both or neither as they saw fit. It's unclear why they even married, although the girls deciphered that love was involved. Neither one of their parents had any idea of saving for the proverbial rainy day. It simply wasn't in her mother's culture and her father, well, without his people behind him, he failed to thrive.

When her mother got breast cancer, Celia's father was devastated: he loved her deeply and he had no money to pay for medicine. She died a few horrific months after the cancer was detected and her father a few months after that, following a period of ritual starvation. He thought he'd let his daughters down. It's true, he did, but not by failing to provide for his wife in her illness – because shit happens – but rather, by taking the coward's way out and leaving them to fend for themselves. They were seventeen and suddenly on their own. In the end, Celia called herself a Native American, a freewheeling spirit obliged to no one but her own tried and true conscience while Ellie took the Swiss-German thing and ran with it, all the way back to Pennsylvania where she enrolled in school and tried to fit into mainstream society. Neither approach was entirely successful, but the cost of not choosing seemed the far greater risk, and hey, they'd found their niches.

People should stick to their own kind. Otherwise they make a mess of things. Take Harley, which Doc decidedly didn't want to do, yet he couldn't stop thinking about the idea and the reasons why he should.

There were more reasons why he should not. One: his love for her wasn't unconditional. Two: he had not legally adopted her which left him holding his love like a baseball trading card. If loss connotes lack then the replacement with something had to be an improvement, right? Instinctively, it sounded correct, but Doc knew it wasn't the case. The replacement part generally had its own faulty wiring, and the melding of it all might cause unanticipated problems more severe than the original ones. Was it universally better to fill the void, or let character ripen in the empty spaces? Was Doc's mere presence enough if all he were capable of giving Harley was a cardboard cutout of a dad?

As for him, Harley forced him to bust down his own moldy and water-damaged walls in places he never knew walls existed. He'd originally agreed to Harley because he'd wanted to sleep with her mother, and now he wanted to take her in to honor her mother, but he hadn't done such a good job until now so why would things change? If everything is communicated telepathically as Celia was fond of saying, what the heck kind of life would he be giving Harley if every time she opened her mouth his brain screamed, "I wish she'd shut the fuck up!" It couldn't possibly be good for anyone.

Then the leaks began.

It started as a drip from the faucet in the kitchen sink. Doc plugged the sink and pulled up a chair, watching to see how fast it dripped. Slow enough, so after a few minutes he stuck a pot under the drip and ignored it until midnight when another drip started, this one directly over the center of his bed. He put a sauce pan under it and moved to the side. In the morning, the water in the pan was convex and quivering, waiting for two, maybe three more drops to send it spilling over the sides. Doc picked it up by the handles with the utmost care, no faster than a sloth. He had almost cleared the bed when he sneezed and soaked the sheets. In the bathroom, Doc dumped the pan in the tub only to find water dripping from the shower head. On his way to the kitchen, he found another leak above the front door in the living room, hitting the floor. Doc grabbed an empty coffee cup from the table and put it underneath. He took the pan back to the bedroom, pulled on a pair of jeans and a polo shirt, brushed his teeth and washed his face, and in that short span of time, the cup in the living room had overflowed. He noticed it when, crossing the room, he slipped on the wood floor. The water had formed a rivulet running halfway to the kitchen that harbored its own leak which had breached the kitchen sink and was busy overflowing the sides. In a few minutes, the tributaries would hook up and form a river. Soon his house would be an estuary.

Doc finally called the plumber who inspected every inch of Doc's pipes, but could not diagnose the problem. So Doc called Celia who did so without leaving her house.

"Given the state of your pipes, I'd say you were leaking some heavy duty emotions.

"Huh?"

"You're awash in repressed grief and your house isn't letting you get away with it."

"English, please."

Doc not only heard, but felt Celia's sigh through the phone like a slap to his ear. "I could tell you a bunch of things. I could tell you that until you release all your guilt and remorse regarding certain events you'll be dealt situation after situation, each a little worse than the one before, all designed to make you wake up and smell the toast burning. I could tell you that the human body is infinitely wise, like your own personal angel that alerts you to the things in your life that are not up to snuff. I could tell you that each acupuncture meridian in the body relates to an emotion. For example, lungs hold grief and the liver holds anger, and air represents thoughts and visions while water, blessed water, represents emotions." Celia sighed. Doc could feel her impatience, snaking its way through the phone line.

"I could tell you all this, but..."

"But..."

❧ ❧ ❧

In an attempt to fit into the community, Celia's mother raised her children Christian like their father, but Celia didn't just want to know about God, she also wanted to know about the Great Creator, the time/space continuum, and the evolution of the Spirit. She figured there had to be a way to combine it all. The first time she felt a fluttering breeze in a closed room, she was hooked. They had accepted her. She wasn't sure who *They* were, but the presence emanated peace and that was enough for Celia. Her mother claimed to see spirits all the time: nature spirits, sprites, fairies, elves, woodland spirits, angels – the whole gamut. Mention a category and Celia's mother had a story for it, but she refused to pass the techniques along. Her life had been hard; she'd always been an outcast and didn't want the same fate for her daughters, but outcast or no, Celia knew what she wanted.

So she read books and practiced on her own every night without her mother's help. One night when she was about Harley's age, she had gone to bed late with no intention of doing anything but sleeping. Within minutes of lying down, her etheric body was flying around her room, and before she knew it, over to her parents' room. Her parents' etheric bodies raised their heads and looked at her, while their physical bodies continued sleeping. Then Celia was in Ellie's room and Ellie's etheric body was waving at her. After months of trying to leave her body, she was flying. Moments later, Celia fell onto her bed. Barely twenty minutes had passed, but Celia's lifetime work had begun. She was hooked, determined to go well beyond anything her mother knew or could teach her.

Unlike Celia's mother, if Harley wanted to know something Celia was prepared to answer questions. The child had a million of them.

"I can't see it, Aunt Cel. Why can't I see it?"

"You're focusing too hard. Just let your eyes go fuzzy. It comes to you when you stop looking for it. The harder you try, the more elusive it is. Now relax your body and close your eyes."

Celia and Harley were in the back yard tucked under a Lacebark Elm, the remnants of their picnic scattered across their woolen blanket. It was too cold for picnicking, but Harley had insisted so they were bundled up with hats and scarves and mittens. Celia was leaning back on her elbows and Harley lying down, looking up at the branches of the Elm. A few dead leaves, the ones that refused to give it up when their time had come, hung there in stoic refusal to fall. She blew air out through her nose – the Harley equivalent of a harrumph – squeezed her eyes shut, took a deep breath.

When she opened her eyes she looked exactly like a toddler on Christmas morning. It was with these eyes, fresh and full of wonder, that she admired the Elm. A few minutes later, Harley bolted upright and her words tumbled out on top of each other. "I saw it! I saw it! There! It was like the tree was dancing with the sky, or pulsing or something, I don't know, like, in and out, and its branches, and those dead leaves looked, like, alive! It's not really moving, right? It can't be."

Celia shook her head. "No, it's not moving. There's so much life inside a tree, but you don't see it moving unless the wind is blowing. What if you just stopped for a moment and listened?"

"Don't you mean watch?"

"That, too, but mostly listen. You can hear it talk to you."

Harley strained her ears, but the call of the birds and Celia's prayer flags, flapping in the breeze distracted her.

"You're trying too hard. Lie back and close your eyes."

Harley complied and just as it appeared that she would drift off to sleep, she smiled.

"Well," Celia asked, "can you hear it?"

"It's almost like...well, there's the sound of leaves when the wind blows and the branches creak. But there's this other sound. Like a hum, like the tree is singing to itself."

Celia clapped her hands and grabbed Harley's shoulders. "Exactly!" She crushed Harley to her and rocked her. "I knew it. I knew you could." Celia stood up and pulled Harley onto her haunches.

"Okay, listen, because this may not make sense at first." She placed Harley's hands on the tree. "Everything has chakras. In humans and animals they run along the spinal column, but in trees, they're mobile which is kind of backwards because a tree looks like a spinal column, right, but it doesn't move." Celia shrugged. "Go figure. But if you scan the surface of a tree with your hands," Celia ran her hands along the bark to demonstrate, "and you feel a tingling sensation, that's one of the tree's chakras. Take hold of it – with both hands because they're about the size of a basketball – and gently nudge it to align with your own chakra." Celia moved her hands over the bark at the height of her solar plexus, turned around and leaned against the tree. "You can do it either leaning against it or facing it. Once you're aligned, you're connected with the tree's energy." Celia leaned back and closed her eyes. "It's really fabulous. You gotta try it."

Harley jumped up and ran both hands up and down along the tree bark. When she found the spot she was looking for, she leaned back against it and grabbed Celia's hand. They stood there, side-by-side, for several minutes. Harley gave Celia's hand a squeeze and flashed a shy smile.

"Aunt Celia, why did you decide to become a shaman anyway?"

"Hmmm. Well, I like the fungible nature of this work."

"Huh?"

"You never know what's going to happen. Sometimes it's like walking through fog. Colors drop away, the air's texture takes on the subtle shape of each thing it surrounds. Images shift before your eyes, shimmering droplets of grey silk. You walk with only sound to guide you and make your way toward a splash in a nearby pond. Is it a duck, or a mermaid?"

Celia stopped and waited. Harley shifted, looked to her aunt, but when no advice was forthcoming, she asked. "What's that mean?"

"What's it mean to you?"

"It doesn't matter what it means to me. I want to know what it means to you."

"Don't you see, Lee? What it means to you *is* what it means. That's the whole point."

Harley graced her aunt with a vacant stare. Light years passed through her golden orbs until understanding touched down and Harley's eyes grew wide. "Oh, like, the world is what you think it is."

"Not like you think it is, but IS what you think it is. That's the whole enchilada. In my line of work, I get to practice that every day." Celia tilted her head back and looked up to the leaves, enchanted. "Besides, I thought it would be cool."

Harley followed her aunt's gaze. "What do you think Mommy would say if she saw us now?"

"Well, first, she does see us," Celia replied, smiling. "And second, she says…." Celia looked out into the distance, past the trees, past the sky, past the sun itself, and squinted until her small smile spread into a wide, river grin. "She says, two thumbs way up."

Don't let anyone kid you. Every death is really a form of suicide. It's just that not everyone gets to leave a note. Here's what I know. Before you come into the world, you've already decided on your parents, the color and pallor of your skin, your socio-economic status, and the particular disabilities you'll be saddled with. By disabilities, I don't mean physical handicaps, although that can be part of it, but emotional disabilities, the ones that tend to derail you, like the inability to commit; fear of abandonment; or lack of trust. It doesn't matter what your issue is – we all have a few whoppers – but everything in your life, your parents, your friends, your siblings, your teachers at school, everything is designed to bring your issues to a head, giving you the choice to work through them or turn tail and run. I had a chance to face them head on and what did I do?

I'm still not sure. The drugs I needed to kill the cancer may have killed me, too. I just kept thinking what if after an arduous fight I still lost? I wasn't afraid of dying, but I was afraid of pain. To fight Death with death – chemo, surgery, radiation – and maybe still lose seemed so ignoble. So I rolled the dice and let Fate decide. I climbed up on the mesa that day knowing that weather was coming and called Death out like the coward he was. Damn if He didn't call my bluff. Hey, at least I chose. Some people never choose. They get stuck, so fearful of change they are, and end up dying a little each day, slow and steady, like rust.

Death by a thousand cuts. Death by routinization.

☼☼☼

Three weeks after the tête-à-tête with Celia, Doc woke from a dream, convinced of his imminent death. He was jumpy and when Celia came to collect Harley from her weekend stay, he relayed the dream in rapid succession.

"I dreamt that Ellie and I were on the mesa and she said, 'I'm sorry, but the tests came back positive.' In my dream I knew what she was talking about even though she never said it. I had breast cancer."

"Men can get breast cancer, but you don't have it." Celia graced him with a penetrating look. "What else?"

"Harley was in my bedroom crying and when I opened the door to see what was wrong, I saw her standing next to the bed, poking me, saying, 'wake up, please, just wake up,' and my face was pale as beach sand and you could see that every time she poked me there was no give to my skin, just a hard surface." Doc slumped over in his chair.

"It's complete transference. You feel guilty that you didn't give her a chance to tell you and this is how you're punishing yourself." Celia dismissed him with a wave of her hand.

"I thought so, too, but then Harley came into my room this morning."

"And?"

"She poked me sharply in the arm, twice, just like in the dream, and when I didn't move she poked me in the ribs. When I rolled over to face her she said, 'I had a dream that you were in a box with a green monster. The monster wouldn't let me see you or talk to you, but I kept begging him and finally he did, but every time I asked you something your hair fell out.' So what am I supposed to think about that?" Doc scrunched his lips together and waited.

Celia's face took on a translucent quality and for a moment Doc thought he could see straight through to the bones of her skull. The space around her began to shift as if she were stepping in and out of the room at warp speed and he had to keep blinking to keep the picture in focus. Celia's horrified look reflected Death itself, as if its energy had enveloped her and started to squeeze. Doc whimpered like a dog and broke the spell.

"What? What did you see?"

Celia shivered. "Nothing." Doc grabbed her arm, but Celia shook him off. He grabbed her again. This time, she faced him.

"Unless something changes, certain probabilities have been set in motion. I can't predict the future, you understand, only probabilities based upon what's happening with you right now."

"And?"

Long pause: "And, it doesn't look so good."

"What do I do?" Doc snapped.

Celia gave him a small smile and grabbed his chin. Doc thought she was going to pull him in for a kiss, but instead, she looked him square in each eye and said: "Whatever it is you came here to do." She collected Harley, and left.

Doc shivered. The door seemed to shimmer in its frame for seconds after they'd left. Doc stared at it, a hand on his hip, his mouth agape, willing it to open, for Celia to walk back in and render some clarity to a murky picture. For the first time in his life, he wished for a divining bowl so someone, anyone, could give him a glimpse, a clue what he was supposed to do next. Celia talked about probabilities, but he only felt comfortable with certainties, concrete problems with concrete answers.

"What the heck does that mean?"

He woke in the middle of the night. The full moon had flipped on its high beams and was making a tenacious push through the blinds, wrapping around his neck like a lover. The sheer torque of its luminosity pushed upon him until he opened his lips to accept the kiss. When he came to full consciousness, he was fully erect with an ache that even Ellie couldn't satisfy. Were forty-five year old men capable of such virility? He shifted his weight, and as an afterthought, propelled himself out of bed and across the room. Doc was not surprised to see the face of darkness in the mirror, looking substantially like his own. The Antler shimmered in the moon's bright beam like the horn of some long-vanquished prey. Perhaps it was the thought of his own immortality that frightened him, but minutes later, Doc was dressed and in the car, speeding off into the night. Somewhere out there was an answer that could be heard only in darkness.

✧✧✧

The grey of the sky against the black open road distorted time and space. Doc drove. If he was being guided, he had no conscious awareness of it. After an hour, he was pulling off the road and down a long driveway, hidden in darkness. How, or why, he wasn't sure, but he finally got out and started walking maybe a quarter-mile or so, listening to the night sounds. It was then he heard it, just once, a deep, noble sound, rooted in revolutions, forged in the fires of individual rights and the protection of homes and hearths, the Great Equalizer, with a sound so distinct, he could name it.

A Remington 760 GameMaster 30-06.

It had a 4" x 16" power scope for really reaching out there – if you could see it, you could hit it. Its nylon stock held five, 30-06 one-hundred and fifty gram bullets that made a hole the size of your pinky going in, a salad plate going out. It weighed about eleven pounds, but felt like a ton when you held it one-handed and adjusted the scope, leading Doc to surmise that whoever was doing the holding had some heft to him.

And he was right. About part of it anyway.

"Whatcha' doin' out in the dark, son?"

Doc caught a glimpse of the Amazonian woman before him as the clouds parted and she stepped into a shaft of moonlight. At 5'11", she was broad-shouldered with a long reach and looked as if she could take more than her fair share of him down.

Doc hesitated, afraid to say the thing that would cause the trigger finger to contract. It only took another break in the cloud cover for him to see he was right. It was a GameMaster and the last time he'd used one he was hunting deer in Western Pennsylvania with his father. Now what to respond to the voice in order for the finger to stay put, maybe even relax itself against the sleek curved metal.

"How'd you know I was here?"

"Bein' that I have title to this property, I b'lieve that earns me the right to ask the questions and you ta' answer."

"I came to check on your well."

"You from Harebrain Oil and Gas?"

Doc laughed. Not the first time he'd heard that, but definitely the first time he'd heard it in the black of night with a rancher pointing a rifle at his third eye. "Yes, ma'am." The rifle did not waiver, nor did the ear-splitting silence of a woman low on patience. "I mean no." He was thinking that it had been a long while since he fired an "ought-6," as he stood there in the chiaroscuro of the on-again, off-again illumination, both sweating and shivering, and wondering if this woman's next move could be his last. "I work for Harburnette, yes. But I'm not here on their behalf. I'm here for my own reasons." The rifle wasn't moving so Doc threw what he hoped would be his trump card. "Ellie was my wife."

The rifle went down. A hand went out. "Well, now, son, that's an entirely different set of teeth. Why didn't ya' say so straight away?"

Doc found himself engulfed by a strong, sturdy arm as it snaked around his waist and ushered him up the drive. It was fifty yards to the house and Doc tried to make out where he was in space and time, but the moon had ditched again and his rods and cones weren't cooperating so he let the strong arm guide him up the gravel drive to where he knew a steaming cup of strong coffee would be waiting for him.

Twila Fuller set her rifle down on the kitchen table, an old farm house staple hewn from a hundred-year old hemlock and in Twila's family for as long. She nodded at a chair and set about putting on a pot of coffee, measuring out seven heaping tablespoons. The aroma filled the air before she'd even set the pot to brew. Twila caught Doc watching her. "No sense drinking it if it's weak. Those Starbucks sissies ain't got nothin' on Twila Fuller."

"Sorry, I'm not in the habit of poking around people's homes in the dark, but I . . ."

"Ah, don't get your drawers all up in a bunch. Was up anyway. Lionel's outta town and I don't sleep much when he's gone." Twila set out two mugs, a pint of half-and-half, and a bowl of raw sugar then leaned back against the kitchen sink to watch the coffee brew. Doc watched her watching the coffee; neither of them spoke for the entire brew time. The coffee pot sputtered out its last gasps. Doc watched it subside to a drip, drip, drip, imperceptibly changing the level in the coffee pot. A full minute later – Doc knew this because he checked his watch three times – Twila poured out two mugs of rich, dark coffee.

"Been married forty-five years."

Doc nodded at this bit of family history.

"You and Ellie are practically newlyweds by our standards." Twila put some sugar and a bit of cream in her mug and waited while the cream mixed itself before stirring. She took a tentative sip, blew out quick air, almost a whistle, set her mug down.

"You know it takes about a million gallons of water to frack a well? These guys don't do it just once. They do it ten, fifteen times a pop. They say it doesn't hurt my ground water, but they're full a' shit." Twila added more sugar to her coffee, stirred longer than need be. "Diagnosed this May past. Hell of a summer, I tell ya'. It's some rare form of some even rarer cancer that I got no history for far back as any of my ancestors care to look. And I can trace 'em pretty far. Been here since the black gold rush of the 1880s. My great-grandfather was a wildcatter." Twila took the bittiest sip and recoiled. "Too hot." She set the mug down. "This fool thing's the second gold rush. Problem is, it's not a bunch of Wile E. Coyote entrepreneurs looking to strike it rich, it's the goddamn corporations." Twila stirred in another hefty dose of cream, turning it into a mulatto cup of Joe. "These are the same people stripping the tops off of mountains with a million pounds of machinery. I mean, what chance's that mountain got against that kinda' metal." Twila took another sip and this time she nailed it and smiled, pleased.

Doc shifted uncomfortably in his seat, then blurted out an answer to an unasked question. "Mechanical Engineer."

"How's that?"

"I'm a Mechanical Engineer. I work for them."

"Well, son, you just proved one of my favorite theories."

"What's that?"

"The need to confess is second only to the need to procreate."

Doc laughed in spite of himself.

"The whole process stinks. The waste of freshwater. All those damn chemicals in the ground. They act like they're pumping into a sealed tube. Like the ground ain't gonna crack." She took a long draw on her coffee – "morons" – then set it down. "And now it's in my glands."

"The fracking enhances permeability. The pressure makes it easier to get at the gas. Pretty much pushes it right up on out of the ground. In case you wanted to know."

"Honey, I been around that block and then some. Could probably tell you a thing or two, Mr. Mechanical Engineer. That's what death'll do to ya'. When you think ya' only got a few months before the lights go out, you can damn well believe you're gonna be looking for another source a' incandescence."

Doc presented Twila with a grim grin. She patted his hand.

"I didn't tell you that to make ya' feel sorry for me, Hon. I told ya' that to light a fire under yer ass. If I'm gonna go, I need somebody to pass the goddamn torch to."

✡ ✳ ✸

Being here's great, don't get me wrong, but there's a slew of things I miss. Things that keep me tethered to the earth like a baby cow cum veal chop. I watch them, Doc and Harley, from my faraway place as they try to connect with each other, to construct a causeway across the marshlands of their hearts. I watch Doc, so freaking lost without me, and I feel something. Not quite guilt because we don't have that here, but a need to do something to help. You know, it's strange. After being here in this place I'd longed to be my whole life I realize I'm still not whole. Pieces of me are walking around in the sunlight, hiking and taking baths and eating ice cream and calling each other on the phone. How can I leave these bits of me behind? So I'm opting for eavesdropping rather than scooting off to another dimension. I mean, what kind of schmuck would I be if I chose enlightenment over Harley's high school graduation? I was so wrong about the lasting nature of love.

Do the dead dream, you may ask? Yes, they do. They dream of living.

☼☼☼

Doc left Twila's and took the highway. The sun's first rays could have been a hallucination. They weren't scheduled to breach the horizon for another forty-eight minutes, but Doc could feel them coming. If he hurried, he could make it to the top of the mesa in time for sunrise.

The wind moaned and buffeted the jeep like a disembodied spirit looking for a host. *Winds of change.* Doc had heard plenty of stories from Celia as well as the locals over the years. The best place to be in a wind like this was inside the house with the windows closed tight lest an evil spirit filter through, infiltrating your body and soul like a bloodthirsty leech. Doc shivered and hit the accelerator.

Forty-five minutes later his mind still hadn't caught up to the decision his heart had come to back at Twila's. A decision that could get him fired or even land him in jail. A decision as viscous as Twila's coffee.

Doc supported Greenpeace even though in their salad days some of their tactics bordered on eco-terrorism. Doc had supported Ellie through her rabid recycling phase, which just happened to last her lifetime. He even showed up every Earth Day to give a demonstration in Harley's class, but this was different. This meant lost production time, and property damage, and workers being laid off while wells came back on-line. This was environmental sabotage and against every corporate tenet ever written. This was Edward Abbey in drag, words lifted off the page and alchemized into 3-D, bits of metal exploding.

Doc was contemplating something that had the potential to drastically alter the course of his reality. Celia told him he had to change, purge, release. This was definitely that. But was it his "that," or was it Ellie's?

Doc lay down on the ground to wait for the sun, and he felt an unexplainable weight resting on his chest. The feeling spread until it covered his whole body. She was here, he was sure – here in the place they'd spent so many hours – and she was lying on top of him.

It soothed him in an eerie way. He didn't know what he'd expected or how he thought Ellie would take form, but since the afternoon at

Celia's the line between life and death had been irrevocably blurred. It was best to keep an open mind. Environmental sabotage was as good a way as any to while away the time while waiting to be reunited with his missing half.

The sun's rays breached first a finger, then a toe, then its whole shiny bald head over the horizon. Doc stared at it until the bottom lip fully separated from the rim then rose to go. Decision made, life path chosen, he was a man on a mission, a man in search of a dream. What he wasn't prepared for was that the dream was looking for him, too.

❖ ❀ ✳

Harley leaned back against the massive oak. She wore boots because it was cold, but no coat. She moved up and down, scratching her back like a bear while her hands held a steady position against the bark. Her eyes were closed, a slight smile on her face. She'd been at it for fifteen minutes or so when Doc yelled out the window.

"Lunch!"

Harley was deep in meditation and didn't hear him.

Doc yelled again.

"Lunch!" When that failed to produce the elicited response, Doc went outside.

"What are you doing? Why don't you have a coat on?"

"Washing my energy."

"Well, dry off. It's time for lunch."

Harley's eyes popped open and narrowed to a squint. It was an improvement, Doc felt, over the saccharine responses of the past.

"What are you looking at? And don't say nothing much," Doc smirked.

"Your aura. I'm not so good at it yet, but yours looks kind of . . . dirty."

"Oh, geez, not you, too."

Harley shrugged. "What did you make?"

"Buffalo wraps."

Harley nodded, took three deep breaths, exhaling each loudly. She turned around and hugged the tree, murmured something into the dark crevices of the bark, then bolted past him. A warm current of air swept by Doc's cheek then dissipated. He felt the chill over his bones in contrast as the cold reclaimed Harley's space. He touched the tree. The bark was hard and unforgiving, true, but there was something else, a current of energy perhaps, that his hands intuited more than felt. He put his ear to the bark. For a moment, it vibrated. Doc shivered, then stepped inside after Harley.

She was sitting at the table, drumming her fingers, waiting, as most teenagers do, to be served. Doc set a plate at each of their places and, feeling indulgent, asked: "So what's this energy washing stuff? Aunt Celia, I suppose."

Harley nodded. "Four hundred horsepower."

"Huh?"

"Four hundred horsepower. That's what it takes a tree to get a drop of moisture from its root system to the leaves. That's thirty or forty feet below the earth's surface to about sixty feet in the air. It's a long way."

"She's pulling your leg. That's more horsepower than my car. Than three cars."

"So?"

"All right, Miss Smarty-Pants. How'd you do the calculations for something like that?"

Harley shrugged. "Aunt Celia read it in one of her metaphysics books, but the Native Americans always knew it. If they were tired from hunting or maybe didn't get enough sleep because the fire went out in the teepee, they could stop and rub their backs against a tree and the tree would share its energy. It only takes ten or fifteen minutes to get juiced. It depends on how tired you are.

Doc sniggered, then shoved a wrap in his mouth to stifle the air of ridicule.

"It's true!" Harley persisted, showing no signs of hurt feelings. "Think about it. Four hundred horsepower is a huge amount of energy to run through something that just sits still all the time. The tree's probably happy to give some away."

"Well, what about winter when there are no leaves sprouting?"

Harley pondered the question. She twirled her hair, furrowed her brow, then realization dawned: "Probably just idling. You know, like when you start your car, but just sit in the driveway and listen to the radio or the new Taylor Swift CD." Harley bobbed her head, although Doc wasn't sure if she agreed with her own theory or was remembering a Taylor Swift song.

Doc's brow did its own furrowing. "What do you have to be tired about?"

"I didn't finish dreaming last night. I'm feeling, like, half-cooked."

Seeing Harley's earnest expression and finding no argument to counter, Doc resisted the smart-ass comment.

Harley took a massive bite of her wrap. "So what happened with you and Mom?"

Doc practically choked. "Huh?"

"Aunt Celia told me Mom came to visit you. A bit ago. What happened?"

Doc cleared his throat and found his voice, but not much to back it up.

Harley shrugged, tried to raise an eyebrow. She swallowed, washed it down with milk. "You know what I was thinking?" Doc shook his head, relieved to be excused from sharing the events of that afternoon.

"I was thinking about a swing we had in the backyard of our old house. You know, one shaped like a box where the swingers face each other?"

"Yeah."

"You can get like, four little kids on there. Me and Mom used to swing on it. There's this Polaroid picture of me. I'm wearing a white dress like babies wear with ruffled panties over the diaper that makes me look like I have a giant butt."

Doc smiled.

"You can tell from our faces that we were really happy. Next to the swing was this huge tire with sand and a little plastic baby pool and a brick BBQ grill. I remember the great smell."

"How? You were like, one."

"I just can. Maybe I smell it through the picture. I swear I can even smell Mommy in that picture. Sometimes I smell her for no reason."

Doc's heart jumped. He hadn't thought that if Ellie was paying him the odd visit, she was probably doing the same with Harley and his competitive nature kicked in. "There's no way you can remember all those details." He was reaching, trying to regain a measure of control over their conversation, but Harley had completely flummoxed him.

"Yeah, well, detail this. Before you, I was a one-woman show. I got a lot of memories under my belt."

Doc wiped his mouth with a napkin.

"Admit it," Harley said. "You didn't like me that much when you first met me. I mean, you probably thought I was cute in a goo-goo-gaa-gaa kind of way, but I probably got in the way of you doin' Mom."

"Harley! Watch your mouth."

"Mom told me about your first sleepover and how I woke up at a most inopportune time."

Doc blushed the color of the shortest ray on the light spectrum from a frisky fuchsia to a bold brick yard red so Harley kept digging: "Remember that first night in the house when you ran off to the bar?"

"How'd you know about that? You were six," Doc asked.

"I remember, is all. And then all that stuff with the baby."

Doc's eyes grew wide. Being upstaged was not a staple in his diet, but here Harley had done it twice in two minutes. "You knew about that?" he asked, almost a whisper.

Harley nodded. "Mom always told me stuff. I was her Main Man."

Doc stared at his plate. Memories flooded his cerebral cortex. "Harley, I . . . ." Doc rubbed his lips together, trying to dematerialize. "Losing that baby almost killed your mom. She was devastated." He wiped his face with a napkin, placed it over his half-finished meal. "She wanted to try again, but I said no. I couldn't stand the idea of what it might do to her. I wasn't thinking about you, Lee . . . I'm sorry."

"It's okay." She squeezed Doc's arm, gave him a little resigned smile. "It's like flowers growing through the cracks in the sidewalk. Life gets through when it's supposed to."

Doc blew out a quick breath through his nose, displacing the concrete in his throat. "Well, what do you know?" he croaked. "Good advice – from a teenager." He touched her hand and half-smiled. Harley blushed. They breathed in tandem.

The San Juan Basin is a 16,000-square-mile area, straddling the border
of Colorado and the northwestern part of New Mexico. It produces
over 1.32 trillion cubic feet of natural gas a year, about 7% of all the
gas consumed in the U.S., and Harburnette wanted to get their hands
on every inch of it. It embarrassed Doc to know he worked for the company that stole the rights – to land, to minerals, to water – out from
under the indigenous people. In the early days they called them land-
men, company employees sent out into rural areas to lease the right
to drill, to excavate, or to extirpate, as the case may be. In the early
days, the ranchers were glad to see them coming. It meant more roads
with easier access to cattle and water and a few extra dollars in their
pockets. In the early days, Doc would have been a landman instead of
an engineer. Today, he was a mere criminal.

Doc had begun his descent into criminality several days before with
a trip to Home Depot. First, he purchased several five-gallon buckets.
The leaks had continued unabated and Doc was forced to turn the
main breaker off when he wasn't home, and when he was home, the
buckets came in handy.

Next, Doc bought half a dozen pre-cut pieces of 2' x 3" lead pipe.
He thought it would take only one pipe bomb to take the well out, but
to be safe he made two. He bought matching 3" caps, some primer,
and glue. The primer was like foreplay, but once you applied the glue
and put the cap on you could never get it off. He also bought a replacement Magneto igniter for his grill and some batteries. At the camping
store he bought a Pelican box, and with a little electronic wizardry, he
was going to buy himself some time.

At home, Doc screwed the caps on and filled the pipe with Triple X
Winchester reloading gunpowder, the very same gunpowder Doc used
to use for his Remington 760 Gamemaster. It came in quart size cans
for filling about 500 bullets, but for this operation, Doc would need
four or five cans. To avoid arousing suspicion, he made the rounds,
buying in small quantities from half a dozen gun shops, no questions
asked. A foot long piece of fuse, a waxed piece of thick string, like the

candles on a birthday cake, green with a waterproof coating, and Doc was ready to put it all together.

The pipe took five cans of gunpowder. Doc pushed the fuse way down and carefully packed cotton balls around the top, leaving a long tail hanging out the end. He used a tooth brush around the threads of the cap to remove the stray pieces of gun powder, about the size of sand, but flat, like pellets. Leave stray pellets stuck between the cap and the threads and the friction might send him home to Ellie sooner than he planned. He fed the tail through the hole in the cap and screwed it down, compressing the powder. He squirted some silicone caulk around the fuse to make it waterproof and assure the fuse stayed in place. Next he used some flat black paint to camouflage it. He placed the Magneto igniter, the timer, and the fuse inside the Pelican box. He'd bought himself an hour.

The night arrived. Doc had scouted and re-scouted the well Site and could get there with his eyes closed. He cut the lights a quarter-mile out, driving slowly over the dirt road. At a tenth of a mile, he cut the engine and hiked in, being careful not to jostle his bundles. A strange mewing broke from the silence like something was dying or maybe being born. Doc ignored the chill that ran from the base of his spine up to the top of his head and set the explosives, taping the lead pipe to the pressure regulator as lovingly as a momma would set her newborn to suckle. Fifty-five minutes later, he watched from his spot on the mesa like the very same mother leans over the crib in the dark, eyes adapting, soaking up the slant of moonlight across the baby's chest as it rises, falls, rises again, listening for the catch of breath at the back of the throat, the small shallow exhale through the nostrils. Doc couldn't hear the well breathing from his perch a hillside away, but what his ears couldn't hear, his heart put in perspective for him. He felt the undulating, the pulsing, as if his own body were the repository, and at the moment it impacted, 3:41 A.M., the fuse ran out and the spark made contact inside its perch in the Pelican box. Doc watched the explosion – a huge flash that hurt his eyes through binoculars: not Hiroshima, but bright white and irreverent. From where he was, it appeared that no one noticed. He saw lights neither switch on nor extinguish. He heard not a single bark from a single dog. Doc watched for upwards of twenty minutes while the fire freely consumed the well, a lovely long-smoldering thing that would keep burning until someone discovered it and notified Harburnette. They'd put it out, rendering it useless. While the fire was still burning, Doc began making plans for his next foray. One well down, four hundred and fifty-seven to go.

I could have done something, maybe stopped the beast in its tracks, but while the fire raged inside me, I was too preoccupied, too caught up in OPD's – other peoples' dramas – to deal with my own, and so I let the beast get the best of me, as humans often do, not because I didn't have the wherewithal to beat it, but because in the beating of it, just what would I be saying about myself? That I was incredible? Amazing? Awesome beyond belief? Well, that just wasn't a mindset I had a template for.

Someone with less body awareness might not have noticed, but I did. It started out as a thought, a feeling, a mere blip on my radar screen. I endured endless self-examinations, but it was a moving target, a shadow of what it would become. They say what you focus on all day long is what you'll get. I spent a lot of time adjusting my bra to fit the inevitable. One day, after months of checking, it had arrived. I had called the beast into form; the power of my wandering and unchecked thoughts had created it. And like Dr. Frankenstein, I didn't dare see it destroyed.

ॐ ❤ ❢

Celia's trepidation about accepting Doc's lunch invitation was creeping around the walls of her abdomen like a hedge fund manager, looking to unload a high-risk derivative swap. "Christ, what am I doing?" She felt it was a mistake so soon after so many things, allowing him to ingratiate himself into her confidence. He could be charming, even disarming with his probing stare and poignant questions. He'd had his own set of mishaps which gave him an insight into the frailties of human existence that few understood, although he kept that part of him under secret service-like security. While Ellie had fallen for him, what would Ellie say about Celia stepping in. Celia was pondering this conundrum when the doorbell rang.

She opened it to find Doc standing there, ruffling her equilibrium with his square jaw and devilish smile, so much that she almost bolted. In that moment, she wanted Doc in the worst way, wanted him to infuse her like a fruity vodka, and her desire was dizzying. She threw open the door to her heart and her living room in the same instant.

Two hours and three margaritas later, their sweaty, naked bodies intertwined, Celia was having some very serious doubts about her sanity. The first time it was for Ellie, after all, and even though she was there, she wasn't really. Any gratification she may have had was diverted like a rerouted tributary, the only thing left behind an obscure bed and bank, drying in the sun with the moss clinging to its sides. *Was it a crime to just want to know? For myself?* Doc lay beside her, rubbing her arm, lost in his own reverie. As if he could read her mind, Doc spoke:

"I had to know . . . you know, what it would be like."

Uncanny how someone so practical could at times be so metaphysical. She coughed, embarrassed by so many things she couldn't even begin to list them, but reluctant to leave the crook of his arm into which she was tucked.

"It was different this time. Without Ellie."

"You were disappointed."

"No."

Doc looked full-throttle into her overwrought soul, Celia could tell. She was used to having the upper hand and now she wasn't sure what she had. She felt like a teenager and he could sense every last insecurity.

"What if we just stayed like this? Let it grow in its weird, organic, surreal way?"

"Doc." She never called him by his nickname. Never called him anything really and it sounded strange on her tongue and perhaps to his ear as well because she felt his body tense and in that instance, she regained a bit of herself.

"When you wake from your dream you'll realize that there's another one inside of that and I'm not Ellie."

"I know that. It's just . . . we could make this work." Celia frowned.

"What?" Doc asked, defensive.

"You're too dry, and I'm not that good with high-maintenance things. Orchids, anything that doesn't need much water to survive. My grandmother had African violets, dozens, on a plant stand by the window. She was desert people; she had desert wisdom in her bones. Those violets bloomed and bloomed. I tried keeping violets. It didn't work out.

"Know what I think?"

"What?"

"That you should move out of the desert before your soul dries up."

Celia raised herself on one elbow. "That may be the most insightful thing you've ever said to me."

"I'm home!" The sound of the door slamming and Harley's footsteps in the hall launched them both from the bed. They scrambled for their clothes.

"I'll go first. Pretend you were in the bathroom or something." She was out the door before Doc could even respond.

The next morning, Celia and Harley floated through Doc's front door, willowy with the smell of a freaky warm winter day on their skin. Doc was snoozing on the couch, but cracked one eye and sniffed the air. "You guys smell good."

"That's the smell of light," Celia said. "photons converting into energy. They're captured by skin cell receptors and brought inside the body, literally lightening it up, converting light into life." Celia smiled. "The photons speed up the spin of electrons. The faster they go, the less gravity attaches to them. If you get light enough, you could float."

"Impossible," Doc said, closing the one open eye. "Gravity is an equal opportunity employer."

Celia waved her hand, dismissing him. "You don't believe anything, but that's what happens when you have a mind like a steel trap and a heart to match." She moved his feet over and took a seat on the couch. Doc rolled over onto his side, his legs hanging over the edge. Harley sat down on Celia's lap and leaned back into her aunt. "It's like this. Sunlight wraps around everything, infusing it. Take a tree. Sunlight hugs the branches." Celia wrapped her arms around Harley's arms and raised them upward. Harley giggled. "When the sun rises, the branches react with sun and chlorophyll and water and they grow. The cool thing is, like the chlorophyll and water, the sun's rays are locked inside which means the tree's branches are also made of light. It's not just a chemical process. The light's still in there." Celia finished the tutorial with a tickle to Harley's armpits. Harley doubled over.

Doc sat up and rolled his eyes. "If it makes sense for you, okay."

Harley tried to retaliate, but Celia grabbed both her wrists.

"You know what I want to know?" Harley asked, struggling to break free. "How did they make up words before there was any talking?"

Celia grinned, wrapped her arms around Harley in a body-lock. "She gets that inquisitiveness from my side of the family."

Celia released Harley who scampered off to the kitchen, leaving Celia to focus on Doc.

"You look like a train wreck."

"You know, you really have a way of making a guy feel good."

"Seriously. You look like hell. What have you been doing?"

"I've been up all night, if you must know. I almost got run off the road by an elk. I almost got shot, and I almost died when I lost my footing hiking up to the mesa and slipped a few stories down a sheer rock face. Scared the crap out of me, but other than that, not much." Doc covered his eyes with his arm.

"What were you doing up on the mesa in the pitch dark?"

"Reconnaissance for environmental sabotage."

Celia took in the scrapes and bruises on his hands, the scratched chin, the bloodied knuckles, the dirt stains on his pants. She smiled, because in this case, looks were deceiving. Peel away the bent and bruised exterior and Celia detected a peacefulness that Doc had not been acquainted with in all the weeks since Ellie died. She patted his knee.

"Whatever it is you're doing, keep it up."

Doc's arm still rested on his eyes so only his mouth was visible. "So where is she?" he asked, without a segue, peremptory small talk, or even an introductory clause that would alert the listener to the fact that he had changed the subject. Celia laughed. All engineer, all the time.

"Who?" she asked, even though there was no one else it could be.

Doc removed the arm shielding his eyes. "Duh. Ellie, that's who. Why do I feel her sometimes? Like she's still here?"

"Technically, she's gone. She lives in the fifth dimension in a place full of light where you travel at the speed of thought."

"Sounds Star Trekkie."

"It is. You want a banana, you think, banana, and that's what you get."

"Really?"

"Really."

"Wow."

"Well, not "wow" if you're not ready for it."

"Why wouldn't anyone be ready for that?"

"Because if you're thinking, 'Holy disaster, Batman,' what you'll get is holy disaster and you have to deal with it because it will be as real as anything else. Every thought you think has to be checked and rechecked."

"Oh. Doesn't sound pretty."

"You especially don't want to be out there in fear because, man, you should see some of the stuff that lives there." Celia leaned her head back against the couch and studied the ceiling. She could feel Doc looking at her.

"Have you?"

Celia nodded. "Part of the job of being a shaman is to hold the vision, so I can assist my clients in shifting their reality. The starting point is their own psyches. Some people are in really dark places at the start." She turned to face him. "It's so much bigger than it seems."

"The important stuff usually is."

Celia smiled. "Wow."

"I do think deep thoughts sometimes." Doc flashed Celia a crooked smile and continued. That still doesn't explain why sometimes it feels like Ellie's sitting right next to me. Even on top of me."

"Sometimes she is. She's full of light, but the earth plane is dense and holds maybe ten percent. Ellie can only stay in this vibration for a short time and then she gets sucked back into the light."

"Does it hurt?"

"No. She's got no body. She's pure light."

While Celia watched Doc ponder the information, Harley walked back into the room, carrying a tray with two Cokes, a sparkling water for Celia, and some snacks. He accepted the Coke she offered, but set it down. Celia opened hers with a phphphssssst .

"Wow, what service," Celia said, gazing at Harley with affection. Harley returned the look and Celia couldn't help but feel a pang of remorse for Doc who always seemed like odd-man-out, a helpless pawn against a millennium of biology. True, he also had a double helical structure joined by base pairs that provided the blueprint of all human life, but he could no more change his genetic structure to make it more simpatico with Harley's than he could paint the Sistine Chapel. At least the latter was a remote possibility.

Harley handed Doc his Coke again, and suppressed a giggle. Then she sat down on the couch next to Celia and opened her own soda. Gas and air exchanged places with a small bit of fanfare, barely a burp. Celia and Harley exchanged glances then watched Doc in anticipation.

Had at least one or two of Doc's base pairs not been absorbed with the nature of themselves, he probably would have guessed that something was up as four expectant eyes waited on him. Instead, one-handed, he popped the lid on the can, breaking the seal and phphph-phphssssttt. Coke exploded all over him; he jumped. Celia and Harley, like the soda, exploded in an effervescence usually reserved for Alka Seltzer. Doc scowled and swiped at his shirt and pants.

"I guess she gets that from your side of the family, too."

"Oh, don't act so pissy." Celia got up and grabbed a few tissues. "She did it to me just the other day."

"When you freeze it a little bit, the bubbles go crazy trying to get out," Harley said. "You want to know why mine didn't do that?" Harley didn't wait for an answer. "Because I opened it a little at a time, starting in the kitchen. That way, the bubbles had a chance to catch up.

"I'm glad you're so pleased with yourself," Doc said, trying to hold the scowl.

Celia and Harley looked at each other, shrugged at the same moment, and broke into fits of laughter.

"Harley, would you go get Doc a towel, please," Celia asked.

Harley nodded and bounded off, leaving Celia and Doc. "She's showing affection, can't you see that? You're silently accusing her of not giving you love, but you don't accept it in the form it's offered." She gesticulated, taking in his soggy shirt and trousers. "This is her offering. A wise man accepts the gift for what it is."

"This," he said, making a wide gesture that took in his clothes, "is not a love offering. This is disrespect, but you want me to sit and take it."

"You ignore the obvious." Celia stood. The admonition of not casting pearls before swine came to mind. She took a breath, checked her anger gauge. "She would have done the same thing to her mother, but

Ellie's reaction would have been much different. They'd probably still be laughing. She also would have left it in the freezer longer – bigger explosion. That's how much she loved her mother."

With that, Celia turned and left the room, leaving Doc in a state of saturation to contemplate the nature of pearls.

✿ ❀ ❁

Harley tip-tied into Celia's room, leaned over her aunt and shout-whispered: "Aunt Celia, I think a spider was spitting on me."

"What?"

"A spider. I tried rolling over and pulling the covers, but I was too scared to go to sleep. Then I looked up."

"What was it?"

"A leak. In my ceiling. Falling like this: drip...drip...drip...." Harley demonstrated drops of water, falling on her head at exactly her third eye.

"Did you put a pot there to catch the water?" Harley nodded.

"Did you move the pillow?" Another nod.

"It's only a tiny little drop? Not much?" A third nod.

"Aww, baby, come here." Celia opened the blanket and Harley crawled in. "We'll deal with it in the morning." Celia started to giggle.

"It's not funny. It was scary."

"Because you thought a spider was spitting on you and you're afraid of spiders, but what if you knew right away it was just a little old leak? Then how would you feel?" Celia rubbed Harley's back to press the fear out of her. "The leak may be an indication of something worse. An emotional block. Things are going great and then, wham! Water pouring on your head."

Harley rolled over and sat upright. "You mean it's going to keep happening?"

"Until you make things right with Doc, maybe."

"What's he got to do with it?"

"I think it's the emotional square dance you two have got going on that's causing all this water to flow out of unlikely places."

"Noooo, Aunt Celia. You mean I have to fix my whole relationship for my ceiling to stop dripping? I liked it better when it was a stupid leak."

Celia pulled Harley into her, stroked her hair.

"What if I don't want to fix it? What if it's too much trouble and work? What if it can't be fixed?"

"I don't think the universe is giving you a choice, honey." Harley looked up at Celia and grimaced.

"If you only take the same road, how will you ever go anywhere new?"

"It's not fair. Just because you know all the right things to say."

"What good's it do me? I can't fix it any better than you can, and I can't fix it for you, but you could start working on it in your sleep. I solve my tougher problems there."

Harley sighed, rolled over and buried her face in the pillow. "Thanks for the dry bed."

"Not a problem."

"I love you."

Ditto, dollface. Celia rubbed Harley's back until she drifted off to sleep.

☼☼☼

The drips from the ceiling had subsided. Apparently, Doc's midnight meanderings, that and his visit with Celia had his emotions if not under control at least in an air-tight Tupperware container. He no longer needed five-gallon buckets, but coffee cups. Still, Celia said that harboring even a little bit of grief was like harboring a fugitive – eventually the law's gonna catch up with you. So a few days after the first well blew, Doc went back to see Twila, hoping she could help him shake the tree, maybe lose some of the unknowing.

She opened the door with a gleam in her eye, sat him down at the kitchen table and poured him a cafe-Twila. She sliced off a thick slab of coffee cake, pushed it toward him, smiled as he ate every bite, then cut him another. Never once did she mention the well. As far as Harburnette was concerned, Twila was a prime suspect and Doc guessed that this made her terribly happy. They ate the coffee cake and drank the steaming brew and spoke companionably about their families and their past while acorns from the giant oak alongside the house bombarded the roof with the velocity, if not the consistency, of heavy mortar fire. Twila already knew a lot about Ellie and Doc felt safe here in her kitchen. He felt he was whispering with a long-time conspiratorial aunt.

She asked about Harley and what Doc planned to do next. His plans were vague. He wanted to mention that he planned to bomb the rest of the wells into infinity, to keep going until he got caught or Harburnette shut down production, but since he wasn't sure whether he had the stomach for the long haul, or worse, prison, he did not mention of them.

"You should go on vacation," Twila announced. She poured another round, and stirred an alarming amount of sugar into her own cup with a thoughtful gaze. "Like a vision quest. You're never too old, and all this staying in one place isn't good for nobody." Twila sipped gingerly. "Sometimes the Soul needs a road trip. Only way to do that while you're still in your body is to go someplace with it."

"I'll take it under advisement," Doc said. "Maybe you can give me some recommendations."

"Well, I got some ideas. I always do."

Half an hour later, filled up on coffee and back-country philosophy, Doc drained his cup and rose to go.

The smile had never left Twila's face.

Doc was lying in bed the next day, looking for the pleasure that should have accompanied last night's job well done. The jolt of adrenaline he'd receive upon completion of his task had pumped him up, no question. But now in the aftermath he just stared at the ceiling, allowing each successive wave of energy to take him over: first the sorry blues from which sprang, if not hope, at least some kicking music; then came the mean reds, that wellspring of action and often, violent tendencies; and finally, the third sister in this unholy trinity, the inky blacks, a hole so dense that light itself got snuffed just crossing the border. He was somewhere between red and black, sitting in a little plastic baby pool of despair, not a black hole, per se, but at least a good thirteen inches of emptiness, and deep enough for despair to have a strong grip on his chest hairs.

Harley rode her bike over after school, fixed him sandwiches and Cokes for dinner. She sat next to him and for that he was grateful, but he couldn't rouse the courage to wrap an arm around her or give her cheek a peck.

"I'm not hungry tonight," he said.

She looked up at him with doe eyes, seemed to intuit it was not her sandwich-making abilities. "That's okay," she said, and ate his sandwich as well as her own. While doing the dishes, she turned her full-on gaze to his half-aware face.

"It won't always be this way, will it?" she asked.

"No, Lee, it won't, but I guess it'll always be some way."

How Zen.

You might think it's weird that I remember this, but when I was a baby, my Mom used to dance me around the living room. Round we twirled, past the built-in bookshelves, holding the dozens of books my mother always had on tap; past the ten-foot windows with their deep recessions; past the brick fireplace with the crack running through the lintel; past the crappy little compact disc changer blaring out the Frank Sinatra/Bono duet, "I've Got You Under My Skin," in all its bass-less glory. Ten, maybe eleven months is all I had under my proverbial hood, but I remember those days like I was thirteen years old. Mom said I couldn't possibly remember, but I do. I had yellow pajamas that snapped together at the waist with a little yellow duck over my heart. My joy paralleled the centrifugal force, tugging at my head and belly while my butt was cradled and safe in the crook of Mom's arm – terror and delight at once. I relive that feeling every time I get on a roller coaster. Those are the things I miss the most about Mommy, the weird stuff she used to do just to make me laugh.

Doc said light travels at a speed of 186,000 miles per second and, at that rate, it takes eight minutes for the first rays of the morning sun to reach your eyeballs. Then Aunt Celia asked if anyone ever did a calculation for the speed of love. I think it travels faster. Mom fell in love with me before she even saw me, before I even touched a toe on earth. Mom fell in love with Doc sort of fast, too, I guess. A couple months, maybe. For him I'd say about eight seconds, as long as it took to get a good look at her and hear her laugh. Even if they can't see auras, I think people can sense them. Mom's always kind of glowed.

I remember their first date. He couldn't stop staring at her, he loved her so much already. He hasn't missed a day since which is pretty amazing, considering she's dead. I feel sorry for him because he thinks that matters. The part about her being dead, I mean. It does, and it totally sucks that I can't, like, talk to her every day, but I know she's there. Sometimes I can feel her. And Aunt Celia says if I keep practicing and studying and being open, like, to new experiences, that sometime

I'll even be able to see her which would totally rock. Aunt Celia sees her. Doc'll never see her. He's just wound too tight. But that's also why I want to see her so I can relay messages and stuff. Maybe it will help him smile more.

I would also like to speed up the learning though, 'cause I want to talk to her about Sam Montoya. She could give me some tips. Right now all I have is Aunt Celia and, no offense, she's great, the most awesome aunt ever, but sometimes a girl just needs her mom.

Sam's mestizo. That's mixed blood. American Indian, English/Irish, and Puerto Rican. It doesn't bother me 'cause I don't see that it makes a difference. I mean, I'm a bunch of stuff, too, right? I think the only way people will ever really stop being suspicious of each other is if everyone gets so mixed up that they don't know who is what anymore. It also doesn't bother me that he's not tall, 'cause he's still dark and handsome, but he thinks about different stuff than I do and that bothers me. Doc says I swoon when I talk about him, so I guess I better watch that. I'm determined not to show my hand to Sam or any other man.

"Whatcha doing?" I jumped. I didn't see him coming which happens sometime, but not too much.

"What's it look like?" Snappy, I know, and be-atchy, but he got up in my space.

"Tossing a ball."

"Ding, ding, ding," I said and touched my nose. Doc looked hurt and I felt bad about it so I gave him a sneak peek at my Internal Processing Department.

"I'm thinking about how Sam does this all the time and how it's so freaking boring and how the heck can he stand it."

"What's he like?" Doc asked.

OMG, does he think I'm going to talk to him about this? I didn't say anything, just tossed the ball up in the air a couple more times.

"Lee, what's he like?"

He does think I'm going to talk to him about this. Shit! I mean, shoot.

"Harley!"

I jumped – again. "I'm sorry. I was spacing."

"That's all right. Tell me about Sam."

What the heck? Maybe Doc's smarter than he looks. I sighed and dove in, because, truth be told, I love to talk about Sam, even if it is only to Doc.

"Well, he only loves me from a distance. The minute he gets close to me, he can't handle it." I used the ball for effect, tossed it in the air again nonchalantly. "He likes the idea of love more than being in love." I threw my arm over the couch and gave him my best drama queen impression – big sigh – as if contemplating the incomprehensible nature of the male species. "Like, he says he doesn't want to hold my hand because it feels clammy, but he doesn't realize that sometimes love is clammy."

Doc was trying not to smile, I could tell, so I folded my arms across my chest and pouted. Of course, I won.

"You're right, Harley. When I think about love, clammy is the first word that comes to mind."

Doc cleared his throat. I knew he was about to wade into the shallow and underused Parental Advice Pool. *Whoa, pardner. Choppy waters.* I was so trying not to giggle.

"Maybe, too, you just have a crush on him and next week you won't even remember his name."

OMG, so not right. "Oh, I totally have an ice-in-the-blender kind of crush, but believe me, even if the ice melts, I won't forget his name." I bit the inside of both of my lips and frowned. I know I looked like an old lady without her dentures.

"What?" Doc asked.

"I'm just thinking. I'm never going to get married. It's too dangerous."

After the third well blew, Doc washed the coffee cups and put them back in the cupboard. After the fifth well blew, Doc put away the shillelagh for good. For the better part of two seasons, he had a pretty good gig going. He'd get up, go to work, futz around with some design change on the new wells Harburnette was drilling – something to make them tamperproof – go out after work with his buds and grouse about their employer, how they don't get paid enough, considering the money Harburnette was pulling in with the new Gas Gold Rush as they'd taken to calling it, and how the damn enviros were mucking up the work with their Abbey-esque forms of sabotage. Once a week, he'd visit Twila and drink enough coffee to power a small hydroplane. Given the nature of it all, it was bound to end eventually. Doc just wasn't prepared for it when it did.

"Who the hell's blowing them damn wells tail over tea cups?" George wanted answers. Although not one to hold a grudge, the curiousness of it all had piqued his interest.

"CNN's even reporting on it now. It's official. We're national." Hank didn't so much care, but his part Sioux upbringing gave him a lackadaisical attitude toward government organizations, quasi-governmental organizations, employers, and rote office-type employment. among other things. Hank took a long draw on his beer, tilting his head back as he did so that the leather strap braiding his thick black hair touched his belt. He licked his lips, set the half-full thirty-two ouncer on the table, and scanned the room. "Should we get a waitress?"

"Hank, man, you got at least a pint left," Doc noted.

"Yeah, but I'd prefer not to run out."

Doc suspected Hank to be the kind of alcoholic that had a shot of whiskey before his feet hit the floor in the morning, followed by a stiff one in his coffee to take the edge off. Doc overlooked all this. After all, a man's demons were his own to wrestle or invite over for cocktails, perhaps a sleepover. Yet he also suspected Hank had done the dinner/sleepover thing so often that his demons had moved in with all their baggage and their in-laws. Doc wasn't sure when Hank went from fun-loving party hound to hard-core alcoholic, but in the space of the two years since Hank's wife left him, his demons had become his favorite drinking buddies. And so it was shocking that after Doc had such a long run as "The Saboteur," it was Hank who assumed the title of "The Rescuer."

Since Harley only slept over on weekends, several nights during the week, Doc would have dinner with Celia and Harley. Sometimes he'd even cook. These small baby steps seemed to incline Celia favorably to him, yet it resulted in Doc being forced to carry on his clandestine activities on select nights during the week. That meant the bomb squad was out at 2 a.m. He averaged one to two wells a week – a brutal schedule which made it difficult to get up for work in the morning – but he was so jazzed by these endeavors that he needed little sleep. Harburnette spared no expense in attempting to catch the perpetrators and, oddly enough, Doc's team was assigned the task of designing a bombproof well. Not that anything was bombproof, but the security system was state of the art, and as the designer, Doc knew how to circumvent the high risk areas.

He'd design and sometimes install a new security system for the wellhead in the afternoon and go out and drink in the evening, all the while cursing the enviros for undoing all his team's hard work, and then follow it up with a well-timed explosion at night at a different well. All in a day's work.

It could have gone on indefinitely if Hank hadn't caught on. Doc had taken to being hypercritical of the saboteurs and one day, Hank called him on it.

"Wasn't Ellie trying to get legislation passed to force the oil and gas industry to disclose what they're pumping into the ground?"

Doc turned two shades of crimson before he trusted his voice enough to answer.

"Yeah. But what's that got to do with me?" Doc said with all the bravado he could muster. He was a terrible liar, coming from a long line of people who, as Twila noted, felt the need to confess like a tidal pull. He wouldn't look at Hank, but his face told the story. Hank nodded, said nothing.

In retrospect, reticence would have served Doc better, his protestations appearing to Hank as the large and ostentatious road sign on the Guilt Highway. Lately, the explosions had occurred at the facilities where security was about to be installed. To the trained eye, it was obvious that someone was taking them out while they still could because once up and running a would-be perpetrator didn't stand a chance. As for Hank, he just had to be paying attention to what Doc was working on and it would be easy to figure out the rest. It wasn't rocket science, although Hank had lived in that rarefied world of brilliance before his wife left him. Since then, though, his brain had gotten a little soggy from all the alcohol. Still, Doc may have died that night if it wasn't for Hank coming to test his theory.

He'd gotten cocky. Doc had set the well for a series of small explosions that would, he hoped, result in taking the whole well down in cascading fashion. With a 1" lead pipe hooked on the upper tier of the rig, a 2" pipe in the middle tier, and a 3" pipe set at the bottom of the drilling rig, Doc had thought a series of explosions approximately ten-seconds apart would provide, not only dramatic effect, but a thorough trouncing. Unfortunately, he'd incorrectly set the timer, resulting in an explosion on the upper tier as he was still walking away. The extreme ringing in his ears resulted in shock, debilitating him to the point of paralysis during the time when he should have been running for cover. That Hank was there to pull him to safety was the only reason Doc was still alive. They both suffered temporary hearing loss.

Hank wouldn't give him up, Doc knew that. They shared too many of the unfortunate threads of life. Both had loved and lost, and although Hank's wife had left him almost two years before Ellie died, Doc had never stopped listening to the crank and churn of Hank's broken heart, trying to mend itself. As such, both men were reluctant to sever such longstanding ties, criminal activity now another one holding them together. Yet Doc knew that his secret was out and he was no longer safe. Hank might take it to the grave, but there was something about secrets once revealed that took on a height and breadth and width of their own.

It's time.

The next day, aided by the fact that his sense of hearing was still diminished, Doc's mind was crystalline and sharp, with all the qualities of a world that had finally sorted itself out. He sat down at the computer to compose his resignation letter. Before the shit storm started. Before something greater than temporary hearing loss became part of his resume. Before the world came to know him as the criminal element he'd become. He didn't mind blowing stuff up. It was blowing people up that worried him. We all want to be heroes. Then the mundane takes a spot on the sofa, the one with the best view of the TV, and the ennui of modern life proceeds to beat the hell out of us, one sound byte at a time. The frog jumps out when thrown in boiling water, but turn it up notch by notch and he thinks he's getting a pore cleanse. Doc would have stuck it out if it was just him, but what about Harley? Plus, he didn't feel like listening to Celia harangue him.

He got as far as "Dear..." and sat back in his chair. Another bit of life's capriciousness biting him in the ass. What the hell am I doing? Before he could further formulate the answer, he was in the car, hurtling through the darkness, much like on the first night they'd met except that night the stars bade him good journey and tonight, well, he just couldn't tell.

❀ ❀ ❀

Harley listened to the sound of her heart, beating a slow and steady thrump, thrump, thrump, the mainstay of youth. As her breath pushed against the walls of her lungs, turning, like Benedict Arnold, from oxygen to carbon dioxide, Harley experienced a burning sensation which she could no longer control, and taking one more inward gasp, tried to hold it all in until her lungs felt about to collapse. She let the air escape into her underwater hideaway where her breath bubbled up like a hot spring.

"Are you lightheaded yet?" Celia asked. She sat on the edge of the tub, watching as Harley gulped air, then regulated her breath. Harley nodded.

"Did you practice circle breathing? You know, the figure eight pattern with the continuous breath?" Harley nodded again. "Did you see anything?"

Harley took a long slow breath, adjusted her bathing suit, and relaxed against the back of the tub. She was developing exponentially these days and her joy and dismay were palpable. Yet as much as she wanted to be treated like an adult, she could have easily stayed a child for another decade or so.

"I dreamed I was driving – which is weird cause I don't have a license – and suddenly these mounds of sand and dirt and snow were everywhere, blocking my path." Celia handed Harley a towel before she got out of the tub. "I put the car in reverse and tried to get through the low parts. I was trying to get to the river, but the whole mess shifted and there was no space in between, just a big bunch of sand and snow and I couldn't get any traction. So what's it mean, Aunt Celia?" Harley stood there, the towel wrapped around her, the water dripping from her bathing suit puddling at her feet.

"From the primordial stew rises the world."

"What's that mean?"

"You know what, Lee? Sometimes I don't have a clue."

☼☼☼

Lloyd let him in. He led Doc down the hall, walking on carpet so plush it swallowed all sound except for that of Doc's beating heart. He could feel Lloyd's grief, stuck to him like Cling Wrap, or like the rank morning after taste after a night of binge-drinking, lounging in a dirty silk robe with its feet on the coffee table. *Been there.* Doc's own trepidation rose like a vapor as Lloyd turned the knob to Twila's bedroom.

The shock hit him like a fist. Twila was lying under a heap of blankets, dissociating mind from body. She cracked one eyelid; arid lips formed the ghost of a smile.

"My body's gone and double-crossed me," she wheezed. Twila's labored breath banged against dark and narrow passageways, hitting blockade after blockade, the exhalations rattling like a million tiny coal cars, tunneling through the dark in search of egress, buckling under the weight.

"Damn doctors don't know squat. I don't care if they've never seen a case this bad before. Hell, if I did what they did all day long, I'da figured something out by now. Got nothin' in the way of intuition, I tell you. Damned insurance companies musta beat it the hell out of 'em."

Lloyd shook his head and smiled at his wife's tirade. He motioned Doc to a seat beside the bed, then left to give them privacy. The waxing moon cast a warm glow over the room. Doc picked up Twila's hand, fragile, like rice paper, and translucent as if the light of the moon were shining through it.

Twila's cells had mutated much like the three hundred heads of cattle they'd turned out on their property for generations: strange growths where there used to be skin, oozing pus, and blood, and death. Twila watched most of her and Lloyd's three hundred heads turn sick and die over the last two years, poisoned water mostly to blame, although Twila believed the airborne contaminants probably hadn't helped. Didn't matter the reason. A way of life was about to become extinct. So was Twila.

Her grip was still strong and she gave his fingers a tug. "Glad you came."

He nodded, not finding a satisfactory response. The boney fingers grasped his then went limp. Doc picked up the slack.

"I'm so sorry, I..."

"Don't make this about you."

"Maybe if I'd have worked faster, or worked somewhere else."

Twila snorted. "If it wasn't you, it'd been some other dang fool working that job. We all gotta eat. You did what you were trained for." She squeezed his hand again. "In the end, you did more than most. You got up and put your coat and shoes on, and did somethin.' Somethin' powerful and scary. Somethin' that you thought might make it all a little more right. There's no sorry in that." She drew a haggard breath as if to punctuate the next words. "But now you gotta stop."

Doc raised his eyebrows in response. The woman was downright scary.

"I'm sorry I pushed you. Now I'm tellin' ya' – stop. 'Fore somebody gets hurt."

He might have told her then about the last time, about Hank and how Hank had saved him, or about how he'd become a criminal just to honor Ellie in death, or about Harley and how he just couldn't figure her out and it was killing him, or how, and it was a big one, how Twila herself had saved him and that if it wasn't for her, Doc'd be the one lying in wait to die, but instead he just nodded and sat there listening to Twila's life force ebb. He held her cold, boney hand until her breathing fell into a regular rhythm and she'd fallen asleep. He kissed her on the forehead, bending close to take a last look at the bold features, now wasted and shriveled by the rampaging cancer.

Her eyes fluttered, locked on his, intent.

"There is no failure, 'cept a failure of the heart and you still got yours," she tapped his chest, "working pretty well, far as I can tell. You had time for an old woman, anyway. Can't be all black in there." She smiled, the sagging flesh, stretching to life for a moment to reveal a mouth full of white teeth. "I think now would be a good time," Twila stopped to pull a belligerent, excoriating breath into her lungs, "to get the hell out of Dodge, as they say. Comprendeme, amigo?" Doc nodded.

"Might want to think about getting a new job, too." She winked, and he saw the old Twila. The visage cracked open a fissure in his heart that had scarred over when Ellie died and for one instant, Twila's light was his.

She died that night. Doc attended the funeral along with dozens and dozens of ranchers and their families all come to pay their respects to this great woman, one of the "stickers" whose family had come in the late-1800s during the first boom and bust era of timbering and mining and oil and construction and who had stayed on to make a living. They worked the land for what it would produce – cattle. So when the time came and they asked if anyone wanted to say anything on behalf of this fine woman, Doc's hand raised itself, his body stood up, and he took over the funeral.

"Twila's great-grandfather was thrilled when the first oil men knocked on his door with a check and a promise. They may not have tamed the harsh out of the land, but at least they made it more hospitable. They built roads and paid well, and the ranchers loved them. That was the heyday when oil flowed like free love out of those great big underground reservoirs. Sweet gas, they called it. Back then a whisper could've coaxed that oil out of the ground."

Doc stopped for a moment and wiped his brow. Someone handed him a bottle of water and he took it, grateful. For a minute he was surprised to find himself standing in front of this crowd, Twila's crowd. It felt more like a revival meeting than a wake, and Twila was lying there, talking through him in a way that all made sense. Everything he and Twila had talked about these last months came shooting up like black gold. All he had to do was pass it on.

"So the energy geeks put in these roads and when you're running 300 head of cattle over 40,000 BLM acres, you'll take all the help you can get. Back then it was a win-win. Now fast-forward to today. The sweet gas is gone and coal bed methane is all the rage. In order to pull it out, you need the wells. Lots of them. Used to be you could drive for miles without seeing a second well. Now you throw a stone and you're likely to hit your neighbor's. If it was just a well, it wouldn't be such a big deal, but it was a well, and a compressor, and a sump pump for the toxic water that comes out once you pump a shit load of brine and chemicals in, and a dehydrator to get rid of the water so you can get at the gas and a storage tank for that water and maybe the pump goes down from time to time and so you need a pump jack to prime it, and you need a pipeline and a road to get it all out of there and before you know it the back country looks like a patchwork quilt and there's spills out the wazoo and underground mishaps that'd make your skin crawl 'cause all that stuff's creeping into the groundwater and soon it's spreading in a great big plume because your neighbor's well a quarter-mile up the road is doing it, too, and before you know it, the cattle are aborting or growing two heads or just dropping over dead, and unless you want to do it, too, you know it's time to get the hell out, but it's hard, you know, because your family's been here so long the land is like a part of you and you just don't know how to say goodbye."

Doc paced the length of the coffin, looking to Twila every now and then for guidance. He thought he saw a look on her face, a look of pride that said more than this she could never hope to ask for. He blinked back his heartache and plowed on, oblivious to his surroundings.

"Then you go to sell the ranch that your daddy and granddaddy and his granddaddy worked, about to leave everything you ever knew behind because you know if you don't then the land – that beautiful land that was once like your momma's milk to you – is gonna kill you. But nobody, not a goddamn soul wants to buy it because they all got the same, and nobody works this land right unless they've lived on her for a couple three generations and since your whole life and every dime you ever made is sunk right down deep into her roots, you can't just up and go 'cause you got nothin' to go with. And so you stay and you hope and you pray and you scream and shout and raise a shit storm hopin' that somebody's gonna hear you, but they don't and you ask God why, but He doesn't say much, just takes another life or two back unto Himself, and the papers report on it, but still nothing changes. They just keep drilling and pumping and stealing and spreading the poison and lying about it, day after day after day, until you and the land, well you're all dried up with nothing left to give anybody, and that's when they walk away."

Doc stopped and drew an enormous breath. He was sweating profusely, every pore in his body releasing toxins for himself, for Twila, maybe even for the land. He looked over at Lloyd who nodded approval.

"And that," he concluded, "is what happened to Twila."

Doc sat down. There was total silence in the room. Some people were nodding and some people were crying, and some people were outraged, and the emotions were all congealing like a newborn consciousness not yet known to itself and then, as if on cue, the crowd breathed a collective sigh and one after another, the mourners began to clap.

When the thunder died down, the room erupted in raucous political commentary. Plans of Action were zinging across the room from every corner. Revival was in full swing and Doc wasn't sure if Twila was gonna jump right out of the casket and chair the meeting. This was his parting gift to her, to rile the masses. Doc blew her a kiss and left the melee of political change Twila had started – not with her death, but with her life – and feeling good about how he'd helped it along; he left Twila, sitting smack dead in the middle of it. He knew that's how she wanted it.

This time, he was sure he saw her smile.

Harley folded her arms across her chest and slumped down into Celia's armchair, a brooding look defining her face. Celia sat down on the arm of the chair and gave Harley's hair a tousle.

"Why so glum, chum?"

"I saw Sam holding hands with Miranda."

"And...?

"That means they're going out."

"Not necessarily. There could be a million explanations."

"Yeah, like what?"

"I don't know. What if she grabbed it when she saw you coming just to mess with you? What if Sam really had no interest in holding her hand."

"Maybe, but..."

"What if, as you were walking by, Sam yanked his hand back and gave Miranda a dirty look, but you didn't see it because you had already passed and he didn't see you because he was busy trying to get his hand back?"

"You didn't see what I saw, Aunt Celia."

"What if I told you Miranda was just trying to get back at you for that stunt you pulled in biology with the fetal pig?"

"Is that true?" Harley bolted upright, interested.

"I have no idea, but it's a possibility. Like Schrodinger's cat.

Harley fell back on the couch and covered her eyes with her arms. "Who's Schrodinger?

"A really smart guy who loved to think about probabilities."

Harley dropped her hands and raised a single eyebrow, coupled with a smirk. The similarity to Ellie was enormous and Celia tried not to laugh.

"Listen. There are only two mistakes you can make in life and both are activated by judgment: one is knowing wrongly, the other is assuming that reality is limited to what you know. Either way, you lose." Celia returned the smirk, sans raised eyebrow.

"I know what I saw."

"You know what you think you saw which isn't always what it is. Listen sister, your thoughts are powerful so don't let them stray. Too many negative ones hanging out together might form their own street gang. Before you know it, you're a victim of your own ass-kicking."

Harley giggled, but remained inert.

"Judgment restricts perception. Take away judgment and life breaks wide open."

"What's that mean?"

"It means – don't be a victim." She brushed Harley's cheek. "You're the next generation to shape the world. For that, you need to keep your eyes wide open."

Harley sighed and sat up. "Okay, I'll try." Harley closed her eyes and after several breaths, a smile graced her lips.

"What did you see?"

"Mom."

Celia nodded. "Soon, you'll be able to see her with your eyes open." She smiled, pulled Harley up from her chair. "C'mon. Let's go get some ice cream."

It was late afternoon when Doc left the funeral and headed to a convenience store where he bought a bottle of Guinness, a bouquet of flowers and some lunch, then headed up to the mesa. Upon arrival, Doc unrolled the blanket, carefully set his flowers down, and proceeded to unwrap his sandwich. He gave thanks for its sustenance. With every bite, he enjoyed the slightly smoky flavor of the turkey, the sharpness of the cheddar, the subtle aroma of the whole grain bread, the crunch and tang of the seeds. Then he opened the beer and toasted Twila and Ellie, the sacred view from his perch, and his part, if not in protecting it, at least in maintaining it for a bit longer.

Lunch over, he lay down on the blanket, sated and content, and using his backpack for a pillow and the brilliant blue sky as a backdrop, Doc spread the flowers across his chest and crossed into the Beta state, looking to make direct contact with his wife.

The past is over, Doc. Not to be harsh, but it's time to quit pining and start living. Don't be like me. I spent my whole life collecting stones: the stone of Anger, the stone of Grief, the stones of Resentment and Jealousy, when what I really needed to do was empty my pockets. I chose fear and worry and look what I lost in the deal: you and Harley.

I'm sure you know, Mr. Engineer, that the atom is the building block of the physical world, and that on a cellular level, we humans are composed of only about 5% atoms. The rest is just empty space. Go figure. We're just big black holes with a few points of light, walking around in designer jeans.

Weirder still, about 70% of our atoms are only water, and that water spends so much of its time detoxing our bodies that we're really nothing more than small wastewater treatment plants. My point is, it's time to flush the system, baby. Don't worry. I'll be waiting right here until you all catch up with me.

BTW, thanks for the flowers.

✿✿✿

Ellie sealed the lecture with a kiss. Doc could taste her on his lips when he came to. He felt an unrivaled lucidity and a lightness that was missing since childhood. He sat up and looked around, dazed and peaceful like one fresh from anesthesia. He breathed in the almost spring air, noted the retreating cold, the slant of the light in the valley below, the sun's rays glinting off the well heads. Then there was the other detail that made the tiny hairs on his forearm come to a rigid and focused attention: the flowers were gone. He looked completely around: no trace. So he cried, and when the tears were spent, he laughed, and when that was spent, he was still.

For the first time since Ellie died their hearts were in sync and Doc knew what he had to do and what he was taking with him.

☼☼☼

When Doc roared into Celia's, parking his brand new Ultra Classic Electra Glide Harley Davidson touring bike in the driveway, the sound of the engine was loud enough to rival the Italian Grand Prix. He thought for sure Harley would have been on the porch before he got his helmet off, but not a curtain moved nor was a window cracked. He sighed and cut the engine, leaving the gateway to his new life gleaming in the sun.

Celia's own gate had stood open for so long that the dirt and gravel and grass had shifted and rearranged themselves such that open had become the new normal. It would take a crow bar to pry it closed now – kind of like Celia – so Doc cruised right in.

He found Harley in the living room plugged into her iPod and doing her best Red Hot Chili Peppers impersonation, jumping all over the room like a Flea infestation. When she finally saw, not heard him, she waved, but kept right on dancing. The volume on her iPod was so loud that she greeted him with a shout: "That song is like a million Smarties with no stomach ache. Do you want to hear it?"

"I already do," he shouted in return. "Where's your aunt?" She pointed up, but kept on dancing.

Doc took the stairs two at a time, found Celia in the master bathroom. He knocked lightly at first, but when Celia couldn't hear him over the Jacuzzi jets, he pounded.

"You almost out?"

"Who wants to know."

"Who do you think?"

Long pause: "I'm communing with my Higher Self right now. She's wearing a gold afro just for kicks. Come back when it turns orange."

Doc rested his forehead against the door with a thud. Finally, Celia relented.

"Open the door then. Just a crack."

Celia's body lay submerged below mountains of bubbles raised by the Jacuzzi's jets. He couldn't see her because the glass doors were completely fogged.

"Geez, how can you stand it in here?"

"My Higher Self wants me to tell you that wherever there's a poison in nature, there's always an antidote within twelve feet."

"Huh?"

There was a long pause, followed by the swirling and giggling of Jacuzzi bubbles. "Consider it a travel advisory. You can just as easily substitute the word problem for poison."

The lump in Doc's throat grew to the size of a golf ball. He cleared it. "How'd you know?"

"Ellie told me."

"News travels fast. At the speed of love, I suppose you'd say?" He could feel Celia smiling through the fog.

"Have you told Harley yet?"

Doc rubbed his hand over his mouth, pondering the soundness of his decision, a momentary doubt creeping in to hijack his will.

"No, I wanted to ask you first."

From the other side of the door came more swishing and splashing followed by, "well, you have my blessing."

Relief flooded Doc's body and his heart pumped like an alternating current. A surge of love spread warmth throughout his entire body. "Thanks, Celia. Other than Ellie, you're the best person I know."

"No, you're the best person you know. You just haven't realized it yet. Now close the door. With you on the other side of it, please."

Doc did as he was told.

When he got back downstairs, Harley was sitting at the computer table with tears in her eyes.

"What's the matter, Lee?"

"I logged on to my Facebook account and Miranda left a message on my wall that said, "Harley Sandberg has no friends. How mean is that?" Harley sniffed. "Sometimes at lunch when I'm talking to her she says, "uh-huh, uh-huh, uh-huh," like she's listening, but really she's not, and the second I start talking again, she asks Gabby or Taylor something. She never cares about what I'm saying, but she pretends she's my friend."

Doc studied Harley's face. The tear-tracks made her look six again. He grabbed some tissues, held them to her like a bouquet of flowers. She dabbed first, then blew upon his urging. She handed him back the crumpled, wet wad, again just like a six-year old, and Doc tossed them in the trash can, inches away. She looked so gloomy that Doc was overcome; he wrapped her in a bear hug. Harley sat there, enveloped like individually wrapped Starburst.

"You ever been to Hershey Park, the Sweetest Place on Earth?"

"In Pennsylvania?" she said to Doc's armpit.

"Yes."

"You know I haven't."

"You want to go?"

"With you?" She arched her back to get a clearer look at the mouth that might be feeding her a line.

"Yes, with me."

"Um, you're shocking the crap out of me right now on so many levels. Can I have my arms back? I need them to think."

Doc released her. "We'll go on the bike.

Harley ran both her hands through her hair. "What bike?"

"The one in the driveway."

Harley ran to the window to inspect the driveway and ascertain this wasn't some kind of cruel joke." When she saw the Electra Glide, her face took on an etheric quality and for a moment, Doc caught Ellie's face smiling at him.

"You're not kidding." A statement, albeit a tentative one.

"By the time we get there, you'll be able to go on that Fahrenheit ride no problem."

"That thing goes up and back so fast, the puke doesn't even have a chance to hit the ground before you finish screaming."

"I'm just going to ignore the visual on that for now. You know, pretend you never said it."

"Okay, sure." Harley beamed, showing all her teeth.

Things just might be turning around.

❧ ❧ ❧

Celia had advised them to wait until the late spring when Harley was done school. Doc agreed; the weeks had flown. Two nights before their trip, Celia and Harley took Doc up on his offer to make a going away dinner. When Celia walked into Doc's kitchen, he was prepping a pair of Omaha Steaks the size of Texas. The packaging the steaks had arrived in sat in a heap on the counter and would take a small dump truck to remove.

"What's that?" Celia wrinkled her nose at the mammoth pile of raw meat.

"Dinner."

"Dinner that came by UPS?"

"It's fresh. It comes packed in dry ice. You hungry?"

"Not for mail-order food, but Harley might be interested."

As if on cue, Harley burst into the kitchen. "What's for dinner? I'm starving." She took one look at the massive meat product, bit her lip, shook her head, and took a seat at the counter. "So listen to this. I'm talking to Lilly and she goes into this half-hour story about her fish and instead of cutting to the chase, she gave me three days of back story when all she wanted to tell me was that her fish died."

"I'm sure you let her know how you felt." Doc said.

"No, I was not sarcastic. I'm still nice to her because she's kind of dumb. I'm only mean to smart people who act dumb."

Doc snickered. Celia peered first at Doc then at the steaks, disdain spreading from her lips to her tapping foot.

"What? You act like I just eradicated a third world country."

Celia shook her head. "I can't do it."

"Do what?"

"Eat those things. It's not like I'm a big vegetarian or anything, but – they came in the mail, for Godsakes. Do you know how many pounds of corn and grain it takes to raise one pound of beef. Like sixteen. That's just the grain. Water's something like 5,000 gallons. You could feed and water an entire village for a week. Besides, cows don't even want grain, they want grass."

Doc's face sagged and he locked his gaze until it was Celia's turn to shift. He really was trying to be a nice guy. Perhaps she could put differences on sustainability aside. She was just about to say she'd eat it as long as he made the salad extra-large when his face broke, and he belted out a guffaw so joy-laden that it sent a ripple through the room, taking Celia by surprise. None of them were physically touching, yet Celia felt the arms of love surround them all.

With one arcing movement, Doc swept the steaks into the trash can. Celia flinched.

Doc shrugged. "We leave tomorrow. You're not going to eat them."

"The waste. Those poor cows."

"Point taken." Doc pulled the steaks out of the trash. "C'mon, Lee. I know a dog who's gonna think today's Christmas."

They bolted out of the house and Celia watched them run across the lawn, laughing.

☼ ❀ ❦

They dined on Chinese. Harley worked her chopsticks, spearing a piece of tofu like a pro.

"The thought of being in the same room as him makes my belly hurt. It's terrifying," Harley said.

"That's because he's such a charged energy force, all focused and intense, not like most 15-year olds," Celia said. "I think it's because of his martial arts training."

"I know, he loves it. It gives him a really ripped six-pack. I'm talking ten out of ten." Harley flipped her hair like she was starring in a shampoo commercial. "I start sweating when I think about it."

Doc cleared his throat. "Are you talking about Sam?" Harley shook her head and plowed on. Obviously, he had catching up to do.

"So I want to invite him over for dinner or to hang out or something when we get back because neither one of us has a car, and any way, you say I'm not allowed to date until I'm sixteen."

"Well, I think that can be arranged," Celia said.

"I want to do it at your house, not Doc's. Otherwise, he'll be sniffin' around all night, peeing on furniture and stuff, and that's not cool."

"Harley!" Celia said.

"Would not," Doc said.

Harley poured herself some tea, then refilled Doc and Celia's cups. "I don't mean literally. I mean, like, territorially."

"Since when did you become the expert?" Doc asked. He grabbed the plate of curried vegetables and dished some onto his plate.

"Since like, forever. Duh. I'm not stupid."

Doc nodded. "I think she's probably right. About the peeing, I mean."

Harley raised an "I told you so" eyebrow at her aunt. "Why can't I just go out on a date?"

"Because you're thirteen," Doc said.

"Almost fourteen."

"Whatever."

"What if I meet someone on the road?"

"I have a gun. I'll shoot him. Just in the leg so he can't follow."

Harley snorted. Usually, when she wanted something badly enough, she could work the weak link. In the past, Doc hadn't paid much attention and most times she could wear down her mother. For some reason, as of late, Aunt Celia and Doc were a united front, exhibiting more cohesion than OPEC. Her only shot was that Aunt Celia would respond to the biological leanings of sisterhood and at the end of the day would vote like Ellie. So she changed strategies and forged ahead. For several seconds, Harley sat, her chin in her hand, as still as a Rodin statue, before piping up: "Why didn't you ever have kids, Aunt Celia?"

"I have you," Celia said, mimicking Harley's position. "You're still not allowed to date."

☼☼☼

That night, Doc and Ellie danced together on the beach. The light of the full moon twinkled across the surf. Ellie stopped and took Doc's face in her hands. "I want you to remember, but no more waiting. You've got too long."

Doc shrugged it off, started dancing again. She kissed him and pulled away.

"I'll be here when you're ready to come home." She turned and as he reached for her hand, she slipped past him like a wave disappearing into the sand. "Ellie!" Doc ran after her, but a giant wave broke on the shore, knocking him to the ground. Water splashed his face and he woke.

Ellie was gone.

☼ ★ 🜚 ✿

Celia sat on the leaf-strewn carpet in the foyer, watching the light change as clouds rolled across the sky. Doc pulled up on the cycle; Celia sighed.

"Harley, Doc's here."

"Be there in a minute."

Celia walked out; the screen door slammed as she crossed the lawn.

"You ready for this?" Doc asked. Celia nodded and for once he noted her resolve was not in a firm and steady place. Tears welled and she buried her face in his shoulder. He wrapped his arms around her, took her sadness onto himself. After a minute, she emerged, fresh-faced and smiling.

"It feels good to be able to do that for you once in awhile," Doc said. Celia blushed. The screen door banged again and then Harley was there before them. She dropped two small bags at the rear wheel of the bike and stepped back.

"Well, I'm packed and ready to go." Doc eyed the bags appraisingly. "No blow dryers?"

Harley shook her head. "Nope."

"Curling irons?"

"Nope."

"Excessive makeup?"

Pause. "Define excessive."

"More than four items.

Harley counted on her fingers, paused before raising her fourth finger: "One thing I have two of so I'm counting it as one."

Doc looked at Celia who shrugged a shoulder.

"Fine.

"Do you have enough underwear and socks?" Doc asked.

"That's kind of personal, don't you think?"

"It's going to get much more personal after the first four or five hours on the bike and we're going for weeks. You need the necessary provisions."

"I got 'em, I got 'em."

"Good." Doc turned his attention to Celia. "We'll call every day." Celia nodded, allowed Doc to wrap her in a strong hug. He leaned in to plant a kiss on her mouth, but at the last minute pecked her cheek. "Thanks – for everything."

Celia gave The Antler a tug. Doc put a hand to her cheek and held it there for several moments before running his hand behind her neck and pulling her in for a full-on kiss on the lips. Then he turned and got on the bike. Celia looked after him, stunned and a bit woozy, before gathering Harley in her arms.

"Your mother wants me to tell you she's so very proud of you. Of both of you."

Doc smiled sheepishly, checked his boots.

"She wishes she could go, but it's time just for you guys now," Celia said.

Harley held Celia's hand and grimaced. A slight shadow, like a cloud passing the sun, concealed Harley's happiness for a moment.

"She did say she'd be watching from a distance. Soon you won't need me anymore."

"I'll always need you, Aunt Celia," Harley said and threw her arms around her aunt like she'd never let go.

Celia stroked her head. "Not to see her you won't, baby. You're there. Just keep your thoughts positive. We need all the light we can get in the world and you're practically a beacon."

"Okay, Aunt Celia."

"Don't just okay me. I mean it."

"Okay." Harley looked up, gave her aunt a sad smile, squeezed her eyes tight. "I'll miss you."

"Me, too, baby."

"Tell Mom I love her."

Celia held Harley an arm's length away, looked her squarely in each eye. "Tell her yourself." Then Celia mumbled the ancient words and drew indecipherable symbols into the air just above Harley's head. At last, Celia was satisfied. "May angels light your way," she said, and with a kiss and a prayer, released her niece. Harley climbed onto the back of the motorcycle. Doc revved the engine, gave Harley's knee a squeeze.

"Ready?" he asked.

"Ready."

"First stop, the Grand Canyon."

"I thought we were going to Pennsylvania."

"It's sort of on the way."

Harley turned to wave goodbye to Celia whose hand was raised, a big, loopy smile lighting her face. Next to her, waving like a madwoman, was Ellie. Harley blinked, but when she opened her eyes, her mother was still standing there, shining brighter than the full moon at midnight.

Harley took a deep breath and her jaw went slack. Tears welled in the corners of her eyes, but instead of cracking, she blew one, then half a dozen kisses her mother's way as Doc eased out of the driveway.

"See you soon, Mom," Harley whispered to the bright, light-field of energy that was now Ellie.

Not if I see you first, honey.

The End...

...and also the beginning, depending on how you look at it.

Made in the USA
Middletown, DE
25 February 2015